MW01294270

LUCKY DAY

ALSO BY CHUCK TINGLE

Bury Your Gays

Camp Damascus

Straight

LUCKY DAY

CHUCK TINGLE

TOR PUBLISHING GROUP NEW YORK

This is a work of fiction. All of the characters, organizations, and events portrayed in this novel are either products of the author's imagination or are used fictitiously.

LUCKY DAY

A Nightfire Book
Published by Tom Doherty Associates / Tor Publishing Group
120 Broadway
New York, NY 10271

www.torpublishinggroup.com

Nightfire™ is a trademark of Macmillan Publishing Group, LLC.

EU Representative: Macmillan Publishers Ireland Ltd, 1st Floor, The Liffey Trust Centre, 117–126 Sheriff Street Upper, Dublin 1, DO1 YC43

The Library of Congress Cataloging-in-Publication Data is available upon request.

ISBN 978-1-250-39865-9 (hardcover)
ISBN 978-1-250-39866-6 (ebook)

First Edition: 2025

Printed in the United States of America

10 9 8 7 6 5 4 3 2 1

CONTENTS

LUCKY DAY

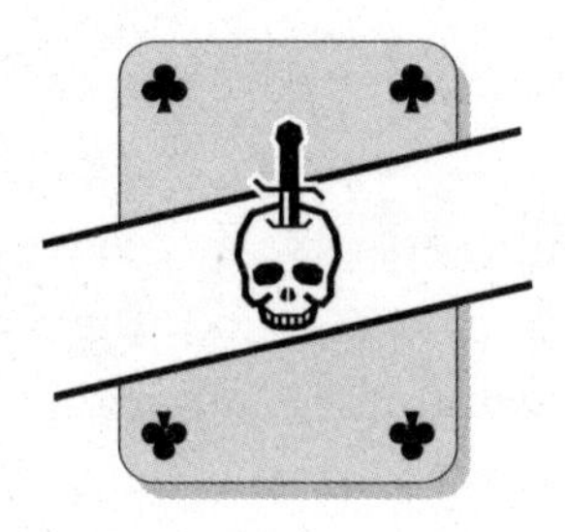

IMPOSSIBLE'S DOORSTEP

Before I'm fully aware of my physical self—before I understand *who* or *what* or *where* I am—I reach out into the darkness. It's a primal movement of comfort, not desperate or worried, just reflexive.

Connection is what we're built for, and while this assertion may sound spiritual at its core, it doesn't have to be. Whether a patch of mold crawling over tile or a pack of hairless apes starting a fire, biological organisms thrive by working together. It's no wonder, then, that as a bodiless, floating thing, my first instinct is to hunt for someone else.

My hand finds nothing but empty sheets. The warmth I'm expecting is mysteriously absent, and this broken pattern does more to jerk me back into focus than any horrible, buzzing alarm clock ever could. Something is wrong. The rhythm of my life has shifted.

I reach a little deeper into the abyss, driven to hunt the cool, clean ocean of this vacant space. "Annie?" I sigh, stretching my body across the bed.

She's not there. My eyes pop open.

Chirp!

I'm greeted by the sound of my phone alarm, a single, piercing digital beep. It's short and efficient, customized so that I won't wake my girlfriend with a full round of the traditional rattling xylophone, but it appears today this effort is for naught.

My eyes scan our dimly lit bedroom. Despite Annie's absence, everything else is as it should be. A faint glow illuminates the blinds to my left, the brand-new day slowly churning itself into existence. Our shelves are organized, the wood floors are freshly mopped, and today's workout fit sits waiting for me on a nearby hanger.

My jaw hurts from a long night of grinding.

"Annie?" I call out, a little louder this time as I find my voice.

My mind leaps back through time, struggling to remember any particular morning that she woke before I did. *I'm* the one who gets up before dawn and walks across the park, then jogs home. *I'm* the one who makes our coffee. *I'm* the one—

A faint shuffle in the living room quells my panic, and moments later a familiar figure steps into the bedroom doorway. My whole world nudges back into alignment. Annie is always a hell of a sight, but this morning her short and messy blond hair feels especially playful, and the constellations of freckles that cover her face seem even more pronounced. She leans against the doorframe and cocks her head to the side, just gazing for a moment. It's the perfect amount of time to let me know that she's thinking something and choosing not to speak it, but her mischievous smile is a strong hint that whatever it is would make me blush.

"Good morning," Annie finally coos.

"What the fuck is happening? *You're* up before I am?" I joke. "And you're *dressed*?"

"Yes ma'am," Annie confirms. She hesitates, then laughs, momentarily shifting gears. "I can't believe you sleep like that, Vera."

I glance down at my rigid pose. While one arm has extended into the empty space where Annie usually rests, the other is tight against my side. I'm lying perfectly straight and flat on my back like a corpse in a coffin, my feet pointed at the ceiling.

I say nothing, consciously relaxing the tightness of my body.

Annie is clad in her workout gear, which consists of a ratty old Cocteau Twins tee with the sleeves cut off and light blue short-shorts that look like they belong on a '70s track star. It's chaotic and fun, like her, and it shows off the sway of her body as she saunters toward me.

"Need some help loosening up?" Annie asks. "There's all kinds of things we could do before your morning walk."

As she reaches the corner of the bed she drops to her hands and knees, exaggerating the movement of her hips. She crawls across the blankets. Unfortunately, as great as Annie looks in this position, my eyes have already moved slightly lower.

"Shoes!" I snap, pointing at the chunky white sneakers on her feet. They're caked in dried mud, soles worn down and laces fraying.

Annie lies flat, stretching out so that her feet stay hanging off the edge of the bed. It's just enough for her lips to meet mine, the two of us holding for a long, warm kiss. Despite the slightly awkward position, we take a moment to breathe each other in, then finally release.

"Later," I say.

Annie nods. "This is *your* day," she reminds me. "Whatever you want."

It *is* my day, and as much as I appreciate the gift of Annie doing her best type-A impression in solidarity, what I'd *really* love is for everything to stay the same. My peace is in the pattern.

"I wanna go for my walk," I inform her.

"Well, *I'm* ready," she proudly announces, standing up again.

I follow her lead, climbing from the tangled blankets. I change into my sleek, charcoal gray workout gear and slip on the running shoes I'd laid out side by side the night before. My jet-black hair is just long enough to pull back in a tight ponytail, clean and manageable. This takes four attempts to get perfect, but the finished product has absolutely no strays.

None.

Annie retreats to the kitchen as I make the bed, taking my time to perfectly crease every edge and tuck in the sheets. I also spend a moment with some water and a paper towel, scrubbing down two faint smudges on our floor where Annie's filthy running shoes briefly trod.

"I only schedule half an hour for this," I remind her as we step out onto our front stoop. "We can't take long."

"I know, Vera," Annie patiently confirms, thankfully more amused than annoyed by my incessant programming. At this point in our relationship, that's a goddamn miracle.

The morning is brisk, but the slowly rising sun already feels pleasant and warm against my skin as we set out on our trek. We head down our front steps then take a sharp turn on the sidewalk, tightly packed apartments and town houses finally giving way to wide open space as our block reaches the edge of the park.

Facing north, a glorious view of the Chicago skyline opens up before us, distant buildings looming over our quaint neighborhood square. This adorable parcel of green grass isn't quite as impressive as the grand 1,200 acres of Lincoln Park across town, but it gets the job done.

Annie goes to cross the street when a sudden movement from the corner of my eye prompts this morning's second instinctual reaction. Again, I reach out for Annie, only this time I manage to grab her collar and yank her back as a blue sedan comes flying around the corner with a loud screech, music blaring.

The vehicle rumbles into a nearby gravel parking lot and comes to a grinding halt across two spaces.

Anger surges within me. For the briefest moment, I consider yelling out or storming over there, but I hold myself back. Somehow, I find the balance to remember the stakes of the day. I need to stay focused and pick my battles.

One action I *do* take, however, is to pull Annie a little closer. I slip my arm around her waist as we make our second crossing attempt, much safer this time.

Glancing over my shoulder, I catch sight of the driver opening his car door. The man hops out, head down and long, ratty hair hanging like a mop. An unkempt beard covers his face. Above him, a large green sign reads: POKER ROOM.

"Asshole," I mumble under my breath, watching as the man hustles inside.

"What?" Annie asks, confused.

It's then that I realize she's already moved on. Instead of looking behind us, Annie's focus is straight ahead. She's charting our journey down a winding cement path, enjoying the lush, emerald green trees that line our morning walk.

"Nothing," I reply, shaking my head.

"You thinking about today?"

"I wasn't, but *now* I am." I laugh.

"And you're nervous?"

I nod. "Always."

"Vera, you should be *excited*. You've been working on this book for *so long*."

"I'm not nervous about the book," I clarify.

Annie considers this, momentarily silent. A dog walker strolls past us. A delivery truck beeps in the distance. The city is waking up.

"You know, you can always wait," Annie finally says. She's extending an olive branch, being the merciful, patient, loving partner that anyone would kill to hold so close at a moment like this, and all those qualities are exactly why I can't take her up on her offer. She deserves better.

I shake my head. "I'm doing it today."

Annie can't help the way my response makes her lips curl up at the corners. The grin is such a genuine display of joy that she immediately glances down, covering it up. She nuzzles her body even deeper into mine, her head pushing hard against my shoulder.

The sun has finally made its grand entrance, sitting low on the horizon and painting the sky with a streak of brilliant pink across what's left of the night. We've reached a little glen at the far end of the park, a place where our path opens onto a small courtyard with some benches and a modest centerpiece fountain trickling away. This is just about where my morning walk transitions into a run.

"Look!" Annie shouts, suddenly breaking away from me and crouching down.

She returns with a grimy copper penny between her fingers, holding it up for me to see.

"Heads," she announces. "It's your lucky day."

"I feel so much better about coming out to Mom now," I state dryly. "What could go wrong?"

When I catch sight of the penny's date, however, the faintest sparkle of childlike excitement ignites within me.

"My birthday year," I say, nodding at the coin.

"What are the chances?" Annie chirps, her eyes widening a bit.

I laugh, moving to press onward until I notice the expression on her face. "Oh, you actually want to know."

I can see now what Annie's doing, but I don't deny her efforts. This is my day, after all, and if my girlfriend wants to pretend she's interested in my probabilistic ramblings for the next twenty-four hours, then who am I to stop her?

"Well, the very first United States pennies were minted in 1793," I explain. "Which was . . . two hundred and thirty-three years ago."

"Then the odds of you finding this coin are one in two hundred and thirty-three," Annie interjects, jumping ahead.

"Not really, no," I counter, unable to help myself. "Most people think like that when they're calculating odds, but we don't exist in a vacuum. It's not just about my birth year, because that's only one variable. You have to factor in us going for a walk between the specific times that someone dropped this penny and the potential future when you pick it up. Also, some years they produced more pennies than others. The fact that we're near a fountain probably bumps up the odds significantly, since people toss coins in, but you *also* have to consider the fact that older pennies are taken out of circulation. On the other hand, the popularity of financial apps and payment services has led to a steep decline in physical currency, which means even less coinage, which means a lower probability of finding small change, and I'm sure the fact that we're in a metropolitan, tech-savvy area only amplifies that effect."

I could go on, but I fumble when I notice the checked-out look on Annie's face. She's trying her best, forcing a smile and nodding along out of kindness and encouragement, but I'm smart enough to see through it.

"Let's just call it one out of two hundred and thirty-three," I offer, my love just enough to numb the discomfort of this approximation. I take the penny between my thumb and pointer finger, then draw it in for a better look.

Annie accepts. "I'm just impressed you knew the first pennies were minted in seventeen-ninety-whatever."

"Ninety-three."

"Yeah, that."

"I used to collect coins when I was little," I explain. "It kinda got me into numbers and probability. There was this book that told you which ones were rare and why. I had a whole collection."

"That's very cute," Annie says. "Are you about to tell me we have a million-dollar quarter tucked away in our closet?"

I shake my head. "Mom made me spend them. Said it was a waste of time holding on to spare change instead of thinking about real money."

"How old were you?"

"Five."

Annie is silent.

"I had these little gold star stickers," I continue with a laugh. "I'd put them on all the coins in my collection. That way, I'd know which ones were for keeping and which ones were for spending."

My girlfriend's expression falters. Her gaze is no longer one of mind-wandering absence, but dialed-in intensity. "Are you fucking with me?" she asks.

"I don't . . . think so?"

Annie grabs the coin from my hand and turns it around, shoving it back in my face so I can see what's on the tails side.

It takes a moment to understand what I'm looking at, but when my eyes finally finish negotiating with my brain I feel an odd sense of disappointment wash over me. On the back of this penny are the barely visible remnants of what appears to be a sticker, the shape eroding over time but leaving a faint white residue. It's been worn down to just three points now, but it certainly would appear that long, long ago, a full gold star was here.

My face scrunches up without my permission, brow furrowing and jaw tightening.

I'm vaguely aware that my reaction is unusual, and this suspicion is confirmed by Annie's rapidly souring expression. She clearly expected me to burst with excitement, like I'd just witnessed the prestige of some decades-long magic trick.

That's not what happens, though. Annie understands that a coin returning after all these years would be rare, but I doubt she has a grasp on just *how* rare that would be. I can't bring myself to use the word *impossible,* because technically speaking it's not correct (and technicality is my specialty), but the scenario she's laid out is certainly standing on impossible's doorstep. These odds are something to be measured in *orders of magnitude,* not ordinary numbers.

Suffice to say, where others might see a miracle, I see yet another moment when I'm forced to be the asshole who rains on everyone's parade.

"That's not mine," I tell her flatly.

"Are you *kidding* me?" Annie shouts, throwing her hands up. "A gold star!"

"I'm sure other people have put stickers on pennies."

"This is your exact sticker," she cries, opening my hand and shoving in the coin, then manually closing my fingers around it.

I shake my head. "It's almost *unquantifiable* how unlikely that is," I inform her. "You don't understand."

She just stares at me, pouting.

"This is literally my job," I remind her.

Annie finally breaks. "You are so *annoying*," she says, rolling her eyes. She leans in and kisses me, quickly untying all the tension I've been cultivating. "You're lucky we're celebrating your book today."

"Are you gonna make me keep this stupid penny?" I ask.

"Up to you," she says, kicking back into gear and continuing past the fountain. "Let's go."

"That's my line," I counter. "I don't know how I feel about you being this on the ball."

"Just wait until tomorrow!" Annie calls back. "I'll sleep until noon and have cold pizza for lunch!"

As Annie continues ahead I hesitate, staring down at the coin in my hand. Taking in this little round piece of copper, I picture its hypothetical journey over the years, imagining it riding in other pockets and dancing through countertop change jars just to return to its rightful owner by some incredible, surreal coincidence.

I suppose there *is* a little magic in that idea, but wonder is hardly the emotion creeping through me. Instead, I can't help the unexpected sense of dread that's slowly twisting my stomach into knots.

Annie is getting farther ahead by the second, so without another moment's hesitation I toss my lucky penny into the fountain.

I don't make a wish.

♣ ♥ ♦ ♠

Gazing into this mirror, most folks would see a twenty-seven-year-old woman in a slick, well-tailored blazer with a stark white button-up underneath, the fabric neat and pressed and *perfect* in a way that's so subtle it barely registers. They'd see a professional.

The secret is simple enough, just taking that little bit of extra time to steam and iron my clothes even if they don't appear to need it—*especially* if they don't appear to need it—because the details matter.

My dark hair is cut sharp at the shoulders, so precise it makes my typically rounded face seem slightly more angular. I like this because it makes me look, not *better* in a broad sense, but neater.

Anyone who burst into this restroom would find a woman who has *something* figured out, defying her youth and becoming a force of nature, or maybe some elemental force of success, years before she'll reach her thirties.

Statistically, I'm way ahead of the curve, and I should give myself a little praise for that, but instead my mind is unable to tear away from a runaway tuft of hair at the top of my head.

What *they* see is a badass self-starter who's already made a mark and will only rocket higher from here; what I see is an awkward cowlick.

I turn on the faucet and get my hand a little wet, then reach up and press down this renegade tassel jutting playfully from the edge of my razorlike center part. I push gently at first, then harder when this doesn't do the trick.

A bit more water seems to help, but by the time I'm satisfied with my hair I glance down to find that my perfect white shirt now features an awkward splash across the front.

"Fuck," I snap, my hazel eyes going wide.

I glance around to discover there are no paper towels left in this tiny restroom, so I'm forced instead to hurry over to a hand dryer. I slam the shiny button with my palm, producing a loud metallic clang followed by the roar of hot air rolling across my chest.

I pull out my phone and note the time. We're still on track to order food by noon, but not by much.

Once my shirt is sufficiently dried, I turn back to the mirror and start the whole process again, checking my hair but also my makeup. I admire my shirt's crispness for a second time, as well as the smooth, fashionable fit of my skirt. The starkness of my outfit looks good against the dark green floral wallpaper behind me.

I intentionally loosen my jaw, which I've been clenching so tightly that I actually notice a faint ache in one of my back teeth.

Whether it's your fit for a book launch party, or a penny traveling around the country for two decades just to end up at your feet, every little thing matters. It's a cosmically grand truth to consider, but the longer I let it marinate, the more terrifying it gets.

I turn and leave the restroom with my shoulders back and my expression playful. From around the corner I can hear my friends chatting excitedly, their voices cascading over one another in the joyful din of this hip Chicago diner.

"Well, where the fuck is she?" someone calls out, teasing and enthusiastic despite the biting words.

I exit the hallway and throw my arms open in an exaggerated gesture to mark my return, my sudden appearance prompting a cheer from the table of my dearest friends.

"There she is!" comes another eager voice, that of my buddy Kevin who's seated at the far end.

I can see now that our waitress is hovering nearby, a notepad gripped in her hand as she dutifully anticipates further instruction. She's already an absolute saint for dealing with a party this large, and I certainly don't want to cause her any more trouble.

"I'm ready, I'm ready," I announce, signaling the woman to start. "Just get to me last."

I sit down in an open chair next to the one member of our brunch who is noticeably older than the rest, a tall, poised woman who bears a striking resemblance to myself.

"Your friends are so nice," my mother gushes in my ear.

I open the menu, scanning my choices and nodding along to Mom's high praise.

Maria Norrie is a ferocious woman, the kind of mother who'd do anything for you, but is also frightening thanks to this exact quality. When I was younger, I was utterly terrified by the prospect of disappointing her—so terrified that disappointment never arrived.

There was *one time* in high school when I'd snuck out to smoke some weed with the kids down the block, a rare opportunity due to the fact that I'd just moved and didn't have many friends yet. Somehow, my mother realized I was gone, and she was waiting quietly in the kitchen when I snuck back in through the side door. She didn't say a word, just stared like a quiet specter of death, and that was enough for me to never sneak out again.

Now *that's* power.

Mom's strict nature left me with plenty of issues, enough to opine my way through three different therapists over the years, but it also shaped me into a well-oiled success machine.

Fortunately, Maria has softened with age, vaguely transitioning into the warm, caring mother I always yearned for, but somehow that's *even more* frustrating in the grand scheme of things.

Regardless, the fear lingers. Maria's been down from Lake Geneva for three days now, and I don't feel any closer to finding my nerve around her. I'm finally starting to realize that the confidence may never come, and I'll just have to push through today's conversation without it.

Mom drives back to Wisconsin tomorrow, and time gives no fucks whether I'm ready or not.

The waitress suddenly realigns my focus, sidling up next to me as she reaches the end of her order sheet. "You know what you'd like?" the woman questions. The name ACORN CAFÉ is emblazoned across the front of her shirt.

I hesitate, staring at the menu and struggling to keep this cascade of options from boiling my already deep-fried brain. It's not just about which food item I should purchase, it's about the thousand other ridiculous things that come along with this seemingly innocuous choice. If I order a large plate, will my mother say something to make me feel weird about it? If I order a salad, will she tell me that I haven't respected the momentous nature of this special occasion?

The book isn't even out until Tuesday, for fuck's sake. We're doing this because she's in town.

Annie, who sits directly to my right, leans in close. "Celebrate," is all she says, then winks.

I turn back to the waitress. "I'll get the breakfast burger," I decide, "and another mimosa."

As the waitress leaves I catch my mother's expression shifting into an immediate frown, her true feelings caught from the corner of my eye. Very quickly, however, something extraordinary happens. Maria's face pulls itself back into position, gradually becoming an accepting, almost excited nod.

"That looks good, Vera," she announces. "I should've ordered that."

It's a new day for the Norries, apparently. Maybe our pattern, after all this time, has started shifting and mutating into something new.

These changes come slowly, so small and incremental that I didn't even notice them until, one day, I woke up with a sweet, semiprogressive mother my friends actually like who doesn't make me feel like trash for ordering a breakfast burger on my stand-in publishing day.

Annie scoots back and stands, quickly drawing the attention of our packed table of friends. There're ten or so of us gathered around this little corner of Acorn Café, but somehow Annie has no problem focusing all the light in the room.

She's got something special, a loud, freewheeling counterbalance to all my rigid plans and patterns. That's why I love her.

"Alright, alright," Annie begins, hoisting her bright orange mimosa into the air as a hush falls over the rest of us. "I just wanted to take a moment and recognize the reason we're all here."

Annie nods toward me, flashing a slightly bucktoothed smile that brims with so much charm I actually feel my breath catch for a moment. As she turns the full heft of her attention my way it feels as though I'm staring directly into the sun, in awe of her power. It takes everything I've got not to turn away and avert my eyes, but the longer I hold this position, the more an uncontrollable smile widens across my face.

Annie loves doing this to me. I told her to play it cool until I had a chance to talk with Mom, but Annie's roguish nature has gotten the best of her.

Still, despite my mother's great intelligence, she's just too old-fashioned to pick up on the subtext of our glances and gestures.

"We're all so proud of you," Annie continues. "It's kinda frightening how much you've accomplished—and I know you hate being recognized for it—but now here we are with the youngest mathematics professor in U Chicago history, *and,* after this Tuesday, a published author!"

"*Statistics and probability* professor," I chime in, "but close enough."

Annie begins to tilt back her drink, then hesitates. I can tell she wants to say something more, to let the aching love within her spill out *just* a little further and give the world a peek. She's on a very sincere wavelength, and the drinks are only adding to the warm, fuzzy feelings that bubble up within her.

Annie's freckle-framed lips part ever so slightly, but I immediately shake my head with the faintest, almost imperceptible movement.

The timing of these things is important, because *everything* is important. I didn't get into this position by fucking around and letting the chips fall where they may. I got here by understanding that every infinitesimal detail can tip the scales in enormous, earth-shattering ways. Nudge Theory is this very idea in practice, but usually the term is used to describe massive corporations cutting corners or politicians edging out the competition by a fraction of a polling point.

In the United Kingdom, analysts found they could convince

people with outstanding tax bills to pay up when they used language specifically designed to make it seem like everyone else had already paid. This small change in wording on their government forms prompted a 15 percent bump in responses. If organ donation programs are an opt-in service, approximately 15 percent of people will join. However, if you're *automatically* enrolled and given an option to opt out, only about 10 percent of people will leave.

To be honest, there's a lot of bullshit in the field of choice architecture, and these very studies have been pulled apart, criticized, and debunked in a variety of ways. It's pop science from airport books rather than hard data, but that doesn't make it obsolete.

It's still worth considering the fact that little movements can have big results.

If Annie spills the beans right now, the statistical odds of my mother accepting our relationship are slim. As much as it hurts to shake my head and move Annie along, the nudge is important.

I mouth a single word to her: *No.*

"To Vera!" my girlfriend shouts without missing a beat, finally throwing back her mimosa with a massive swig. This prompts the rest of our crew to follow suit with cheers of their own.

Annie returns to her seat.

"That was really sweet," I offer.

Her response is a forced smile, the sign of someone who's trying desperately to keep her real emotions at bay, at least for the time being. She knows Maria will be out of our hair by tomorrow afternoon, at which point she'll drive back home and we won't have to think about it anymore.

Unfortunately, that's just not good enough. I can't bear to see her feeling this way, to see that incredible light within her dimmed and trembling.

I'm so focused on Annie that I barely notice a brewing chant from the rest of my friends. It's a single word repeated playfully, at first, and then with growing intensity as they start rapping their palms against the table and clinking their glasses.

"Speech! Speech! Speech!" they rumble, louder with every passing round until, eventually, other patrons start glancing our direction.

"*Okay!*" I finally shout, leaping to my feet in an effort to calm them down.

The table relents, falling back into silence as their eyes come to rest on mine.

I take a moment to look from one smiling face to the next, then clear my throat. "Thanks. Uh. Wow," I stammer, still collecting my thoughts. "I guess I'll add that the real people we should be recognizing today are the two point eight million American fraud victims who are taken advantage of every year."

Expressions falter slightly, but my friends manage to hold it together. They care about the *publication* of my book, but not the book itself.

"Yeah Vera!" Kevin shouts from the back, his lone voice forcing me to crack the faintest smile.

"I know it seems kind of silly how much this stuff matters to me," I admit. "Everett Vacation and Entertainment have done an incredible amount of damage to good, hardworking people, and I'm just so glad this book is finally coming out. They say the house always wins, but . . . this is a win for us."

From the seat to my right, Annie reaches out and places her hand against my leg, a gesture of reassurance and pride.

"We love you!" someone cheers.

The whole table laughs.

"I love you, too," I reply. "I know I haven't been the greatest friend while working on this book. I'm not making excuses, it's just . . . I'm sorry. Thanks for sticking with me and helping me push through to the other side. I won't forget it."

I raise my glass and tilt it back, allowing yet another glorious swig of sugary citrus mimosa down the hatch. I can certainly feel it now, and while I don't typically enjoy the sensation of being drunk, this buzz is actually helping me to chill the hell out and enjoy today for what it is. We're here to party, after all.

Maria leans in, pulling my attention to the left. "I like your roommate."

I tense up, searching for any extra weight within her declaration. The word *roommate* is historically loaded in queer circles, but I can't fathom my mother being aware of that fact. If Mom *is* dropping hints, that could potentially reframe the conversation I've been dreading this entire trip, but as I hold her eye I sense no bridge being extended between our worlds.

She just likes Annie, which is fair. I do, too.

"I'm so happy for you, sweetheart," my mother continues. "I told everyone back home about your book. They're all buying a copy."

I laugh. "Thanks, Mom. I'll need all the help I can get."

Maria hesitates, shifting in her chair a bit. "Someone tells me you've found a little helper right here in the city. A new boyfriend?"

Here we go.

I scan the table, hunting for the culprit who might've accidently slipped some confidential intel to my mother. My friends aren't used to keeping things tight-lipped, as we don't typically have someone's parent sitting in on these tipsy little brunches.

Whoever it was didn't leak the whole story, but at this point it might not matter. Maybe this is the opening I've been looking for.

I can feel my body flushing with heat and my heart speeding up, as though I'm cresting the hill of a rollercoaster.

"Fiancée, actually," I finally announce, forcing the pithy correction through my lips.

Maria's eyes go wide. "Sweetheart, no. What? That's so . . . impulsive."

The two of us stare at each other for a moment, a looming sense of dread creeping through my veins. Years of examples have taught me to fear the rest of this interaction, but then again, this is the new and improved Maria Norrie, a woman who has shed the trappings of her own toxic upbringing and entered a tolerant, enlightened era.

She's angry, I can tell, but she's doing everything she can to brace against those crashing emotional waves. The ship of her mind is taking on water, but she's also sealing off various blast doors, accepting defeat in some ways but insuring her survival in others. Eventually, Maria seems to ease herself into calmer tides.

Instead of rage, a flicker of curiosity glimmers behind my mother's eyes.

"Well, who is he?" she asks, glancing around the table.

Oh boy. All hands on deck.

There's a lump in my throat, some last stand by the part of my brain that would rather put off this conversation forever. I force my words past it.

"Who is *she*?" I counter.

Mom's expression shifts rapidly, bouncing through three distinct emotions. At first she actually smiles, a hint of laughter bubbling up within her upon hearing what would only make sense as a silly little joke. Next comes fury, with a hint of disgust, a brief flare of heat before her better self can jump in and wrestle back the reins.

My mother lands somewhere I didn't expect, however: denial.

"You've always been impulsive, but not *that* impulsive," Mom states, breezing past my admission as though it never even occurred. "You need to get serious about finding a real relationship, Vera."

"I just told you I'm engaged," I say, doubling down.

Mom leans in closer, lowering her voice to the point that I can barely hear her. "You're not gay, sweetheart. You're experimenting."

I shake my head. "No, Mom."

Her denial is unrelenting. "This is normal in college."

"I'm a *professor*," I scoff.

My mother lets out an exasperated sigh, pulling back a bit to reassess the situation. She looks at me, then Annie—who is deep in conversation with someone else—then back at me. A scowl has worked its way across her face.

"I don't see my daughter for six months and suddenly she's a gay?" Mom exclaims, a little too loud and oozing with skepticism.

"Bisexual," I snap.

Instant relief floods her body as her doubts are finally confirmed.

"Vera, bisexuals don't exist," she counters, her voice tinged with laughter.

I've somehow managed to remain calm this entire time, but there's something about my mother's choice of words that immediately sends my already wobbly house of cards crashing down. Maria has said things to me containing exponentially more vitriol than this throwaway line, but maybe that's what makes her statement so brutal. She really, truly means it.

What I've built with Annie is deeply important, but it will never be enough to satisfy people like my mother. A furious and belligerent rejection might've felt better in this moment, because at least I'd know she was taking me seriously.

"Are you fucking *kidding me*?" I suddenly growl, emotions boiling over and making themselves known.

"Language," Mom retorts.

"Get the fuck out of here," I spit, loud enough for the whole table to awkwardly stop what they're doing. The cheerful conversations that had once disguised our little sidebar have now fallen away, revealing the raw, seething nature of our confrontation.

Mom says nothing, frozen in place.

"Go," I rumble.

It's only now that I can see the tears welling in her eyes, the emotional whiplash between these timid revelations and my sudden anger proving too much for her after all.

Mom stands abruptly, grabbing her bag and turning so hard that her foot catches the leg of our table and generates a sudden, rattling bang.

Now the whole restaurant is watching, din falling away to highlight the horrible sound of my mother's frustrated sobs. As cathartic as it felt standing up to her like this, the second I see the emotional torment it's causing her my demeanor shifts. I snapped back in an effort to defend myself, and that's not something I regret, but it was never my intention to hurt her in return.

"Aw, fuck," I groan, scooting back my chair and hurrying after Mom.

She's already made it halfway out the door.

Annie reaches over and squeezes my hand as I go, one last moment of reassurance.

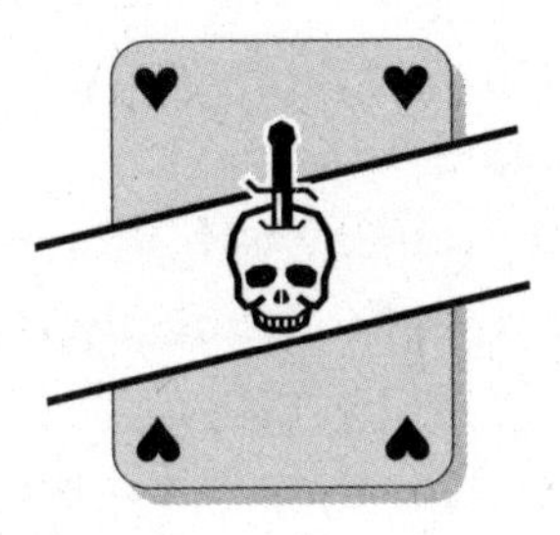

MONKEY WITH A TYPEWRITER

I barrel out of the restaurant, frantically calling after my mother as she hustles away from me down the sidewalk. The late morning light is crisp and golden, shining between towering buildings all around us as I jog to catch up with her.

There's plenty of other people out here on the bustling streets of downtown Chicago, but in this new setting my mother's wild sobs are drawing much less attention than they were at the restaurant. The folks passing by don't give her a second glance, too concerned with their own metropolitan business on this clear spring day.

Someone is giving a speech at the park across the street. A busker sits on a nearby corner, drumming enthusiastically on his upturned bucket. Two tourists ask someone for directions, then point at their phone map in a state of confusion.

There are thousands of stories unfolding in this city, and ours is just one more.

"Mom! Stop!" I scream, finally giving my voice enough authority that she has no choice but to listen.

My mother halts in the middle of the sidewalk, her tall form looking somehow meek and small next to the towering brick wall beside us. She slowly turns around to face me, struggling to regain a shred of emotional control.

"I'm sorry," Mom blurts. "I'm *trying* to support you, but this is so much, Vera. It's *so much*."

"What is?" I ask. "I'm fine, Mom. Actually, I'm *great*. Look at this life I've made for myself. You really think this is something you need to cry over?"

She glances away momentarily, her lips tight and quivering. In this unexpected moment of silence, I notice Mom's eyes drifting across the street to the park, her gaze wandering over a broad assortment of gathered protesters.

"The world's changed a lot," she says. "I've changed with it, I really have, but there are some things inside us that are . . . consistent. People have patterns, Vera. This little phase is something *everyone* goes through, at some point, but you can't let it derail you. You're on a great path."

I scoff. "I understand patterns, Mother. That's literally my job."

Mom's eyes widen a bit, her jaw somehow tightening even more. "Your father had his little midlife crisis, too" she hisses. The anger she's worked so hard to contain is now boiling behind every word. "Everything was *just right*, then he left us."

"I'm twenty-seven," I remind her.

"You're on a *perfect* track. One little slip is all it takes before . . ." She trails off.

"Before?" I ask.

"The partying. The late nights. The *sex stuff*,"

"Mom, I *love* Annie," I exclaim, cutting her off.

"No, you don't!" she growls, shaking her head as she grows even more confident in her denial. "You'll see. I know you think you do, Vera, but girls these days are just looking for something. I've heard *all* about it on the news, this bisexual thing. More and more young people identifying as bisexual or *transgender*." A literal shudder courses through her body. "These things aren't *real*, Vera."

My mother hesitates slightly, even more kernels of some deep, primal fear popping within her.

"This is going to affect the rest of your life," she finally continues.

"It's who I am!" I yell, cutting her off and relieving myself from this torrent of utter bullshit.

"It's not," Mom snaps, giving me the distinct realization that we're running in circles now, spiraling down a drain without a plug in sight. "This isn't the little girl I raised. I love you so much, Vera. I want you to be happy, but *you* of all people should know this is a *trend*. I have to put my—"

Mom stops abruptly, her swollen red eyes drifting over my shoulder as her expression shifts into one of bewilderment.

I'm annoyed, of course, but when Mom's sight line remains transfixed on the scene behind me I can't help turning around and looking for myself.

It's started to rain, which is certainly unexpected given the blue skies above. The drops flicker as they cascade down, glinting like silver and bouncing awkwardly when they slap the pavement. They're slightly larger than usual, and oblong in shape.

My mother and I are tucked under an overhang, so the patter isn't striking us directly. However, just off the sidewalk I can see these droplets dancing in the street, and as I lean out a bit I quickly discover they're not droplets at all.

A tiny creature stares up at me in bug-eyed terror, no more than two of three inches long. It looks just as surprised to see me as I am to see it.

It's a fish.

This shower of tiny aquatic creatures continues whacking the pavement as every single pedestrian stops in their tracks, covering their eyes for protection but unable to keep from gawking skyward with awestruck curiosity.

It feels as though the whole world has paused to observe this bizarre moment, reveling in the majestic oddity of it all. As important as this conversation with my mother is, the tone has been completely upended by, for lack of a better word, magic. For the briefest moment, Chicago is quiet and still. The protesters across the street have halted their demonstration, and the bucket-drumming falls away. Nobody asks for directions.

This reprieve is broken when a few larger fish slam against the pavement, the impact killing the creatures instantly while their smaller friends continue flopping around in a futile struggle to breathe. A scream rings out, echoing through the streets, then another. The novelty is fading fast, ripped away by the escalating cries of human pain and scaly flesh against concrete.

A sudden crash causes me to step back, not entirely sure where the sound came from until I catch sight of a stark crimson blur rocketing toward my mother and me.

It's a swerving truck in cherry red, wheels screeching and body lurching as it cuts sideways across the opposite lane. I barely have time to comprehend what appears to be a massive king salmon resting halfway through the shattered window of the vehicle as it barrels toward us, the natural consequence of a giant fish crashing through your windshield.

With only a few yards of distance between us and the truck there's barely enough time to call out a warning, let alone pull Mom out of the way.

I leap back as the truck slams into the wall next to me, its runaway movement instantly halted with a sickening metallic crunch. My ears are ringing and I'm not sure why, but as I stagger from side to side I gradually realize the endless drone is the truck's horn being pressed and held.

The part of my mother that rests above her collarbone is bent awkwardly over what used to be the truck's hood, now a twisted mess of metal and glass. Her body shouldn't be able to contort this way, but it does. She's face down, her perfect hair now splayed and wild thanks to the blood and debris.

I rush toward Mom, shrieking in a way that's utterly foreign to me. I'm barely aware I'm even producing these sounds, focused instead on some tragic attempt to render aid.

Maybe she's fine. Maybe she's fine.

Of course, there's nothing to fix here, nothing left of her to repair. I'm going through the motions in a state of desperation, clinging to anything I can.

I frantically try pulling back the metal that surrounds my mother, but it's no use, and standing this close only serves to show how much damage has already been done. My feet stick a bit as I move around the vehicle for another approach, a bloody pool blooming across the sidewalk below us.

I need to do more. I have to help her.

There's nothing I can do, though, and now the cosmic gravity of this realization hits me so hard that I drop to my knees, unable to stay upright despite my best efforts.

My brain is screaming for me to *do something,* to fix this somehow, but my body is too overwhelmed for these commands to register. Other than the tears running down my face and the heart slamming within my chest, I barely feel *here* at all.

"This—this is a nightmare. This is a fucking nightmare," I stammer, my hands covered in blood as I struggle to push myself back up.

I say these words out loud as if that might somehow give them more potency, make them really *count* for something, but according to the car horn that's still blasting away in my ear, my declaration doesn't change much.

It doesn't change anything.

I start to say it again, this time even louder, but when I open my mouth nothing comes out but a ragged, horrible scream, an unfiltered expression of torment that I can't hold back any longer.

When my cry finally fades, I notice a full chorus of tortured howls still drifting through the air, spilling out from all around me. The voices echo down from skyscraper windows above, ring out from just across the street, and erupt right there on the corner. I stop and listen, unable to ignore the sound of these haunting shrieks as they chime in from all across the city.

This is so much more than a nightmare.

A deafening boom suddenly pulls my attention upward, and I barely catch sight of rolling orange flames as they lap against the side of a building across the park. Smoke billows like a towering black snake, winding into the sky.

But this tower of smoke is hardly the most haunting image that looms above.

A massive parade balloon drifts past, blocking out the sun as it glides between the skyscrapers. I've seen these helium-filled creations on television before, but never have I witnessed their astonishing size in person.

The balloon soars some three or four stories up, a colossal green dinosaur in a gray astronaut suit. This gigantic figure stares down at me with a wide, sharp-toothed grin, which might be fun and friendly if not for the horrific adornments that dangle just below it.

At first, I'm not entirely sure what I'm witnessing, my mind unable to accept this uncanny display. The problem is not just how *macabre* the scene is, but how astronomically *unlikely*. There are at least twenty ropes hanging from the parade balloon, the strands typically used by handlers to lead inflated characters along a route. Instead of guiding this balloon, however, it appears the chaperones have gotten swept up in their own ropes.

A host of lifeless bodies hang from the floating dinosaur, their corpses drifting down the street like puppets as they bounce against lampposts and twirl in the air. Every cadaver has a tangle of rope above it, somehow wrapping itself around each neck to create a sloppy noose.

I'm frozen in a state of mind-numbing shock, watching this ghoulish monstrosity pass by.

More cars slam into one another; honking, screeching, then crunching as they ricochet like pinballs. Pedestrians flee in a crisscross of belligerent panic, heading one direction before swiftly altering course when some new disaster blocks their path.

As a young couple sprint past me, a circular manhole cover blasts straight up, blown off its hole in a hissing discharge of steam. The metal disk carves through the running man's face like butter, cleaving flesh as it rockets skyward. The man reels in confusion, understanding that something's wrong but unaware his face is now a pulpy mess of red carnage and shattered bone. Somehow his eyes remain intact, but without their lids or brows his expression is one of permanent surprise.

The woman is shrieking.

The man reaches up and touches his face, gazing down at his hand for a moment and then collapsing to the pavement. His companion falls to her knees in a strange recreation of the moment I just had with my mother, only this time the mournful tableau is of lovers torn apart.

Lovers torn apart. This phrase echoes through my head over and over again, growing louder with every round as it slowly transforms into a piercing alarm bell.

Where's Annie?

I snap back from my trance, the tether between brain and body tugged into place as my feet kick into motion. I turn, stumbling at first and then finding my footing, my shoes leaving a trail of bloody tracks as they slam into the pavement.

It's a straight shot to the diner.

With a loud clatter I burst through the front door, barely able to stop myself as my wet soles slide and catch on the tile floor.

The café patrons have emptied out and left utter chaos in their wake. Tables are overturned and food is scattered everywhere, painting the walls and floor with splatters of ketchup, mustard, and spilled cola that still fizzes and pops as it pools across the remaining upright surfaces. A few of the windows are broken, the shattered glass streaked with blood like someone leaped through in desperation to escape.

"Annie!" I frantically call.

Another explosion—this one even closer—causes dust to cascade from the ceiling and the restaurant lights to flicker menacingly.

This unexpected rattle prompts a companion noise to drift from the back hallway. It blooms from the tucked-away corner where I'd emerged some twenty minutes earlier to join my friends at a celebratory brunch that seems so silly and trivial now. I hear excited, awkward shuffling, like someone rummaging through an old box of childhood toys in their attic.

"Hello?" I shout, taking a few cautious steps deeper into the mangled corpse of Acorn Café.

Behind me, a haunting song begins to ring out, the familiar retro rock number drifting through the streets. It sounds as though it's coming from everywhere and nowhere all at once, like every radio in Chicago has been tuned to the same station, tilted toward an open window, and cranked to maximum volume.

The first few bars of "Good Luck Charm" by Elvis Presley wash over me, smeared with ghostly reverberation as they rattle across hundreds of glass-covered buildings. "*Don't want a four-leaf clover, don't want an old horseshoe,*" Elvis bellows atop a country-tinged shuffle and walking piano line. "I want your kiss, 'cause I just can't miss, with a good luck charm like you."

I creep a few steps deeper, my eyes laser-focused on the back corner from which the odd shuffling emanates.

"Annie?" I call, a little softer now.

The rummaging abruptly stops, prompting my heart to skip a beat. My muscles clench tight.

In the distance, Elvis's voice has been joined by an air-raid siren.

Suddenly, there are pounding, frantic footsteps as a figure comes barreling past the corner. It's not Annie, but I immediately recognize this terrified face as another one of my brunch friends, Kevin.

"What the fuck is going on?" I shout, but he's too panicked to answer, too desperate and wild-eyed to register my words.

He's running so fast that he slams into the wall, bouncing off it then scrambling toward me as another figure comes lumbering behind.

I stagger back when I spot the enormous chimpanzee galloping after Kevin on its knuckles, massive teeth bared in a violent snarl. The outlandish sight of this ravenous primate is only heightened by the costume that covers its furry body, some strange Renaissance outfit featuring puffy white sleeves and a gaudy tunic that might be downright comical if not for the fact that it's covered in blood. The animal's holding something rectangular and black, a little larger than a shoebox.

"Run! Go!" Kevin shrieks, the words a tangled yelp as he leaps over a toppled café table in his mad dash for the door.

Kevin's panicked face stays locked in my mind's eye like a photograph. There's no doubt in his expression, no question whether this whole thing is real or just some wacky hallucinatory vision of the world's end. Up until this point, I think some skepticism still lingered within me, the lurking thought that I might be seconds away from bolting upright in bed, covered in sweat.

Kevin knows this isn't a dream, though, and now so do I.

The chimpanzee whips its arm forward, the force of this movement so powerful and animalistic that I flinch before I even understand why. There's a horrific crunch as Kevin slams onto the café tile, out like a light. The typewriter clatters to the ground next to him, its bent keys angled violently to the side after colliding with the back of his skull.

I let out a horrified shriek and stumble back, my scrambling legs pushing me all the way to the door and then out onto the sidewalk.

The air-raid siren has stopped, but Elvis is still bellowing. "*Don't want a silver dollar, rabbit's foot on a string.*"

The chimp leaps forward, baring its vicious maw as it navigates a maze of overturned tables, but the creature stops when it reaches the tangled body that now lies face down on the restaurant floor.

Blood is swiftly pooling around Kevin's head, and a long, aching groan escapes his lips in an expression of guttural, primal pain. He reaches toward me and struggles to drag himself onward, still hoping to put as much distance between himself and the chimpanzee as possible, but it's too late. The animal is already on his back.

The chimpanzee grabs its busted metal typewriter with long, muscular arms, lifting the heavy tool into the air and then bringing it down against the back of Kevin's head with a nauseating crack. It strikes Kevin's skull with unflinching strength, again and again and again and again, until the sound of the typewriter transitions from wet brain matter to the hard tile below.

I don't stick around to see what happens next, already sprinting in the other direction.

I find momentary cover behind an overturned semitruck, the contents of its shipment now spilled across the intersection in a massive pile of tiny wooden horses. They're painted in swirling shades of red, white, and green.

A strange recorded voice emanates from within the truck's cab, speaking in an odd monotone cadence and wobbling slightly as the station cuts in and out. It appears this is the only broadcast that isn't playing "Good Luck Charm."

"*Thirty-seven. Eighteen. Thirty-two,*" the woman on the radio says, then pauses as a digital chime sounds. "*One hundred and fifteen. Thirty-six. Fifty-two.*"

I press my back to the side of the truck, my eyes darting frantically as I struggle to catch my breath.

"*Thirty-seven. Eighteen. Thirty-two. One hundred and fifteen. Thirty-six. Fifty-two.*"

The words keep repeating over and over again as the chaos around me builds. A man with both arms severed at the shoulders sprints past, his body covered in shimmering gold paint and leaving a crimson-and-aureate trail in his wake.

Four squealing pigs hurry along in the other direction, plastic wings on their backs and cherubic angel masks strapped over their faces to produce a disturbingly humanoid appearance.

"Thirty-seven. Eighteen. Thirty-two. One hundred and fifteen. Thirty-six. Fifty-two."

Another massive explosion above me, twice as high as the tallest buildings but so loud and frightening that I actually duck and shield my eyes. Flaming debris blooms across the great blue in either direction, spreading out in the shape of farfalle pasta before gravity takes hold and starts pulling the pieces downward in a fiery rain.

Smoldering hunks of metal slam the pavement all around me, forcing me onward.

I leap from my cover behind the truck, making it no more than two steps before the whole world flips on its side and a horrible thump rings out, followed immediately by a sharp crack as pain radiates through my elbow.

The ground disappears as air blasts from my lungs in a hearty puff. I'm moving sideways now, traveling much faster than before. Red and blue lights flash across my field of vision, and somehow through all the chaos I realize that I've ended up on the hood of a police car. A cracked windshield spiderwebs out below me, its brand-new concavity cradling me like a bucket.

In the driver's seat, one of the masked pigs sits oafishly, sniffing the air without a care in the world. A headless police officer rides along beside the pig, the front of his blue uniform painted dark with fresh blood. He's strapped in tight, a seat belt across his chest and an upward-tilted shotgun between his legs. Brain matter and skull fragments decorate what's left of the roof above him.

Inertia holds me in place as we rocket from one side of the street to the other. There's a sudden bump when we launch over the curb, nearly bucking me off, then another resounding crunch as all this energy and movement stops on a dime. The windshield is no longer a cradle but a catapult, joining my voyage forward while the rest of the car stays locked against two pillars of concrete.

The crash ejects me in a spray of beaded safety glass, the windshield finally giving way. My body hurtles onward, flipping end over end through an open doorway. I land with a thud, then a roll, then a long slide across a smooth tile floor that alternates between red and black.

Eventually, I come to rest against a tall freestanding shelf, the structure rocking slightly as it absorbs what's left of my momentum. A faint sigh escapes my lips, the subconscious expression of every new ache and pain that has suddenly befallen my body.

The more I collect myself, however, the more amazed I become. Yes, I have bruises and scrapes, and my head is throbbing and my lungs are tight, and the blood filling my mouth is a sign that I bit my tongue during that last tumble, but overall I feel strangely fine. As far as I can tell, there are no broken bones or fractures, and certainly no irreversible bodily harm.

Not yet, at least.

As my gaze refocuses to the dim light of my new surroundings, I'm swiftly hit with the realization that I've spoken too soon. The freestanding shelf that towers above me has only one item on display: a giant framed mirror that now teeters precariously on a single hook. If it falls, those shards won't be as kind as the laminated safety glass of a car windshield.

I scoot away from the shelf and sit up a bit as my surroundings find a gradual clarity. Cruiser lights still flicker through the open door. They dance across the shadowy interior scene in a rolling pattern. Combined with the checkered tiles, this surreal illumination makes it feel like I'm at the center of a massive roulette wheel.

It's not actually a roulette wheel, however. I seem to have found myself on the first floor of a department store, though most of the space is shrouded in darkness. This is the home goods section, specifically where one might procure a vanity. Rectangular glass panels completely surround me, but even more concerning is the fully mirrored ceiling that hangs above, reflecting back my own horrified expression as I survey the massive crack that's jutting across its surface.

Outside, Elvis has finally transitioned into another track, the crooning voice of Dean Martin's "Who's Got The Action?" announcing itself over the dramatic noise of a world falling apart. Dean's voice soars over the din, accompanied by a chorus of clown horns, chainsaws, wolf whistles, bonks and boings, gunfire, and so, so much screaming.

One of these howls, in fact, is closer than I realized. Drawn by the crash, a grotesque figure staggers out from behind one of the shelves. The silhouette is vaguely humanoid, the general shape of a woman in a dress, but her arms are slightly longer than a person's and two massive antennae jut out from her face at awkward, violent angles. My breath catches at the sight of this creature.

The monster shrieks for a moment longer, whipping her head back and forth in frustration, then pauses abruptly. Her wailing stops as she holds this pose.

The figure takes a few steps forward, finally emerging from the darkness to reveal something even more horrible than any supernatural beast. This is a human being in terrible pain, disfigured in a way I could've never anticipated with a million different guesses. The antennae are not antennae. Instead, it appears this woman has had black, three-foot-long parasols shoved into both eye sockets. These closed sun-umbrellas are shockingly deep, destroying her eyes but also likely piercing her brain in a lobotomizing scramble. It's hard to say how much of *her* is still left, but it's enough to keep her body wandering around.

What I'd initially taken for elongated arms are actually normal hands gripping enormous kitchen knives. I understand the weapons—if this woman has retained any concept of what's going on around her, she's probably terrified.

Another massive rumble shakes the whole building, the reflective crack above us springing another crooked branch.

"Hey!" I call. "I know you're scared, but if we don't get out of—"

I can't even get the words out before the woman is sprinting toward me, arms flailing and blades glinting in the rolling flashes of red-and-blue light. Her screams echo through the department store.

I yelp, rolling to the side as the woman crashes into the shelf where I lay just seconds before. She hits it hard. The whole interconnected aisle rocks back as her knives clatter and clink against the metal.

I scramble away, but she senses this movement and comes swinging after me, her blades whipping past so close that I can feel the air displacement. Behind her, the shelves have tilted enough to finally catch the other side of their weight distribution.

The whole mirror aisle comes toppling down, a thousand years of bad luck cascading over the floor like a crystalline wave. It slams into the next aisle with a deafening crash, knocking that one back, then the next, and the next.

All the while I'm clambering through the darkness, desperately trying to put as much space between myself and these falling shelves and slashing knives as I possibly can. As if that weren't enough pandemonium, another mighty rumble shakes the building, rattling various appliances from their ledges and causing the giant crack above us to reach out even farther.

When the mayhem finally settles, I find myself trapped in a corner, tucked between the back wall and a heap of toppled shelves that run parallel for several yards. This new passage is a rough one, haphazardly aligned and sparkling with shattered glass, but worse yet is the simple fact that there's only one way out.

The woman with parasols for eyes stops jerking around for a moment, wobbling back and forth at the mouth of my escape route. Much closer now, I'm amazed at the sheer amount of blood that pours down her face and neck, staining the front of her dress in a giant crimson bloom.

She takes a few lurching steps toward me, her knives glinting in the flickering cruiser lights. This new passage is only five feet wide or so, close enough that I might bump into her while creeping past, or worse, find her blades deep within my gut.

I look over, considering crawling through the shards or making my way up over the busted shelves, but those potential escape routes are just not possible. The mirrored ceiling above us is an absolute mess, too, a labyrinth of cracks just aching to pour down on us in a sharp, artery-slicing rain.

Fifty-six percent of patients who are rushed to the hospital for a carotid artery wound are dead on arrival.

She takes a few more steps toward me, whipping her blades through the air. The parasols jammed into each eye socket bob and weave as she rolls her head back and forth, groaning loudly.

I'm pressed against the back wall, and somehow in this moment of panic a crackling shockwave of strategy comes rippling through my mind. I'm used to this feeling of inspiration being one of strict calculation, taking my time and playing the odds, but right now it doesn't feel that way. I'm not sure the odds matter anymore. Instead, raw instinct propels me forward, a drive for survival that lurks within my subconscious depths. There are certainly calculations here, but they aren't numerical.

The parasol-eyed woman is no more than five feet away now. She cocks her head to the side, listening intently.

Crack!

Across the mirrored ceiling, more giant lines spring from the heart of the web. It's seconds away from tumbling down.

My primal self takes hold, maneuvering without thought, strategizing by feeling. I reach out and grab a salt shaker from the ledge next to me, then hurl it against the opposite side of the aisle. The woman springs into action, lunging toward the clatter, and at this exact moment I rush past her. She jerks back, swinging a giant knife toward my neck and missing the soft flesh by a matter of inches.

I'm running, pumping my arms and legs with all the strength I can muster as a mess of swiping blades follows closely behind. At the end of the passage, I make a sharp turn toward the exit, and thankfully my pursuer continues onward into the darkness.

This is only half the battle, though. I don't let up, weaving through the toppled shelves and shattered glass. To my right, an escalator is barreling upward at quadruple speed, blood streaking the railings and chunks of flesh wedged between the steps. Nearby, a man I hadn't noticed before is stumbling through the shadows of the apparel section. He's dressed as a mime, silently fighting to pile a mess of hanging intestines back into a giant slit across his belly.

The rolling flicker of red and blue lights guides me onward, leading me through the chaos. Five more steps. Four more. Three more.

Another shudder finally causes the ceiling to give way, massive panes of glass splitting apart and tumbling downward in jagged chunks. I leap through the open door, rolling over the hood of the busted police cruiser. Plummeting sheets of mirrored glass crash down behind me, and somewhere deep within the department store a woman's frustrated screams are cut short.

I'm back on the street now, and things have gotten even more frenetic in my absence. A man in rabbit ears hangs by his wrists, dangling from a nearby lamppost. He kicks and squirms in the air, his feet severed as arterial spray pumps out onto the sidewalk below.

To my right, a cannon of rainbow confetti explodes, booming so loudly that I instinctually duck. A woman rockets past me, thrown from the massive barrel. She hits the opposite concrete wall so hard that it pushes her head and spine down into her torso.

My inner voice bellows a simple, one-word command: *RUN.*

I start moving, sprinting down the middle of the street as more chaos unfolds in a diabolical tidal wave. I'm vaguely aware that the fish have stopped falling, but that peculiar weather phenomenon has only been replaced by even more horrific and uncanny sights.

A flaming skeleton rolls past as I weave between overturned cars, the blazing body perched atop a vending machine that zooms down the avenue.

I don't stop running.

A woman sprints parallel to me for a moment, her body absolutely covered in arrow punctures. She looks like a pincushion, shot so many times that pure adrenaline is likely the only thing keeping her alive. The woman startles another survivor as she dashes by, prompting the frightened man to accidently fire off a bow he's been using to protect himself. It pierces her yet again.

"Oh my God," the man fumbles. "I'm so—"

Before he can finish, a rocket of green sparks whips past my head and plugs his open mouth. The firework emits a high-pitched whistle as it illuminates his skull with emerald flame, the man clawing at his face in an attempt to yank the explosive from his throat. He's a few yards behind me when I hear the pop.

I don't stop running.

Somewhere up ahead a crash rings out, glass raining down as a motorcycle launches through an office window four or five stories up. A ghastly rope of humans is dragged behind the vehicle, all of them shrieking with terror and confusion as they plummet toward the pavement below. I barely even look, just track this movement from the corner of my eye as I weave across the street to avoid them.

The falling bodies are dressed in shocking, vibrant colors, thumping against the concrete in rapid succession. It's only after I'm past the carnage that I realize they were dressed as clowns.

I don't stop running.

The noises start tapering off. Bells and whistles give way to the steady thumping of my heart, and eventually even that seems to fade. My legs are burning and my jaw is clenched so tightly that I think a tooth might crack.

If it did, would I notice? Would I care?

Miles and miles pass. I run until the city disappears behind me, and even then, I keep on pushing. The pain of physical exhaustion continues to bloom across my body, consuming me, and I'm amazed when this sensation transforms into a sort of overwhelming numbness. It feels as though I've disappeared, nothing more than an empty body in perpetual motion.

I don't stop running.

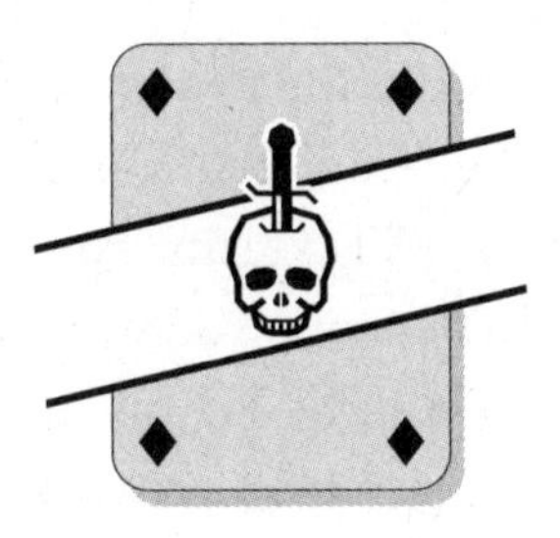

CHARRED BABEL LIBRARY

The ceiling looks the same this morning, but I feel slightly more detached from it as I crack open my eyes and peer up at the dull eggshell coloring. It's not a huge shift, but it's definitely there, and for a brief moment I bask in the tiny bit of solace it provides me.

After four years of lying here, these small changes feel monumental.

Somehow, just when I think all the care I have for this world is gone, I manage to care even less. To some, this might sound like a devastating, soul-crushing punishment, but to me it's a sweet morsel of relief, a step toward the cliff's edge.

Have you ever peeled off a sticker that was attached to something for years? A dainty gold star on a penny, maybe? At a certain point, the sticker starts melting into its base, whatever adhesive chemical that made it tacky gradually undergoing yet another mutation. Ripping off the sticker just leaves an outline, a ghostly white pattern in the vague shape of some colorful image that came before.

The memory of that image is an annoyance now, nothing more.

If you want to remove these scraps completely, get ready to spend your time scrubbing and tearing at every little piece, and even then, a bit of residue will likely remain. The leftovers get stuck under your fingernails. You realize you'll never remove this old sticker completely, never truly disconnect, but that doesn't stop you from yearning for the clean, cold surface you started with.

Here in Lake Geneva, Wisconsin, sprawled on the couch of what was once my mother's living room, *I'm* the ghostly outline.

After the first rip I thought I'd be lucky enough to vanish without a trace, but it doesn't quite work like that. Now I just hang around, a stubborn pattern holding the place of some other person.

To make matters worse, this time to think has made me just as terrified of the prospect of a clean break, no better at dying than I am at living. I'm getting closer to disappearing, though. Little by little, I'm working my way toward the inevitable. This path toward oblivion happens in the tiny moments, only hindered by a few rare, pestering feelings that flutter out of the ether and, if they're brave enough, beg me to matter. I don't listen.

Lately, I've started noticing the way the shadows stretch across my ceiling when seasons change, started perceiving some kind of face in the darkness, but before I get too invested in this quaint little observation I always manage to shed my hope.

It doesn't matter if it looks like a face.

It didn't matter when the grass started growing too long, wild yellow weeds reaching through the cracks in my driveway. It didn't matter when a bird flew through the bedroom window, blood splattering everywhere as it croaked and chirped and eventually died. The bedroom smells now, and I started sleeping in the living room, but nothing really *changed,* did it?

The bird was a year ago, although I'm not exactly sure. Maybe it was two years ago, or maybe it hasn't even happened yet. Time is a lot more malleable than we'd like to admit.

It takes a special kind of cosmic trauma to get to this place, but to me it's a fucking *blessing*—a wake-up call. Other folks might get bored puttering around their house all alone, letting the haunted structure fall into decay as the world rolls on without it. Eventually, they'd find something to pass the time, whether it was cracking open a book or turning on the radio or, yes, imagining faces in the shadows that stretch across their ceiling.

I don't do any of those things.

Yes, you do. If nothing matters, then why keep the lights on, Vera? Why pay the bills?

It's a good point, but the answer isn't quite as dramatic as one might hope for. I'm just too afraid to stop completely.

With Mom's life insurance and a little help from the May 23 Survivors Program, I still pay my electric bill and keep the water running. Taxes are still collected on this property, and the garbage trucks swing by every week despite the fact that I never put out my bins for collection.

Trash lies strewn across the floor, rotting away alongside me. Every once in a while, I'll gather up a bag and toss it into the backyard where a new pile has formed, surrounded by the overgrown, weed-filled garden my mother used to care for.

I can't be bothered to bring them around to the front on garbage day, especially since I haven't known what day of the week that is for a very long time.

The living room ceiling remains as subtle and featureless as always, a grand expanse of nothing I can't help sinking into. There're a few faint bumps and ridges up there, but for the most part it's just empty space.

A beautiful, endless void.

My stomach churns. I consider getting up and making some ramen, but eventually decide against this. Maybe when it gets dark. I could just sleep until then.

I'm about to close my eyes again when I notice an unexpected movement to my left, something stirring in the garden. From here in the living room I can see the backyard through a set of farmhouse-style French doors, their wooden surfaces featuring large squares of glass. I don't look out there often, but now I find my attention drawn to the base of the door where this slight movement continues.

It doesn't matter what it is, I remind myself. *It just doesn't matter.*

I stare at the ceiling in protest, stubbornly refusing to acknowledge my own curiosity.

Finally, however, my body can't help glancing over, this visceral drive to quantify the unknown just too much to bear. There, sitting inches from the glass, is a scrawny, scruffy black cat.

I lock eyes with the timid creature, lying here in silence as the two of us take each other in. I can only imagine how terrifying I look through the window, a gaunt, blanket-wrapped form with a wild bird's nest of long black hair.

The cat doesn't seem to mind, however. It reaches out and places its paw against the glass, swiping a few times before changing tactics. The mess of fur starts rubbing its head awkwardly against the pane, really getting in there as though scratching some itch it otherwise couldn't reach.

I don't smile. In fact, I don't react at all. Instead, I roll back over and stare at the ceiling, waiting until the annoying little beast meanders on its way. By the time I glance back at the door, the cat is gone.

I lie around a bit longer, the shadows in the living room stretching in the same quiet way they've done a thousand times before. Eventually, the painful ache at the pit of my stomach becomes too persistent to ignore, hunger gnawing away at me until I'm finally forced to peel my body from the couch and shamble into the kitchen.

My legs and feet sting a bit, facing serious atrophy after years of neglect. I open the pantry to find the jumbo-size flat of ramen I've been working through. The plastic wrap is shredded and open on the right side, each meal pulled out one by one rather than removing the packaging because, of course, that would take too much effort.

Unfortunately, this technique also makes it difficult to know when I'm about to run out of food, and that's exactly what has just happened.

I search through a few other cabinets, finding nothing but stray condiments and a handful of canned goods that have long since gone bad and I haven't found the time to throw out. Eventually, a deeply unfortunate realization washes over me: I've gotta go to the store.

The hassle of taking out my car isn't just about gassing up or maintaining the battery, which somehow always manages to fire off a charge on the very rare occasions I need it to. No. The problem I have with using my car is the same problem I have every time I walk past the gun sitting on my dining room table. Being around something so powerful, so capable of violence, forces me to confront just how nice a clean break from this life might actually be. It's an interesting pickle to be in. Too scared to take the leap, yet avoiding situations that might make that leap a little easier.

For a moment, my eyes flicker over to the dining room, lingering on the weapon that sits collecting dust right there in the middle of the table. I hesitate, staring at it like it's some religious artifact, then continue going about my business.

I wander onto the front porch and down the walk, making my way through a yard full of wild grass and weeds that reach so tall they might as well be wheat.

The car battery works, *hallelujah,* and soon enough I'm making the two-mile trek through suburban Wisconsin. I can only hope that someone traveling the opposite direction does me a solid and yanks their vehicle into my lane at the last second. The seat belt hangs loose by my shoulder, unused.

When I reach the grocery store I find a gathering in the parking lot, a large tent set up at the far end of the giant cement rectangle for a religious service of some kind. The competition for physical houses of worship has grown stiff as more people scramble for meaning after the Low-Probability Event, so new denominations have been forced outdoors.

I'm not sure which one this tent belongs to. These days, there are too many spiritual saplings to keep track of, especially for someone who actively avoids the outside world. More established modern sects—like the Mormons, Jehovah's Witnesses, or Kingdom of the Pine—have also ballooned in size, but they've smartly locked down the indoor community spaces. Meanwhile, the world's largest religions have kept buying land, breaking ground on a record number of behemoth megachurches over the last four years.

I park and get out of my car, head lowered as I focus on the task at hand. I refuse to shuffle through this hot summer air any longer than I have to. The conversations of strolling families drift past me as I walk, offering little hints of the outside world that I immediately push away.

None of it matters. Not a single word.

As I approach the sliding glass doors of the grocery store, however, an unexpected vision stops me in my tracks. My breath catches at the sight of a ragged, witchy woman creeping along behind me, and I'm genuinely panicked until I realize this is actually just a reflection of myself. My hair is so much longer than I remember, dark and wiry as it hangs down my back. My clothes don't fit anymore, either, the body under them wasted away. I'm so distracted by my own decaying visage that I hardly notice when the door doesn't slide open for me. After a good fifteen seconds, however, the surreal feeling of something *not quite right* begins to manifest.

I take a curious step forward, hoping to activate the door's automatic sensor, but get nothing in return.

I don't exist.

A young couple walks past me, triggering the door to open with a soft hiss.

Once inside the store, my mission becomes intuitive. I buy the same things every time: a large flat of chicken ramen, a box of crackers, and whatever basic house supplies I might need.

Grabbing a cart, I try my best to ignore the massive National Lottery display that sits to my right. Years ago, this section might be relegated to a single vending machine sponsored by the state, but things have certainly changed. The whole entryway of this store is now an immense, multicolored advertisement, with a separate checkout counter for those who've only come for their routine games of chance. Colossal golden letters hang proudly above this section with a simple proclamation. LUCK IS REAL, SO WHERE'S YOURS? it asks.

Down below this, in slightly smaller letters, is a darkly twisted addition. *A percentage of all profits go directly to the May 23 Survivors Program and victims of the Low-Probability Event.*

I suppose I shouldn't complain too much. As the child of a May 23 casualty, I get my checks just like everyone else.

Hoping to not be here long, I quickly get to work. I head for the ramen section first, opting for three flats instead of my usual single purchase. This should keep me from needing another trip any time soon.

The mission goes well enough, and I'm only distracted once as my attention drifts over to a fully stocked butcher's case. We're all made of the same flesh and blood, the exact same rotting proteins that rest cold and carved in the meat department. The difference between myself and a frozen steak sold at $5.93 a pound is that *I've* still got electricity pulsing through my brain—but that's only temporary.

As I turn to head for the checkout line, however, I suddenly feel a potent, nagging thought bubble up. It paws and whimpers and mews, begging for my attention.

What about cat food?

What *about* cat food? I'm here for necessities, just enough to keep some blood pumping through these veins while I disappear a little more.

It suddenly occurs to me that I'm standing directly before a wall of pet supplies, somehow ending up here through keen work from my deep, subconscious mind. I'm frozen in place, unable to escape the aching feeling that washes over me.

It's an ancient sensation left covered in dust and cobwebs that has somehow rumbled to life, awkward and bumbling after years of neglect. Whatever it is, it's still got a little bite, and I allow this warmth to work its way through my body even more.

I can sense a tear welling up in the corner of one eye, gently rolling down my cheek before I briskly wipe it away. A *tear*?

"Fuck" is all I can manage to say, clearing my throat awkwardly.

A flash of Annie's smiling face suddenly tears through my mind in a colorful explosion, a beautiful image that hurts so bad it nearly brings me to my knees. I recognize now what this sensation is: it's the feeling of actually caring about something.

I've gotta get out of here.

I spring into action, ignoring the pet food aisle and hustling onward to the front of the store. I catch a nearby security guard closely tracking this sudden movement, but I honestly can't blame him. I'd be skeptical of a witch, too.

I arrive at the closest register and start checking out, doing everything I can to forget about the cute little feline wandering around my backyard. When the woman behind the counter announces how much my tab is I can't even hear her, my head buzzing as if it's full of hornets.

"What?" I snap.

"Seventeen dollars and eight cents. Would you like to add a ticket for this week's National Lotto?" the woman repeats, mumbling slightly as she meanders through scripted language. "When luck is real, *anyone* can be a winner."

The National Lottery uses six numerical selections, each ranging from one to a hundred and fifty, so I briefly acknowledge the first string of digits that pop into my head—*Thirty-seven. Eighteen. Thirty-two. One hundred and fifteen. Thirty-six. Fifty-two.*

Unfortunately, the random radio transmissions of an overturned semitruck aren't going to provide me with a fairy-tale ending today. One of the few things I *have* managed to do through the malaise is check in on the National Lottery records, searching to see if this combination has *ever* come up.

It hasn't.

"No thanks," I say, handing over more than enough cash. I don't wait for any change, just turn and head for the exit.

"Okay?" the woman sighs.

Soon enough, I'm barreling out into the sunlight, headed straight for my car. When I arrive, I toss the food in and then collapse into the driver's seat, my heart slamming and my lungs feeling as though they can't quite catch a full breath.

It's here I remain, aching to reach out and turn the keys and get the hell out of here, but for some reason I just can't compel myself to do this simple task. I stare out the window instead, gazing past the parking lot and the cars and the trees beyond and the clouds that drift slowly overhead in an otherwise bright blue sky. In another life, I might think something like: *It's a beautiful day today.*

Slowly, I look down at the keys gripped tightly in my hand, realizing that my palm is starting to burn as I squeeze them into oblivion.

I relax my grip, then climb out of the car. There's still one more thing to pick up.

♣ ♥ ♦ ♠

I start leaving out small cans of wet cat food, setting them just outside the door where I saw the critter snooping around. The first night my offering goes completely ignored, but eventually I begin to notice little nibbles here and there.

When the food finally disappears I put out another portion, along with a small bowl of water.

It's a good while before I actually see the cat with my own eyes, but soon enough I start to notice her skinny little frame creeping around in the tall grass.

I call her Kat. This skittish feline is as wary of me as I am of her, each of us skeptically testing the waters of this new relationship. From the animal's perspective, a giant human lurking in the darkness of this dilapidated home could easily be setting a trap, playing the long con and coaxing her closer and closer until, one day, poor Kat is snatched up and devoured. The threat to Kat is bodily harm, a visceral and direct consequence after her careless mistake of letting me in. Of course, I'm not going to hurt the tiny creature, but she doesn't know that.

The cat's threat to *me,* however, is much more complicated than the instinctual urge of biological survival. Opening myself up to *hope* has implications that go far beyond any physical suffering I might incur.

For the first few days, I somehow manage to ignore the consequences of our developing connection. It's not that I've talked myself into caring about this absurd mess of a world, it's that I've blocked out my thoughts entirely. I put out Kat's food on autopilot, letting my body do the work while my brain rests quietly in the back seat.

Eventually, however, I start getting curious when I don't see the bag of bones coming by for her evening snack, and a wave of relief washes over me when she finally emerges to lap up a soggy puck of compressed chicken.

Instead of worrying about things like whether I'm gazing at the ceiling with enough indifference, I start watching Kat as she roves around the backyard, stressing over her frail body despite the fact that I'm feeding her on a regular basis. *Maybe she needs a different kind of food?*

The water on my stovetop starts boiling, pulling my focus toward it. I unwrap a package of ramen and toss it in.

Outside, a fresh portion of cat food sits undisturbed, but it's only a matter of time before my friend comes along for her evening meal. The animal is later than usual. That's not a problem for me, though. The only thing on my calendar tonight is waiting for a pot of noodles to cook.

Surrounded by kitchen drawers, I find myself sizing up a particular handle. This built-in storage is positioned by the front door, the first thing I see when I turn the corner and head for the fridge.

Most people would call it a "junk drawer," but in a house like this, that phrase could apply to any cabinet or cubby.

I stare at the drawer for a moment, remembering what lurks within. After disconnecting myself from all the worldly attachments I could manage, forgetting this formerly ubiquitous device was simple enough. It used to mean so much, used to melt through any spare time I had like a perpetual flame, but when there's nobody left to call, it gradually transforms into little more than a flat rectangle of glass and metal.

Now, however, the thought of that luminous glow against my face sounds kind of nice.

Even more potent is the simmering curiosity that pumps through my veins, a stomach-turning temptation. I'm skeptical that I'm ready for that kind of high dive just yet, but for some reason I just can't tear my eyes away from the drawer. Instead of backing down, I walk over and grip the handle. I slowly open it up to reveal an assortment of letters and bills, spare keys, coins with some buttons mixed in, a garage door opener, and one final item that immediately gives me pause.

My old cell phone rests at the dead center of it all, screen dark and silent like some ominous tomb that's crawling with spiders and skeletons.

I glance over my shoulder, peering onto the back stoop to find Kat's food has still gone unclaimed. She's taking her time tonight.

With the caution and wonder of an archaeologist adventurer, I reach into the drawer and pull out my cell phone. Its charger is still attached at the base, so I plug it in and turn it on.

You haven't been paying your bill, I remind myself.

Or have I? I honestly have no idea, but if an automatic payment was set up then I suppose this thing could've been draining my account every month. I never thought to check.

The screen turns on and immediately messages start coming through, flooding down the proverbial wire after a four-year backup.

I stroll to the dining room table and sit down, shutting off my stove on the way. All the while, my eyes stay transfixed on my phone, unable to tear away from this tiny digital screen. I see a list of contact names, their messages left unchecked. The name *Maria Norrie* catches my eye and I stop abruptly, just staring at the glowing pixelated letters that rest in the palm of my hand. I press the play button and hold my phone against my ear, listening as my mother's warm voice comes drifting out from the tiny speaker.

"Hey sweetheart, just got to the hotel," she announces in a singsong tone that nearly rips my heart in half. "I brought some wallpaper samples from my kitchen remodel. By the end of the trip, I think we can get your apartment looking presentable."

There's a brief pause.

"I really am proud of you, Vera. I don't quite understand this book of yours, but I know my baby's gonna help a lot of people. I've been telling everyone to go buy it. Okay, I'm heading over there soon."

The message ends, leaving me to wrestle with a self-inflicted parental encounter from beyond the grave. I sit quietly at the dining room table, waiting for the pain and sadness to hit me like a tidal wave and sweep me away, but for some reason that sensation never comes. The emotions are strange and bittersweet—a little difficult to figure out, actually—but they're less *overwhelming* than I expected.

Unfortunately, the more my mind lingers on those days before the Low-Probability Event, the more uncomfortable I become. Maria's last voicemail was vaguely passive-aggressive, but it was kind. Our final *unrecorded* conversation is the one that really stuck the knife in.

Vera, bisexuals don't exist.

That's what she told me, and while this invalidation might seem specific to one aspect of my life, my sexuality, it amounts to so much more. Maybe she's been right all along and I just didn't realize it yet, because the events that followed certainly indicate my mother was onto something.

I scroll up a bit, making my way past a mixed bag of voicemails from people I haven't talked to in years. I remember checking some of these, back when they were fresh, yet responding to none. After an international tragedy on that kind of scale, it makes sense for people to start reaching out, but it just wasn't in me to reach back. The fact that the messages are calls and not texts says a lot about the mood of the day, about the desperate need for personal connection.

I stop on a message from Annie, knowing it'll hurt like hell but pressing play regardless. I hold my phone up to my ear.

"Where are you?" she's screaming. "Are you okay? A fucking *bomb* just went off downtown or something. Vera, please tell me you're okay."

The belligerent hooting of a wild animal—probably the chimp—pierces through my phone and prompts Annie to shriek in return.

"Oh my fucking God!" is the last thing she says before the line goes dead.

I scroll up and select the next voicemail, this one arriving an hour later. During this message, Annie's breathing is heavy and exhausted. She's found shelter somewhere, the chaotic background noise from before now blissfully absent. Annie is choked up, the utter dread in her voice making it difficult for her to get the words out.

"Vera, are you there? Vera. Please be alive. Please be alive." She's repeating these words into her phone as a desperate mantra, not necessarily leaving me a message any longer but sending out a prayer. "Please be alive. Please be alive."

At the time, there were plenty of texts from her saying as much.

I scroll up a bit more, watching as the messages become pointedly homogenized. They're all from Annie now.

I select a random one to play.

"So, I just talked to Jeff," she begins, her tone distinctly different than before. There's a long, long pause on the line as Annie gathers her thoughts. "You're . . . alive?" she finally states, landing somewhere between an announcement and a question.

I can only imagine what it must've felt like to go through all that trauma and mourning just to discover the love of your life has simply run away, faded into the background without so much as a goodbye nod. As selfish as it sounds, never calling her back hurt me, too. I didn't just disappear on Annie, I disappeared on myself.

Death will stop you in your tracks, but sometimes being alive can be just as arresting. When you finally realize that *absolutely nothing matters,* that your whole life has been dedicated to quantifying a universe that can't be quantified, a sort of waking death occurs.

I turn off my phone again, suddenly questioning why I chose to put myself through such a harrowing stroll down memory lane, but it doesn't take long for the answer to arrive.

As tough as that was to get through, I'm left feeling oddly fulfilled, the weight that's constantly crushing me somehow alleviated the slightest bit. Yes, it hurt to hear those phantom signals from some distant, almost unrecognizable past, but there's something cathartic about letting these sensations back in and confronting them after running away for so long.

Caring again was a frightening prospect, but I feel like the effort is starting to pay off.

I head back to my ramen and drain the pot, finding just the right amount of liquid before tossing in a powdered flavor packet and mixing it all together with my spoon. I pour the soup into a bowl and, standing here in the kitchen, I take my first bite.

Even my boring dinner tastes a little better than before. I can't help it as the faintest hint of a smile begins to make its way across my face. The full expression never quite arrives, but as I gratefully enjoy a bowl of cheap soup, I can sense the edges of my lips giving it their all. For today, that's good enough.

I'm halfway through my meal when I notice Kat still hasn't touched her food.

Curious, I shuffle over to the back door. I open it and study the yard, a glorious sunset blooming over the distant horizon in plumes of purple and orange. This is the first time I've actually noticed the sunset in what seems like forever, but unfortunately the concern bubbling up within me makes it difficult to enjoy.

"Kat?" I yell, stepping onto the cracked patio as my eyes patiently scan the tall, yellow grass and accompanying weeds.

I receive nothing in return, just the quiet rustle of an evening breeze through dry blades. "Hey! Kat!" I continue, stepping out a little farther. "Dinnertime!"

My attention suddenly catches on a tangled black shape lying sprawled in the garden. The scrawny, furry body is instantly recognizable, but the stillness is unexpected.

Kat's face is twisted toward me, her mouth slightly open and her tongue protruding awkwardly through tiny teeth. Even without touching the body, I can somehow sense the stiffness of her meager frame, no longer the curious, skittish creature I'd grown to care for.

How did this happen? Why did this happen? The cat was eating. The cat was thriving. I was saving her!

Unfortunately, I already know the answer to all my blubbering, sanctimonious drama, an answer that's been waiting in the wings this whole time, poised to emerge and remind me of the same devastating lesson over and over and over again.

Maybe I needed it, needed this massive spike of bitter nihilism pounded into my skull a little further so it might actually stick. I'll never know how Kat died—whether she was always sick, or allergic to the food, or bitten by some venomous snake, or maybe she just happened to drop dead when her tiny kitty heart stopped for no reason at all. With a bit of detective work and some elbow grease I could probably get to the bottom of this mystery, but now there's one greater fact stopping me, hanging above me like a flickering neon sign.

It doesn't matter how the cat died, because

nothing

fucking

matters.

I let go of the bowl in my hands, half-finished soup plummeting to the concrete and erupting across the ground in a splatter of noodles and broth. The bowl shatters and my spoon bounces clumsily into the grass.

I let the ache *really* sink in, then finally turn around and make my way back into the house. I slam the door behind me and pace for a moment, then glance over at the gun on my dining room table. Time stretches as I imagine what its weight might feel like in my hand. All it would take is a single step in that direction, one little movement to get the ball rolling and then it's cruise control from there. The prospect is daunting and scary, yet so plainly simple.

This is it, I think.

My foot yearns for momentum, tensing up just enough to flex but not enough to pull me onward. I stand like this for hours, until the sun has fully disappeared and the vast empty night swaddles me in a blanket of darkness. Only then do I realize this is not, in fact, *it.*

Not yet, anyway.

Instead of heading for the dining room, some deep survival mechanism compels my body to turn and collapse onto the couch.

I lie here on my back, staring up at the ceiling once again. The lack of texture is welcoming, a vast pale nothing that goes on and on like the surface of the moon. In the glow of the neighbor's porch light, the subtle patterns above me don't look like a face anymore.

They don't look like anything at all.

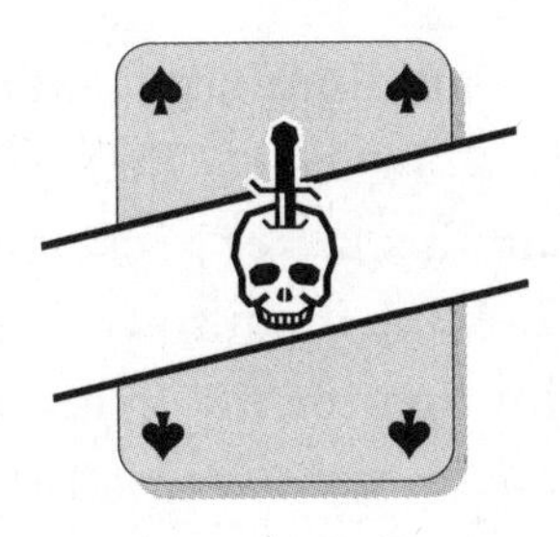

LUCKY SEVENS

Three confident knocks ring out, a closed fist pounding against my wooden front door. This happens every once in a while, a solicitor coming by to drop off a flyer or push a sale, and my response is always the same: I just lie here until they go away.

There's a long pause before, eventually, my visitor offers up three more knocks. This is usually the point when they give up and move on, but moments later the exact opposite happens.

From the corner of my eye, I catch an abrupt movement, the front door swinging open as someone steps into my home.

"Heeere's *Johnny*!" the voice of a self-assured man calls out. "Just kidding, this is Agent Jonah Layne. Is Ms. Norrie home?"

I sit up from my usual spot on the living room couch, shocked by the fact that someone has so flagrantly invaded my space and not sure how to react. "What the fuck?" is all I can think to say, my voice cracked and gravelly from a lack of use.

The man and I lock eyes, staring awkwardly at each other for a moment. It's been years since I put my social skills to use, and I'm not entirely prepared for the sudden arrival of human contact. This Agent Layne, however, seems perfectly capable of holding a conversation; he just wasn't expecting the disheveled, withered woman who sits before him.

"Did you just quote *The Shining*?" I ask.

"Carson. I've been slamming clips online," he replies. "You ever actually watch those old shows? Pretty good."

The man reaches into his jacket pocket and pulls out a badge, stepping forward and holding it out so I can see a fancy metal oval in the oppressively dim light of my living room. I hadn't really noticed how dark it was in here with all the shades drawn, but now that I'm actually tasked with analyzing something, I become quickly aware.

"Cops really *do* just barge in wherever they want, don't they?"

"I'm not a cop," Agent Layne informs me. "I'm with LPEC. Can I ask you a few questions?"

The man is tall and broad-shouldered, objectively handsome with dark hair and unusually brilliant blue eyes. He's clean-cut, sporting a perfectly tailored suit that displays ten times more care and fashion sense than your average government agent. He's probably in his late forties, but there's something youthful and energized about his demeanor.

We've only exchanged a few words, and I already find him deeply annoying.

"No, you can't ask me a few questions," I state flatly.

Agent Layne stands for a moment, his eyes drifting slowly across the room as he takes in the tragic mess of blankets, filth, rotting ramen bowls, unopened cat food, and piles of garbage.

"You, uh, got somewhere to be?" he asks.

A joke. I don't laugh.

Eventually, the man's eyes come to rest on the weapon that sits perched at the center of my dining room table, still collecting dust. The two of us remain silent for an uncomfortably long time, as if Agent Layne is daring me to speak first.

Eventually, Layne gives up and turns his attention back to me. He holds out a brass-colored sphere that's been quietly palmed in his hand.

"Your doorknob fell off," Agent Layne informs me, then sets the knob on my counter.

"You wanna hang around in my house? Fine," I proclaim. "The gnashing molars of time will chew us both up."

Layne cocks one eyebrow slightly.

"I don't know who the hell called in a welfare check or whatever this is," I continue, "but you can tell them I'm neither alive nor dead."

"What are you?" he asks.

"I'm a meat-shaped holding pattern."

There's a long pause.

"I mean, meat doesn't really have a *set* shape," Agent Layne flatly replies. "And this isn't a welfare check, I'm with the LPEC, like I said."

His words finally sink in. Despite my best efforts, I can't help the sudden spark of curiosity that crackles within me. The Low-Probability Event Commission is a government agency formed immediately following that tragic day, May 23, its creation passed by unanimous vote in both the House and the Senate. Few things will bring a country together like 7,954,000 bizarre deaths or serious injuries occurring in unison across the globe.

Of course, nearly every country on the planet was affected by that day in some way, but based on what I gathered from random newspaper headlines in the grocery store checkout line, an unusually large portion of the victims was American.

"So you can just walk into my house?" I ask. "There's no probable cause."

"You're thinking of the cops again," Agent Layne reminds me. "LPEC operates without oversight. Desperate times and all that."

"Desperation is the natural state of an animal under the wheel," I reply. "We're all under the wheel. The *problem* comes when you forget that a wheel keeps going around and around and around. The *problem* is that we've already been *crushed*."

Agent Layne stares at me for a long, long beat. "Are you always like this?" he finally asks.

"Like what?"

"*Weird* is the word I'd use."

"I got significantly weirder after a monkey dressed as Hamlet beat my friend's skull in with a typewriter."

He takes a deep breath. "I'm sorry," Agent Layne says. "I'm not here to be a dick. It's my job to help people."

I erupt with a fatalist scoff. "Good luck with that. We're all fucked."

Agent Layne frowns slightly, nodding along but clearly disagreeing. There's a sickening air of hope that seems to permeate the man's skin and hang above him like a fluffy white cloud.

Agent Layne strolls over to the nearby blinds. "Mind if I open these up?" he asks, then proceeds to open them before I can answer.

"You want so much for it all to make sense," I say, vaguely sympathetic to this golden retriever of a man on his quest to do good no matter the cost. "It's never going to make sense. There's no master equation. There's no hidden key. It's just tragedy and bullshit and chaos."

"You don't think there's a scientific explanation for May 23?" Agent Layne asks.

"I was talking about *life,*" I clarify, "but no, I don't think there's a scientific explanation for the LPE."

"So . . . divine then? You don't seem like the punishment-from-God type."

"*Order* was a god you could actually count on . . . until it wasn't," I say. "There's no explanation for that kind of shift."

"What about bad luck?" Layne asks.

"Bad luck isn't an explanation, it's an excuse," I scoff. "Either way, it all leads to the same result. There is no God, and there is no science. Nothing matters. Including this conversation."

Now it's Layne's turn to get a little irritated, letting out an exhausted sigh. "You want me to leave?"

"I *don't care* if you leave," I groan.

He's staring out my back window now, his gaze wandering across the yard until it stops abruptly. He's spotted the dead cat.

"Back when you were teaching, you came down pretty hard on Everett Vacation and Entertainment," Layne states, his abrupt shift in topic piquing my interest for a second time. "*Despite their claims to the contrary, it is not only improbable but statistically impossible for Everett's flagship property, the—*"

"*Great Britannica Hotel and Casino to operate at a profit,*" I jump in, finishing the quote. "You read my book."

"I did," Agent Layne confirms. "I'm investigating EVE. That's why I came to see you."

The second he says this my heart skips a beat, his words striking a chord. I find myself reeling a bit, shocked by the arrow that has somehow pierced my steadfast emotional armor. I've spent years training myself not to care, to keep myself from falling back in love with a world that will only grind me to dust in the most tragic, painful, and most of all *pointless* ways possible. However, Agent Layne's arrival tickles something different in me, something that's still furiously *angry* after all this time.

"The FBI *and* the Nevada Gaming Commission have already investigated the Great Britannica Hotel. Multiple times," I counter, remaining skeptical.

"Remember how I walked right through your front door without giving a flying fuck?" Layne retorts. "That's how I'm prepared to walk into that hotel. The LPEC operates without government oversight, so any red tape is gone."

My heart is pumping a little faster now, terrified by the prospect of slipping back into this world for another round of disappointment and tragedy.

"I'll pay you to assist me," Agent Layne says, "but something tells me the money isn't gonna be what sells this."

He's right.

"You literally wrote the book on these pricks, and I think that makes you an asset," Layne continues. He reaches into his jacket pocket and pulls out a faded poker chip, balancing the little token on its edge and placing it on my living room coffee table.

The words WE BET ON YOU are emblazoned across the front, the text arching above a weathered depiction of the Great Britannica Hotel and Casino.

"That's an old chip," I observe.

The man nods. "It is. I haven't gambled on anything in a very long time, and by the looks of it, neither have you." He straightens up, staring at me with intensity now. "Did you like that line?" he asks. "I practiced that."

Despite his playful commentary, Layne maintains the conviction of this moment for much longer than one might expect. His eyes haven't strayed from mine, still probing for something hidden under the surface.

"You're angry," Layne says.

I can feel my body tremble slightly, simmering with equal parts rage and sickening hope as I connect the dots. Layne is here because he's uncovered something that connects the casino to the Low-Probability Event. I've been furious with these monsters for years, watched as they got away with everything, but it appears I was tugging on a very, very long string.

"Yeah, I'm angry," I finally growl.

"Me, too," Agent Layne replies. "Let's do something about it."

General Mitchell International Airport is a circus of color and movement, a landscape so manic that I find my eyes glued to the floor despite the dark sunglasses that already cover my face. After all that time spent on my own, witnessing this many people in one place is even more overwhelming than I expected.

I glance up every so often to keep track of Agent Layne, who marches ahead of me with unshakeable confidence. He's brisk in his stride, but he makes sure to slow down whenever I drag too far behind.

Layne has headphones in, bopping along to something upbeat and rolling a small carry-on suitcase behind him. He's paired his suit with bright white high-tops that give the distinct appearance of some professional athlete who's just arrived at the big game. Layne's strange, cheery nature has not grown on me. In fact, I find him more irritating by the second.

In contrast to my companion's smart look and neatly packed luggage, I'm boarding the plane with absolutely nothing. If it were up to me, I wouldn't have even changed clothes for this, but Agent Layne insisted that a shower and some basic clean apparel were in order. He claimed they wouldn't let us board the plane otherwise.

I threw on some well-worn boots and a simple black jumpsuit, the first thing I found crumpled at the bottom of my closet. The jumpsuit certainly doesn't fit anymore, hanging off my body like a garbage bag, but who's watching? Who the fuck do I need to impress?

On one of my brief glances away from the floor, I notice a massive banner, a brilliant image looming over the concourse.

FLYING INTO THE FUTURE, NEVER FORGETTING THE PAST is written in huge red letters across the top of the hanging display. Below it sit the logos of several airlines, and under each logo is an extensive list of names. The banner also features the image of a pilot and a flight attendant, each placing a supportive hand on one shoulder of a kneeling, crying woman.

On the day of the Low-Probability Event, all six of the active Boeing 777 passenger planes crashed in unison, suffering midair collisions with one another over Chicago, Dallas, and London. I know because I saw the aftermath of Chicago's fireworks with my own eyes.

A flash of the luminous, soaring debris suddenly fills my mind, recalling the distinct hourglass shape of paired aerial explosions headed in opposite directions. I can still see those burning fragments as they spread out across the bright blue sky, smoking trails stretching like fingers before plummeting downward.

Every passenger on a plane marked with lucky triple sevens died that day. What are the chances?

You'd think that kind of horrific, unexplainable event might cause the air travel industry to come tumbling down, mirroring one of its precious metal tubes that burst into flames over several metropolitan cities.

I'm sure there was cause for alarm, CEOs panicking and investors screaming down the wire till their voices were hoarse. But time is a tide that always returns, quelling any blaze and cleansing financial panic.

Now, you'd hardly know that tragic mishap even happened. Everything returns to the same dreadful shape.

Layne and I manage to arrive at the gate, board, and take off without exchanging a single word. He tried making conversation at first, but I wouldn't bite, and eventually he just shrugged and dove into a book titled *Origami for Beginners*.

The captain's voice crackles over our plane's announcement system. "We're currently cruising at an altitude of 33,000 feet, with an airspeed of 450 miles per hour. We've got a breezy flight for you to Las Vegas. The weather is just fine, but we expect a bit of turbulence, so please keep your eyes peeled for that 'fasten seat belt' sign. Thank you for flying Heeler Airlines."

I lean back, staring at the seat ahead of me as I settle in for the ride. Agent Layne glances over from my right, his eyes wandering curiously across my stoic face. Eventually, he closes his book and pops out his earbuds.

"Are you really just gonna raw dog this flight?" he asks. "Not even a magazine?"

I don't respond.

Layne shoves his headphones back in, shaking his head and chuckling to himself. When the beverage cart rolls by, Agent Layne orders a Shirley Temple, which is so bothersome that I can't help reacting with a twisted look of alarm.

"You want one?" he questions.

I shake my head, grimacing at the twee joy on my companion's face, then return to my meditative state. I push my dark sunglasses farther up my nose, blocking out as much light as possible.

Layne takes a long sip, savoring it and then letting out an obnoxious *ahhhh* sound. He smacks his lips.

I try not to consider why Agent Layne had such an unusual order for a grown man, but I can't help myself. Soon enough, my mind is working its way through a variety of options, mostly oscillating between *sober* and *has unique tastes.*

Finally, my curiosity wins out. "Why'd you order a Shirley Temple?" I ask, vaguely disappointed *this* is what toppled my wall of silence.

Layne smiles, removing his headphones. "You mean, like, in the existential sense? Why sustain myself when my body will inevitably decay and die and the universe will succumb to heat death?"

"I didn't say that."

"Yeah, but it's something you *would* say," he quips, then holds up his glass of red fizzy liquid for a better look. "I ordered it because I've never had one before."

The plane around us suddenly drops, plummeting so quickly I barely have time to react with grateful excitement. I can only hope we keep falling, so that I might suddenly find myself blessed with an escape from this endless torment.

Thank you.

All the passengers, including Agent Layne, let out audible gasps, fingers digging tight into armrests and muscles paralyzed with fear. Layne somehow manages to keep his drink from spilling, showing off the reflexes of a man who's had a glass in his hand much more often than he lets on.

"Holy fuck!" Agent Layne hoots, somehow still jovial despite his utter terror. "I hate this!"

But our vehicle doesn't plummet from the heavens, nor explode in an inferno of twisted metal and flesh. Instead, it just rattles for a moment as the lights flicker, bobbing and lurching like a truck on an old gravel road and then gradually pulling it together for a steady but secure tremble.

A flight attendant hops on the intercom system. "Alright, folks, that's the turbulence our captain was talking about. We're gonna drop to a lower altitude and find our way through this. Nothing to worry about, but as you can see, we've turned on the 'fasten seat belt' sign. This should be all cleared up in about ten minutes."

Agent Layne's eyes are closed and his mouth is quivering as it struggles to work up to a grin. I can tell he's having trouble staying positive. "I hate flying," he announces. "I appreciate the adventure, but I still fucking hate it. That feeling of falling, you know?"

"Depending on the year, there are between point zero one and point zero three deaths for every hundred million flight miles," I reply, unable to help myself. It's been a very long time since I had the opportunity to throw out statistics like this.

Layne glances over. "What does that mean?"

"It means you'll be fine. It's way more dangerous to take a train. At least, it used to be," I reply. "Who the fuck knows anymore."

Agent Layne nods, listening intently. I can tell he's thinking hard about something, carefully choosing his next words now that he's found a conversational opening. "So, you believe in statistics again?" he asks.

"I don't *believe* in anything."

"You're coming with me, though," Layne counters. "So you must believe in something. Revenge, maybe?"

It was stupid of me to open this door, to start a conversation with someone I really have no intention of getting to know. I wouldn't say I was enjoying the silence, but it was certainly better than whatever *this* is.

Ever since the Low-Probability Event, I can't help noticing this world we've built for ourselves has rotted away and left a shell in its place. We're all going through the motions, still pantomiming out our little play by making small talk on a plane or getting to know a new coworker, but deep down nobody gives a damn. They never did.

The plane stops trembling and I lean back in my seat, disappointed.

"Typically, the way these partnered investigations work is by asking questions and sharing ideas about the case with each other," Layne says, settling in again, "but since you don't seem like the 'asking questions' type—unless it comes to my beverage order—I'm just gonna pretend you are."

Layne clears his throat, then shifts into a new, higher-pitched voice. It's clearly meant to represent me, but the impression is terrible. "What is it that suddenly has the LPEC interested in a casino management firm?" he squeaks from the corner of his mouth.

I don't smile in return, utterly stone-faced.

Agent Layne's grin drops. He leans in a bit and returns to his normal cadence. "I'm glad you asked. Lots of weird theories about that day, right?" he continues, speaking with the confidence of someone who's rehearsed this explanation for weeks and is finally called on to make his grand performance. "Some think it was a terrorist attack. Religious folks say it was sinners receiving divine judgment. I even read an article claiming everyone who died that day had dated a Taurus during years divisible by three."

I'd seen this last theory on the cover of a grocery store newspaper. "Did you follow up on that?" I ask dryly.

"A question about the case!" he shouts, delighted. "I did, in fact, follow up."

"And?"

Agent Layne shakes his head. "To be fair to the wilder theories, it's a large sample group to sort through. Nearly eight million people killed or severely injured in freak accidents; all basically occurring at the same time right down to a twenty-minute block. When you control for population density, there was still a much higher frequency of incidents in metropolitan areas. Nine out of ten casualties were American, even if they were killed abroad, and ninety-nine percent of the victims who died that day were adults, which I always thought was especially weird. Very few kids."

Layne pauses when he says this, his expression flickering slightly as some deep internal trauma bubbles up within. It's a side of Agent Layne I haven't seen until this very moment, but before I get a chance to synthesize its meaning, he forces these feelings back down and locks them away.

"I used to play a lot of cards, so that's where my mind went once I entered the picture. You can't legally gamble until you're old enough, right? I started looking into some of the victims and, lo and behold, I think I found a pattern."

"Which is?" I press.

"Every single death involved someone who visited the Great Britannica," Layne replies. "Most of the serious injuries had a connection, too."

"Hundreds of millions of people have been to that casino," I counter. "Did you also check if the victims drove cars or brushed their teeth at night? Maybe they all ate food?"

Layne manages to keep a straight face, but I can tell he's a little disappointed by my reaction. "So . . . you don't think there's a connection?" he asks.

I stare at him for a moment, suddenly realizing that I'm not entirely sure.

For as strict as my mother was, she *did* like to gamble. I don't recall her taking any trips to Las Vegas, but then again, would she tell me if she did? Would the draw of the Great Britannica—this magical place where the odds are in your favor—be enough for Maria Norrie to betray her only child? Would she go there for a weekend of fun, knowing damn well these were the very people I'd dedicated years of my life to taking down? Would she lie by omission, not because she understood the weight of the situation, but because she thought I'd get "too emotional" about something that "wasn't a big deal"?

Why, yes. Yes she would.

"That's even dumber than the Taurus theory," I finally reply, turning away from Agent Layne.

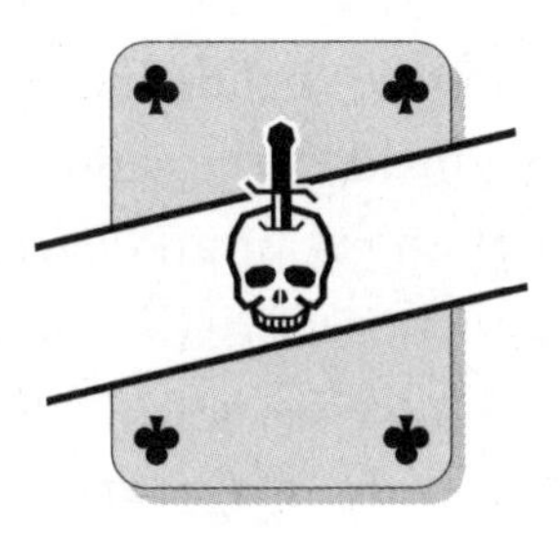

THE DEEP STACK

The Great Britannica Hotel and Casino towers above us, rising against the stark blue Nevada sky in a brash symbol of mankind's conquest of nature. This place, like all of Las Vegas, is an abomination. It's a giant middle finger lifting above the barren desert and announcing to the world that humankind's endless subjugation of it cannot be stopped. There's not enough water out here in the middle of nowhere to sustain human life? Fuck you. We'll bring our own.

The British-themed structure sports a massive Big Ben replica as its majestic centerpiece, and a digital Union Jack flag waves valiantly on a gargantuan digital screen nearby. It shines down on us as we make our way across a large pedestrian bridge that reaches from the parking garage to the casino.

Messages dance across the screen. THE ONLY CASINO WHERE WE BET ON YOU! boasts the first one, followed by another flash of text that reads, TWO FOR ONE LUNCH BUFFET FOR ALL MAY 23 SURVIVORS PROGRAM MEMBERS WITH PROOF OF MAGIC SHOW TICKETS!

Below this grand display a modest protest is happening, three figures hoisting signs while others kneel in prayer. A man with a megaphone is braying something about God's punishment and the insidious sin of gambling, but he goes decidedly ignored.

Tourists scamper past Layne and me like ants in the blazing

heat, desperately searching for shelter and sustenance. It's honestly a little scary trying to get inside the casino as bodies smash against one another, lining up by the door and eventually waved through by a regiment of very patient security guards.

This building is constantly at capacity, and they're notoriously strict about staying up to code. We've arrived at the most popular casino in the world, after all.

In fact, the only reason we're waved through so easily is Agent Layne's badge.

The moment we enter this building I find my senses overwhelmed by a cascade of brilliant lights and sounds. Slot machines hum and buzz with frantic rhythms, cocktail waitresses weaving through them as patrons sit in dumbfounded silence. Beyond, a table of craps players erupts in applause.

Statistically speaking, craps is one of the best bets at a casino, offering fairly good odds to a player who knows what they're doing. For instance, the house edge on a standard pass line bet is only 1.41 percent.

Of course, that's not the case here at the Great Britannica. While most casinos only double your money on an opening roll of seven or eleven, this establishment *triples* it.

Slots here are equally tipped against the house. Your average machine will have its RTP—return to player—easy to find. Usually, all it takes is pressing the help button to reveal a number between 92 and 97 percent, the higher the better. Slot machines in the Great Britannica, however, have all been adjusted to sport an RTP of 105 percent, astronomically good odds that you won't find anywhere else on earth.

Blackjack with six decks usually has a 0.64 percent house edge. Here at the Great Britannica, it's a little more than 2 percent in the player's favor. Keno typically sits between 25–29 percent house advantage, but within these walls, those numbers are closer to 3 or 4 percent in the opposite direction. They've bumped up their roulette payout from a thirty-five times multiplier to forty.

The odds here are so good that you might as well be taking money out of an ATM. At least, that's how it *should* work, but the way things *should* happen and the way things *do* happen are not always in sync.

All these changes are closely monitored by the Nevada Gaming Commission, which would have no problem shutting this whole place down if they found evidence of someone bending the truth.

Suffice to say, the Great Britannica is still open.

"Day party at Loch Luck, best wave pool in Vegas!" someone calls out, shoving two passes in my face. He's dressed too nicely for his wild demeanor, hired specifically to get the young and fun tourists excited about catching a tan. "State-of-the-art technology lets you feel the beat in the water. DJ Luck Norris is playing."

"Ugh," I moan, grimacing and pushing away the man's hand as I continue onward. "No."

The promoter falls away, but its only now that I realize I've lost track of Agent Layne.

I stand awkwardly on the casino floor, my eyes hunting the tumultuous scene in search of any hint I can find—a tracker in the wild. I was so good at keeping up, and Layne was so diligent about stopping for me to catch him, that we developed a second nature. Unfortunately, it appears this location is simply too chaotic for us to travel at different paces.

I wander down an aisle of slot machines, awash in their twinkling glow. Wheels of golden light flicker across my dark sunglasses. Nearby, comically big levers are yanked down, prompting wheels to spin and churn. I ignore the lights and sound, gazing past them in hopes of catching Layne's tall, suit-clad figure on the outskirts of the carnival.

Beyond the pandemonium are a few calmer sections of the casino floor, a gift shop on one end and an empty buffet on the other. These eateries are typically buzzing with life, but right now it appears they're making the transition from lunch to dinner, momentarily shuttered while the king crab legs get a much-needed refresher.

It's here my inspection stops, as I notice a single patron who sits quietly in the darkened restaurant. He's tough to spot with all the caustic brilliance that jangles and flashes between us, but I suppose I've always had a knack for catching the little details.

The restaurant lights are dimmed, but it's just enough to watch as the man goes about his business. The figure is tall and exceptionally lanky, his face gaunt to the point of sickly. His skin is disturbingly pale, approximately the shade of my eggshell ceiling back at home, and his eyes are dark and tired. He looks so exhausted that I actually consider whether he's wearing effects makeup from a nearby show, although I can't for the life of me imagine what use Cirque du Soleil could have for his frail body.

The man is hunched at his table and tearing through a thick, juicy cheeseburger, the bun gripped tight in his hands as sloppy cascades of yellow fat spill over sizzling meat and splatter across his plate. The man takes a bite, chews for a moment, and then takes another before he has the chance to swallow. He's utterly ravenous.

Someone absolutely devouring a massive burger isn't unusual, of course, especially in a town as gluttonous as this one, but it's not *just* a burger that rests before him. Colossal platters of food sit piled high around the man, filling his table with a feast so excessive that a family of four, plus their dog, might have trouble taking it down. Towers of pizza slices are heaped on one plate, the layers of dough and sauce transforming into a wobbling monument that, shockingly, appears to have a few pancakes mixed in. Maple syrup oozes down the sides of this baffling culinary atrocity. Another stack features a pile of sushi and mashed potatoes, their disparate flavors melting into each other.

My attention is frozen, captivated as the near-skeletal man continues plowing through his food like a wild animal. I feel strange about watching, as though I've caught someone in the secret throes of a deeply intimate act, but I can't seem to pull my eyes away. I'm so wrapped up in my voyeurism, however, that I'm entirely unprepared when the man turns to look right at me. His sunken eyes are bulging out of their sockets and his emaciated face is oddly expressionless. A vivid streak of sickly orange sauce is running down his chin.

In another life I might've looked away, but not anymore. Instead, I hold his haunting stare.

"There you are!" Agent Layne suddenly appears on my right, drawing my focus as he approaches from an aisle of slot machines. "They're ready to see us now."

"Oh, uh—sure," I fumble, struggling to collect myself.

His eyes narrow. "What's up?"

"I just . . ." I start, then shake my head. "Never mind."

"Okay, well, I need you sharp up there," Layne reminds me. "You know a lot more about these people than I do."

"Knowing more is just accepting the grand cosmic truth that there was never anything to know."

"That's great," he chirps dryly. "So, are you coming up? Or do you just wanna put out a weird vibe down here for a while?"

"I'm coming up," I confirm, despite the best efforts of my darker instincts.

I follow Agent Layne through the sparkling mess, cutting toward a quiet bay of elevators nearby. From the corner of my eye, I catch another quick glimpse of the thin man, but his attention has now returned to his dimly lit banquet.

"Are you a gambler?" Layne asks.

"You mean, do I sit in a loud room surrounded by degenerates wasting away and burning through money like it's kindling for no other reason than a fruitless endorphin hit every time I get a few cents back?" I retort.

"I actually just meant 'Are you a gambler?' But sure."

"No."

"What about here in the Great Britannica?" he presses. "The odds are in your favor, right?"

I don't answer.

We stroll past two poised security guards, Layne offering a respectful nod as I ignore them completely. My companion presses a button and the elevator door opens. We step inside.

"What about you?" I ask from behind my dark shades. "Are you a big gambler?"

"Used to be," he replies. "I was good at it, too. Great poker face. After a few bad beats I decided maybe cards weren't for me. Lost with two straight flushes in a row."

I can't help chuckling at this. In Texas Hold'em, your chance of getting a straight flush is 3,590 to one. The odds of actually *losing* after this only multiplies the rarity, and the chance of this happening twice in a row is, well, on impossible's doorstep.

"Was that during the Low-Probability Event?" I ask, already knowing the answer.

"Just before," he replies. "When things started coming loose."

"Two bad bets. Guess you got off easy."

Layne gives me a half-hearted smile. "I didn't."

The elevator stops and opens directly into an enormous penthouse suite. The ceilings are high, vaulted at least three stories up, and the stark white room is relatively empty besides a desk sitting quietly at the opposite end. The desk is quite large, but it still feels stunted by the gargantuan size of the office.

To be fair, it's unlike any *office* I've ever seen, but that's because the sheer opulence has transformed it into some kind of otherworldly space. The whole opposite wall is a multipaned, floor-to-ceiling window that showcases the glittering Las Vegas strip. Beyond is the grand Nevada desert, and even farther off in the distance, the vista transforms into a rolling cascade of yellow mountains.

Somehow, you can *see* the heat of the outside air as it dances across the panes of glass.

To the right is a massive white wall upon which a video game has been projected. It's a digital field, lush and green but stylized to feature sharp-angled polygons. Clay pigeons spring into view on this massive projection, promptly blasted into oblivion as point designations flash above and a rolling scoreboard leaps higher and higher.

"Ha! Y'all see that?" comes an enthusiastic voice with a thick Southern drawl. "Hot *damn*! I'm a good-ass shot, aren't I?"

At the center of the room stands a woman in a white cowboy hat and an equally stark blazer. A bolo tie is cinched high against her neck, and tan cowboy boots cover her feet. She's wearing jeans, likely meant to signal some hardworking blue-collar upbringing, but they're too crisp and clean to be convincing.

Layne steps forward, pulling out his badge. "Ms. Denver White, I'm Agent Layne and this is my partner, Vera. We're with the LPEC and we're here to ask you a few questions."

The cowgirl doesn't even turn to check Layne's badge, her eyes still locked on the screen before her as more clay pigeons spring into view. She points a large plastic rifle at the projection and blasts a few more targets out of the air.

"Just Denver is fine," she says, "but alright, shoot."

Agent Layne clears his throat. "I'm here as a courtesy to you. My position as a Commission agent grants me access to every file in the Great Britannica archives. I could've just strolled into your IT department, but I came here first."

She finally pauses her game, dropping the fake weapon to her side. "Y'all knock yourselves out."

I watch intently as she turns to face us, struggling to pick up on any shift in the cowgirl's demeanor but finding her incredibly difficult to read. She's certainly not worried about our investigation, that much I know.

Plenty has been written about her youth and her gender, both rarities in the world of billionaire CEOs, but the visceral difference between Denver and the corporate old guard is even more stark in person. She's thirty-three years old, but up close she looks even younger, with extra-large eyes framed by long, caramel brown hair that curls around her shoulders.

Of course, this casino operation is just one head of the Everett Vacation and Entertainment hydra, and EVE (along with Heeler Airlines, Harold Brothers, and a slew of other massive corporate juggernauts) is owned by Hex International. In other words, Denver White is not the queen of the mountain, but she's got a pretty impressive little hill to rule over.

Denver holds out the gun as an offering. "Y'all want a turn? I can change 'em to birds or aliens."

Denver uses a button on the side of her fake rifle, each press of her finger dropping a new digital skin across the enormous screen. Her first tap changes the setting from an open field to a beautiful lakeside, while the floating clay pigeons transform into birds. Next is a gray, crater-pocked vision of the moon's surface, an otherworldly locale where the targets become flying saucers.

"Area Fifty-One is right down the road. Y'all sure you don't wanna blow away some little green fuckers?" Denver continues.

I glance over at Agent Layne, and it suddenly occurs to me that he's actually considering a game.

"No," I state bluntly, pulling him back into focus.

Layne barrels onward. "This is different from your previous dealings with law enforcement. I just wanna make sure you understand that. We'll have access to everything, not just the files that a warrant deems relevant."

I'm abruptly struck by just how odd this meeting is. Why are we even here? Why not just take the files in an unexpected raid instead of giving the Great Britannica time to cover their tracks? Agent Layne's history at the poker table might hold a clue. If I'd shown any semblance of interest this morning then I'd probably know for sure, but right now my best guess is that Layne is aiming for shock and awe. He's giving an aggressive display of power to knock them off-balance and encourage mistakes.

Which is why he brought me along. I know these people well enough to pick up on their tells.

"Licensing deals," I jump in suddenly. "Investments. Payout records. Human resource reports. Real estate holdings."

With this final phrase I catch a pang of tension on Denver's face, the faintest glimmer of something lurking just below the surface. It could be nothing, but I make a note.

The cowgirl straightens up quickly. "We've got nothing to hide from y'all. This casino's got the best damn odds in the world, because we *believe* in our customers. At the Great Britannica, *we bet on you.*"

Denver leans in a bit when she hits those last four words, adding a little wink at the end.

Standing here in my dark sunglasses and ill-fitting jumpsuit, I've been trying my best to stay aloof, to float above it all and not get bogged down in any emotions that might bubble up during this conversation.

Nothing really matters, after all.

Unfortunately, this blather of corporate buzzwords has finally caused my frustration to boil over. I've been after these assholes for *far* too long to leave my emotions completely at the door.

"But you still turn a profit?" I suddenly snap, a little more aggressively than intended.

To my dismay, Denver just turns away and dives back into her video game, hoisting the rifle and blasting apart a few bobbing, weaving spaceships.

"Sugar, the reason we're the most *profitable* casino on the planet is because we actually care about our patrons," she explains over her shoulder. "If you're looking to gamble, why *wouldn't* you go to a place where the slots are cranked up in the player's favor? Where blackjack pays four to one?"

"Because players hit blackjacks significantly less here than at other casinos," I retort. "It always seems to even out. Kinda mysterious."

Denver still doesn't turn to look at me, but even from the side

I can see her expression curl into an amused grin. She's certainly not afraid, but I've struck a chord.

"If y'all think we're rigging our games, you're free to look for evidence. Go on ahead!" she laughs. "You won't find anything rotten. We're good girls here at Everett, but knock yourselves out."

Denver suddenly jerks her rifle to the side, tearing through five pixelated UFOs in quick succession. "Yeehaw! Get fucked, E.T.!" she hollers.

Agent Layne and I exchange glances.

"Alright then," Layne states with a nod of confirmation. "We'll make arrangements with your IT department."

We turn and head back to the elevator, pressing the call button as the cacophonous sounds of exploding digital spaceships and laser blasts wash over us. It's a relief when we finally board the lift, glass doors closing behind us and blessing our ears with a silent reprieve.

"Feels kinda strange having a cowgirl run a British-themed hotel," I state flatly.

Agent Layne considers this a moment. "The world's a strange place."

We don't speak another word as we walk back through the casino, but my thoughts are racing. I can't help the feeling that something's amiss, an important puzzle piece not quite fitting the spot it's been wedged into.

Still, my silence persists. To participate would be an admission, not just to the world at large, but to myself. It would mean that, on some small level, I care.

That I'm invested.

That I'm interested.

Of course, flying halfway across the country is a pretty good sign that I'm not *entirely* checked out on this bizarre journey, but for some reason this potential moment of inquisition seems like a much bigger leap. Layne asked me to come and I said yes, simple enough, but letting genuine interest get the best of me takes this whole thing to another level.

Agent Layne stops at the IT office while I hang back, but after ten minutes he returns and we continue onward.

We reach the rental car and climb in, shutting the doors and starting it up to get some much-needed cold air blasting in our faces. Layne doesn't put the car into drive, however, just sits there for a moment as the vehicle gently hums below us. He reaches into the middle console and pulls a long piece of red licorice from its oblong package, chewing one end of the rope while the rest of it dangles from his mouth like a limp cigarette.

"You wanna catch a movie at the Sphere?" Agent Layne asks between bites.

"What?"

"That giant orb with the video screens on it," he explains. "I've never been. It's gonna take about three hours for the tech department to send all that data over, so we've got a little time to kill."

That strange feeling at the pit of my stomach unfurls a little more, begging for my attention. "I don't care," I sigh.

In my peripheral vision, I can see Agent Layne gazing over at me, an odd look on his face. He stops chewing the licorice, deep in thought. "Unless, of course, there's something you want to ask me?" he finally says.

My eyes immediately dart over and lock with his, a question bubbling up and out of my throat despite my best efforts to keep it tucked away. "Why would you tip them off like that?" I erupt. "It makes no sense. You're giving them *three hours* to go through their files and delete the sensitive documents? I understand trying to rattle them and all, but it's not worth giving away your position like that."

Layne's expression is frozen solid for an unusually long beat, then it begins to melt ever so slightly. His tight lips begin to curl up into a wide smile, then he eventually breaks out in a full-on toothy grin.

"Fuck yeah!" he shouts, pumping his fist and then patting my shoulder in a fit of job-well-done enthusiasm. "Look at us, a real detective team! I love it! I gotta get you out to a card room some time, you were fucking *reading* me."

"What is even happening?" I reply.

Layne cackles with laughter. "Alright, alright, sorry," he says, withdrawing his hand and settling down a bit. "You're absolutely right, it's a terrible strategy. Obviously, I could've told you that, and I *would* have told you soon enough, but you *figured it out for yourself*!"

"I hate this."

"No, no," Agent Layne replies, shaking his head. "Don't sell yourself short. You've got great instincts."

I can't keep deflecting his praise, so I meet this one with silent acceptance. Despite my best efforts, it feels alright. "Why, then?" I finally ask. "Why not get the data and *then* cause a ruckus?"

"Because I already did," he replies, pulling out a thumb drive and wiggling it playfully between two fingers. "Two weeks ago. LPEC cyber division has some real monsters behind the keyboard."

He casually tosses over the drive. "It's a shitload of information to sort through, we're talking years and years of material, but it'll be a lot easier once we cross-reference the files," Agent Layne explains. "Just focus on the folders they delete from this batch."

I hate to admit it, but it's kinda brilliant.

"People tend to remember the cards their opponent lets them see, the big pocket pairs or the risky gutshot straights they catch," Agent Layne muses. "The thing is, sometimes you can learn more from the cards they *don't* show."

Layne puts the car in drive as the end of the licorice rope disappears into his mouth.

HEAD LIKE A HOLE

The papers are spread out before me in an explosive pattern of rectangular stacks, pages and pages of information fanned across the motel room floor like a blooming flower. I often sit at the middle of it all, jumping from one stack to the next in a flurry of frantic energy. Other times, I'm tucked away in the corner of this dark room, hunched over the laptop I purchased with government funds from Agent Layne.

Layne also took the liberty of filling my closet with new clothes that fit a little better and, to quote him directly, "don't stink."

I finally changed this morning, mostly out of appreciation that he didn't force any funky colors on me. The wardrobe is all black, just fresher.

Despite this moment of progress—if you can call it that—the feelings welling up tonight are far from heroic. I'm exhausted and frustrated, my head throbbing after three full days of working through the troves of information from Everett.

Agent Layne's comparison maneuver was helpful, targeting our audit quite a bit. Huge swaths of information were "accidently corrupted" in the data center, and nearly all the real estate records were "lost in a fire."

Unfortunately, as suspicious as it is to lose so much of your data before you hand it over, the big reveal is that there's nothing illegal happening at the Great Britannica or its parent company. There never is.

For the last thirteen years, this casino has clawed its way to the top of the heap by loudly making one simple claim: customers will come if we put the odds in their favor, and we will cover our losses with auxiliary purchases that are driven by our popularity. It's no wonder they can charge ten times the room rate compared to anywhere else on the Strip and stay booked for years in advance. In fact, the closest thing they've had to a scandal is when *other people* were subletting their suites and making a killing.

This is an absurd business model—something that shouldn't work, statistically speaking—yet no matter how deep I dive into their affairs I always reach the same answer: they're playing by the rules. Every third-party trial of their return to player models is immaculate. Every gambling commission investigation is clean.

If you sit down and play a slot machine at the Great Britannica, the program is *actually* set for a payout in your favor over time. In practice, however, the casino still turns a profit, because the house always happens to win a little more than fate should allow.

Imagine you're in a coin-flipping contest against the Great Britannica Hotel and Casino. You agree to flip it one thousand times, giving yourself a point for heads and the casino a point for tails. You've checked this coin and it's the real deal—in fact, *you're* allowed to be the one flipping it—and because there are only two possible results, the more you flip it, the closer your total results will get to a fifty-fifty split.

If you play this game against a friend, you'll come out right down the middle. If you play this game against the Great Britannica, they'll win.

This is a cold hard fact, one I still don't understand despite looking at it from every single angle. I've even considered the possibility of deep, multitiered corruption at the gaming commission, but the logistics of maintaining these results across every single casino game would be impossible. Political corruption also doesn't explain the bountiful third-party studies that all reach the exact same conclusion: these games are fair.

All kinds of people have covered this disparity between practice and results, from documentarians to podcasters to politicians. We've shouted from the rooftops, reminded the world that even though this blackjack payout is *technically* higher, you end up getting great cards a little less for some fucking reason. People just wanna win every once in a while, get drunk, and go home. It's enough to take a girl from a four-year depression to a four-day rage binge just to get some fucking answers.

Remembering the way Denver reacted when I mentioned real estate, I've played close attention to those particular records, poring over every tract of land Everett has purchased over the last decade. They own five casinos on the Strip, three of them obtained during this period, but the Great Britannica remains their star attraction. It's also the only establishment they own with inflated odds; the other casinos operate normally.

With all this cash rolling in, EVE has also started putting their money into one of the safest bets there is: raw land. What this could possibly have to do with their scam, I have no idea, but it was enough to remove those files from their official information drop. These acres of desert were purchased at a fair price and either held or developed into yet another profit-generating venture. Sometimes this means a fancy new commercial zone, other times it's a blanket of suburban homes at the edge of the desert, their bright green lawns thriving as they suck up every ounce of water they can get.

On this afternoon's deeply frustrating journey into the data I've started to pace, hoping it might do something to relieve the potent headaches that bubble up and grip my brain like an ever-tightening vise.

This is what happens when you start to care, I remind myself. *You feel like shit.*

In the other room I can hear Agent Layne watching reruns of

the nineties television drama *Dark Encounters,* a show about two FBI agents investigating paranormal crimes.

He's gone through all kinds of TV programming while he waits for my analysis, from black-and-white cartoons to nature documentaries. I can hear his reactions through the wall that separates our rooms, mostly loud and boisterous laughter. These outbursts are coming from the body of an adult man, but they're absolutely childlike in their inflection. It feels like this is the first time he's actually watched television.

As I think this, a sudden gasp erupts from the other room. The music swells. "Oh no!" Layne yells. "The moleman's in the cave!"

I inspect the papers spread out before me, taking one last stab at finding some hidden pattern before my patience finally snaps.

Fuck this.

I march toward the door of my motel room, throwing it open as I emerge into the brilliant sunlight. We're a few short miles off the Strip, yet it feels like we've moved several thousand light-years closer to the brilliant, blazing sun. Shimmering waves of heat roll off the asphalt parking lot below in a manner I can only describe as *deeply annoying.*

I throw Layne's door open with so much force that the knob busts through the drywall on the other side and sticks in place. "Hey, I'm done!"

Agent Layne sits up from his reclined position on the hotel bed, genuinely startled. He's wearing a plastic yellow drinking hat with a translucent straw that swirls around the dome in wild corkscrews, the tube starting at a cup of carbonated liquid on the side of his head and leading to his mouth.

"I thought you didn't drink," I snap.

Layne parts his lips, letting the straw fall out. "I never said that. This *is* a virgin mojito, though, from the go-kart track down the street. You want some?"

It's now that I notice a box leaning against the wall next to his bed. It's labeled FIRE SPINNING BASICS: POI AND HOOPS.

Rage flares within me. "Can you stop seizing the day *for just one fucking minute*!" I scream.

Agent Layne seems genuinely confused by my outburst, glancing over at the box and then back to me. "Did you find something in the files?" he asks, ignoring my question.

"No, I'm done," I snap. "I quit." I don't stick around to offer any words of condolence or clarity. Instead, I turn and head back into my room, yelling as I slam the door behind me, "Book me a flight back home! Or don't! I don't fucking care!"

I trudge through all the papers once meticulously laid out on the motel floor, stirring and tearing them haphazardly until I reach the bed. I turn and fall back onto the mattress. The second my attention locks onto the subtle pattern of the ceiling above, I feel a potent wave of relief wash over me. It's a comforting sight, a home away from home that I can easily sink into and drift away.

I hear Agent Layne shuffling around in his room, followed by a gentle knock on my door. I don't reply, but he enters anyway, standing quietly for a moment. The plastic hat is nowhere to be seen.

"You're the best at reading the data," he proclaims. "I need you."

"You work for the federal government," I remind him. "Shouldn't you have like . . . a whole floor of people doing forensic accounting on this stuff?"

Layne hesitates. "It's easier to keep track of things this way" is all he says in return, an odd nonresponse that I have no choice but to accept.

"There's nothing to help you with, anyway," I continue. "Everett turned everything over, just like they always do. It shouldn't work, but it does, and that leaves us *where*? Nowhere. I have *twice* the records that I had back then, and it's still not enough for a *goddamn thing* to make any fucking sense."

Agent Layne pauses, watching me. My eyes remain fixed on the ceiling, but even as a blur in my peripheral vision, I can tell he is troubled by something.

"I know what's waiting back at home," he finally states.

I say nothing in return, just sink into the bed a little deeper.

My companion lets out a long sigh, considering something. "Alright," he finally says.

Agent Layne leaves, closing the door behind him and returning to his own room. I expect the television to turn on at any moment, but it never does. Instead, I'm greeted by a seemingly endless ocean of silence, nothing but the soft rattle of the window-mounted AC unit rumbling away as it struggles to keep up with this incredible heat.

I can feel my eyes getting heavier, the wings of exhaustion finally wrapping around me in a warm embrace.

Gradually, the faintest whimpering starts drifting out from the other room. It sounds like Layne is crying, muffled and soft through the paper-thin walls. It's an unexpected reaction, but in some deep, subconscious way it makes more sense than anything else I've witnessed from the man. I get it.

My eyes close, and in the darkness behind my eyelids I see Annie. I imagine how desperate she must have been that day, watch her calling me over and over again. I picture the way her freckled face must've twisted in horror when she learned I was still alive, the love of her life simply choosing to ignore the world. Unable to reconnect. Unable to do *anything*. Tears well up and roll down my cheeks. I'm separated from Layne in the other room but mirroring him just the same.

Before long, I drift off to sleep.

Another swift knock at the door, this one much harder than before. My eyes fly open and I sit up, noting the sky outside my window has shifted hues. It's much later in the evening now.

I stand, wearily strolling over and opening up to find Agent Layne.

"You don't just walk in anymore?" I question.

"I'm working on it. And I was thinking about what you said," he admits, "about how you have all the information now, but it still doesn't make sense."

There's a shift in Agent Layne's tone, a new note to his personality that I haven't witnessed until now. He turns and gazes off into the distance, his eyes trained on the horizon line as lush colors swell across it like a bruise.

"You don't have *everything,*" he continues, turning to lock eyes with me once again. His usual happy-go-lucky smile has disappeared. "Here's the thing: once you see this, there's no going back."

I stare at him blankly. "You think I care about going back? I don't care about anything."

"I think you do," he retorts.

"You're wrong."

Layne hesitates, considering something for a very long time as he stares out into the desert. "Can I trust you to keep your mouth shut?" he finally asks, welling up a bit as an unexpected surge of emotion washes over him. "I like you, Vera. You're a real fucking nut, but you're a good kid."

The tension is suffocating now, sneaking up on me and wrapping itself around my lungs before I even noticed. It's only now that I realize how heavy this conversation really is.

"I don't know what I'm agreeing to," I reply.

"Do you want me to drive you to the airport, or do you want to see what the LPEC is out here dealing with?" he asks. "I just got a call. You're welcome to tag along."

I join Agent Layne's survey of the distant horizon line. "Is it on the way to the airport?" I ask.

He nods.

"Then I guess it won't matter if we make a pit stop."

♣ ♥ ♦ ♠

We're hurtling down a four-lane straightaway, driving into the dying sun as Layne pilots his exotic, mint green rental car toward the great unknown. He usually seems thrilled to be behind the wheel, but tonight his expression is oddly somber. The stereo is off, which is rare.

Layne keeps glancing over at me, frustrated by the fact that I still refuse to put on my seat belt. He's been demanding I use one since he first drove us to the airport, insisting that I—of all people—should "know the statistics."

I *do* know the statistics. In the front seat, the chance of a fatality is reduced by 45 percent when you wear a seat belt. That's exactly why I quit using it.

He should just be grateful that the safety warning beep has finally stopped.

In the distance I watch as the silhouette of an enormous jet makes its descent into Harry Reid International Airport, tourists frothing at the mouth as they scramble for their chance to throw it all away in the name of a grand night to write home about. This city can do that to you, pushing even the most modest traveler toward one more spin of the wheel, one more drink, one more lap dance. I don't judge. I suppose it's nice to have a place where once-in-a-lifetime debauchery is so strongly encouraged. I just happen to recognize that it's a futile battle.

Congratulations, you've earned yourself a great story! I'm sure it'll still be getting laughs in two hundred years when the oceans are boiling.

We're all headed to the same place, rocketing down the same highway toward a blazing sun that's waiting to swallow us up. Every story, every memory, every thought will disintegrate as our drop-top convertible slams through the surface of roiling lava and detonates in a grand bouquet of cosmic flares. Metaphorically speaking, of course.

In reality, our deaths will be boring and the sun will burn out with much less fanfare than when it arrived. It's all worthless.

"Let's party," my companion suddenly announces apropos of nothing, as though he's somehow picking up on my unspoken apathy. I don't even need to say these things out loud anymore; the energy permeates my skin.

Layne reaches out and turns on the stereo, which is connected to a particularly grating playlist on his phone. Sound thunders from the speakers, an upbeat neo-soul tune that's so utterly saccharine I'd swear it's making my teeth hurt.

"This is . . . not good," I inform him, my official review.

Agent Layne glances over at me and actually manages to crack a smile. He starts bobbing his head. "Driver's choice."

We work our way through four equally disturbing pop songs before eventually pulling off of the road and heading onto a dirt drive. An arrow-shaped sign points us toward Cornicello Trailer Palace. Agent Layne turns off the stereo once again.

Despite his best efforts to shift the mood with some good-time jams, it feels strangely inappropriate out here in the heart of the desert. Something in the air is off, a blanket of darkness too thick for even this bumbling himbo to cut through.

The sunset has faded from the sky above, leaving only a faint indigo afterglow over the distant mountain range. The twinkling lights of the Strip loom large behind us, and before us sprouts the cold, almost greenish illumination of the trailer park.

As we draw closer, I notice a gathering of confused residents corralled by the side of the road. A woman in a suit is speaking with them, trying her best to calm down the crowd.

They appear to have been torn from their beds in the middle of the night, and are not exactly thrilled about getting marched down the lane just to stand in bewilderment at the edge of the desert. Half of these folks look terribly distraught, screaming and crying as they plead with the government agent who's struggling to control them. Others, in contrast, are ecstatic, cheerfully hugging. Some residents appear to be a mixture of both, not quite sure what to do with themselves.

I turn my attention back to the front windshield as we pull through a rusty old gate that marks our arrival. A fire truck and an ambulance are rolling out as we make our way inside, and yellow crime-scene tape surrounds the perimeter.

The mobile homes are placed in five long rows, a wooden fence bordering the grounds and three overhead streetlamps valiantly fighting to light the area with their fluorescent glow. The trailers appear to be fairly well kept, but I notice one or two of them feature curious black singes across their sides or charred into the front porch. One of them has been fully burnt out, nothing more than a scrap-metal skeleton.

We cruise a little deeper to find there are two police cars positioned haphazardly in front of one of the mobile homes, as well as a single black vehicle marked with the words LOW-PROBABILITY EVENT COMMISSION.

Layne parks, then reaches over and pulls a gun out of the glove compartment. He slips it into his holster.

"Oh," I say. "It's that kind of stop."

"You never know what's coming," Layne replies.

We climb out and another agent quickly approaches, flashing Layne his LPEC badge and offering a firm handshake. "Agent Layne, I'm Agent Goodwin. So glad you're here. It's an honor."

"Who's been inside?" Layne asks, scanning the handful of police officers standing around in frustrated confusion.

"Just two—local PD," Agent Goodwin replies, nodding at a pair of shapes lurking in the shadows on our right. "As soon as dispatch got word of what they found, they called us."

"And the bodycam footage?"

"Gone," Goodwin replies.

The two officers skulking nearby look deeply shaken by something, pacing to calm their nerves. A pair of cigarette cherries track their back-and-forth movements through the shadows.

Layne hesitates, then nods at the men. "Can you take care of that?" he asks.

Agent Goodwin looks gravely disappointed by this question, but not surprised. He doesn't protest. Before Goodwin turns to leave, however, he catches sight of me and freezes again.

"Is that—" he starts, a surprisingly pained look on his face.

"She's a consultant," Agent Layne states.

Goodwin takes a deep breath. I track the strange expressions that work their way across his face, struggling to interpret the bizarre subtext that has suddenly developed. Goodwin is trying his best to stay even-keeled, but his clenched jaw is a dead giveaway that there's something more going on here.

"Is there a problem? Layne presses.

"She's just . . ." Goodwin starts, then fumbles and shakes his head. "No, sir." With that, he turns and heads off to speak with the nearby officers.

"I used to have that job," Agent Layne explains, his eyes trained on the agent.

"What the hell was that about?" I ask.

"You'd have to ask him," Layne replies, then pushes onward. I follow his lead, hurrying behind as the two of us slip under some black LPEC tape—different from the yellow crime-scene border—and approach the trailer. We've entered the *inner* inner circle.

The police officers behind us can't help watching with rapt curiosity, not accustomed to this kind of exclusion.

"I thought the Low-Probability Event Commission just went around interviewing lotto winners," I state.

"Sometimes," Layne replies, hesitating a moment as we stand outside the trailer. This pause goes on for much longer than I expected, a moral dilemma weighing heavily on my companion's mind.

"You okay?" I ask.

"Just considering whether or not you should come in," he says. "There's no going back from this."

"I can handle blood."

"It's not that," Layne insists, shaking his head. "The LPEC is strict about consultants. You'll be tracked and followed for a while. Your emails will get read. Someone's gonna check in on you."

"Sounds like a civil rights nightmare," I say. "You sure you're allowed to do all that?"

"I can do whatever I want," he replies, every ounce of good-natured fun drained from his tone. His expression is carved in stone. "No red tape, remember?"

I realize now he's not hesitating for himself, but waiting on me to make the call. Once again, it's apparent that much more is happening just below the surface, a decision with consequences reaching far beyond the immediacy of tonight's little pit stop. Layne seems genuinely worried about me, making damn sure I understand there's no turning back once I take the leap.

Apparently, he's forgotten who he's talking to. I'd walk through that door if there were nothing more than a guillotine waiting behind it.

"I haven't checked my email for four years, so if LPEC wants to sort through it for me that'd be great," I finally retort. "Let's get this over with."

Layne nods. He cautiously opens the screen, then the door, pushing his way inside as I follow behind. We find ourselves in the dark common area of a classic 1970s mobile home, a small rectangular living room where the only light to guide us is the flickering glow of an infomercial dancing across a nearby cathode-ray television. The TV's eerie hum washes over everything, bathing the scene with a strange discomfort. The volume is cranked up loud, jangling music pumping through cheap speakers while a woman rambles on and on about kitchen knives.

Layne motions toward a figure sitting upright at the dead center of a nearby couch. This form is positioned directly before the screen, perfectly still as the TV's dancing illumination offers a peculiar sense of ghoulish movement.

A startled gasp escapes my throat as I struggle to understand what I'm looking at.

It appears to be the body of a man. The figure is wearing blue jeans and a red button-up flannel, his hands on his knees and his posture stiff. His face, however, is unrecognizable, because his face is not there.

"What the fuck is that?" I murmur, the words tumbling out of my mouth with an involuntary huff.

Morbid curiosity and primal dread now battle within me, driving my body in opposite directions, but fascination wins out. I step a little closer.

This scene is grotesque in a way that defies my understanding of the universe, an abomination of basic physics, and the compulsion to understand it is rooted deep. A floating hole—about eight inches across—covers the man's face, tilted ever so slightly to the left and leaning back haphazardly. Due to its awkward angle, this cosmic disk slices through most of the man's sensory organs, his eyes, nose, upper lip, and left ear consumed by the slowly rotating mass. Only his right ear and the bottom of his jaw remain, the latter hanging just below the edge of the circle.

A good third of the man's skull is missing, a hefty portion of his brain along with it. Despite all this, however, there's not a drop of blood to be found; no sign of earthly violence, nor exposed flesh.

Layne turns, drawing his weapon as he moves to check out the back room, seemingly unfazed by what we've discovered. For once he's all business, which only adds to the strangeness of the moment.

I creep a little closer to the body, still yearning to understand the cosmic makeup of the floating, churning circle.

The disk is constantly—but very slowly—rotating on a central axis, and its surface bubbles and roils like a shiny black liquid. Flashes of dazzling silver come and go within the brine, moving with the same natural flow as ocean currents or bird flocks—but this particular description fails to capture the otherworldly nature of its fluctuation. It's possible that a tide could surge like this, but only on some distant planet at the edge of the universe. Birds could hope to match its swirl if they flew backward, or upside down.

Enthralled by the movement, I step forward. I'm just a few feet away now, peering into the darkness of the strange void. I can feel the abyss pulling me toward it.

The edge of the disk is shimmering blue and approximately one centimeter thick, although the exact boundaries of the object are vague. It looks as though the world itself is flapping against the celestial platter's slowly churning edge, subtly contorting like the trembling haze over a hot Las Vegas parking lot.

"Oh my God," I sigh.

Something powerful and unseen is spilling from the opening, bathing me in the sensation I've been so desperate to find. It's not a profound force of energy on display, but the opposite. This is the sweet embrace of the grand celestial nothing.

It's empty space.

I lean in.

The corpse erupts to life, arms flailing and throat screeching wildly, bluntly revealing that he's not a corpse at all.

I cry out in alarm, falling back onto the carpet and scrambling away as the body jerks and spasms. The man with the half-missing head can't seem to pull himself away from the disk that has so brutally sliced through his face; everything above the neck is glued into position, while everything below whips into an utter frenzy.

Layne rushes back into the room, his eyes wide as he catches sight of the convulsing form. He immediately springs into action, turning off the television set and doing his best to calm our new friend.

"Hey, hey!" he cries out, kneeling before the figure. "Can you hear me? We're here to help."

The body doesn't stop jolting around, kicking and scratching. His chin pumps awkwardly as guttural noises blubber from his throat in a panic, tongue hanging clumsily to one side while the rest of his face remains swallowed up by frothing oblivion.

"This—this is what you wanted to show me?" I stammer, glancing over at Layne while the figure continues to grunt and shake. "Jesus fucking Christ!"

Eventually, the faceless man calms down. His hands start curiously exploring the area, finding their way up to the vacant space atop his head. He pushes in and out through the churning liquid of the floating disk, searching around inside and then pulling back to reveal empty palms.

Agent Layne finally stands up and backs away, collecting himself. "These holes pop up every time a Minor Low-Probability Event occurs. Little tears in the fabric."

I can feel my blood freeze, a chill of utter horror surging through my nervous system. "Did you just say a *Minor* Low-Probability Event?" I snap. "There's only one. It happened four years ago."

Layne hesitates a moment. "Afraid not."

A wave of nausea washes over me, visions of that day flashing through my mind in a terrifying highlight reel. I see my mother's blood flowing across concrete toward me, the crimson liquid wrapping around my shoes. I see corpses swaying in the wind as they're carried away by a massive dinosaur parade balloon.

The emotions bubbling up are too much, finally compelling me to turn and rush from the trailer. I barge through the door, the screen whipping back with a loud clatter as I stumble down the steps.

What the fuck. What the fuck. What the fuck.

The world is spinning with such velocity that after three steps I'm forced into a wobbling halt, leaning forward with my hands on my knees. It's a struggle to keep my balance.

I still haven't fully processed the events of that terrible day, but there's always been a vague safety net in knowing that all that chaos was behind me. Now, that net is full of holes: swirling platters of black and silver with a sizzling blue edge that never quite finds its shape.

What did Layne say? *Little tears in the fabric.*

Agent Layne eventually exits the trailer behind me, strolling over. "You okay, bud?" he offers.

I ignore his question. "Do we need to get out of here?" I gasp. "Is it safe?"

"Safe? I thought you didn't care what happened," Layne retorts with a laugh.

I bolt upright and turn toward him, an unexpected rush of anger flaring within me. "Do we need to get out of here?" I repeat.

Layne shakes his head. "These small holes only create one event, or a quick combination of events over a small timeframe," he explains. "There might be a stray animal loose or something like that, but by the time we get here the show is usually over."

Before Agent Layne has a chance to continue, Agent Goodwin approaches. His demeanor has shifted a bit, eyes slightly wider and breathing ragged. "Direct witnesses are handled, sir," he says. "We're dealing with the others right now. Appreciate you calling in a bigger team for this one."

I notice now the police cars are gone, but right outside the trailer park a few more LPEC vehicles have arrived. Agents are taking statements from the crowd huddled nearby, pulling each of them aside for private discussions.

"Lots of loose ends," Layne replies with a nod. "Keep on it, this one's a mess."

"What do you wanna do about him?" Goodwin continues, nodding at the trailer behind us.

Agent Layne considers this. "Just sort out the others for now. I'll call you."

"Yes, sir," Goodwin confirms.

Layne steps a little closer to the agent, his already serious tone taking on even more weight. "Do not let anyone else inside that trailer," he commands. "Nobody. If you do, it's on you."

Goodwin's eyes flicker over to me for the briefest moment, then back to Layne. "Understood. Yes, sir." With that, Goodwin turns and marches back toward the crowd of frightened residents.

Layne and I stand in silence for a moment. He reaches into his jacket pocket and pulls out a small rectangular box of jelly beans, pouring a single green candy into his hand. "You want one?" he asks.

I shake my head.

"Some taste good and some are gross. Kinda fitting," he observes, popping it into his mouth. Agent Layne chews for a moment, his brow furrowed inquisitively and then gradually relaxing. "Lime!" he chirps, then swallows.

Layne tucks the box away and nods at one of the charred trailers nearby. "Let me show you something."

Before I get the chance to respond, he's strolling ahead, leaving me to scamper after him. This particular mobile home has a huge black streak on the front porch, the burn fully engulfing an aluminum folding chair and then running up the side of the metal Airstream.

"Half the people in this park held winning National Lotto numbers for tonight's drawing," Agent Layne casually states.

I suddenly recall all the blissed-out expressions I'd seen on the way in. Tonight, all those lives have completely changed—rent covered for years, loans paid off, lifestyles acquired—all because of six little numbers.

A thought occurs to me, my body tensing up a bit. "Do you know what the winning draw was?" I ask. A series of digits begins to roll through my head, returning to me like an old friend. *Thirty-seven. Eighteen. Thirty-two. One hundred and fifteen. Thirty-six. Fifty-two.*

Agent Layne flips through his field documents, scanning the pages. "Yeah, sure," he says, then starts reading aloud. "Twenty. One hundred and six. Seventy—"

"Never mind," I interject.

Layne reads the document a little further, then chuckles to himself. "You'll never guess where the headless wonder worked."

I have a feeling that I know the answer, but Agent Layne fills it in for me. "Just got hired as a blackjack dealer at the Great Britannica."

The poor guy. Trying to make ends meet, and now this.

I glance around the trailer park. "So, half of these people are filthy rich now? I bet the other half are pretty upset."

"Not really," Agent Layne chirps. "Spontaneous human combustion. They all burst into flames."

In another life I might glance over to see if he's joking, but at this point my needle barely moves for his horrific reveal. I see now that a pair of severed feet sit directly before the chair, side by side in sneakers and white athletic socks. There's a surreal neatness to them, straight and tidy, but that quickly disappears by the time I reach the scorched ankles, flesh and bone quickly transitioning into black char and gray dust. Other than the feet, there's no body to be found.

"No idea what the divide is just yet," Layne continues. "Could be folks born on an even day got popped. Maybe it's sorted by age. Sometimes it's just random. You never know who's getting the lawn clippings flavor."

"The what?"

Agent Layne pats his jacket pocket, jelly beans rattling within.

My companion hesitates a moment, breathing deep and then letting it out. For the first time, I notice the pungent smell of burning flesh and melted plastic haunting the air. I'm not sure what you'd call this flavor.

Inside, the man with half a head has started up again, moaning and groaning as he flails about, trapped in place by some bizarre celestial tear.

"Aw, fuck," Layne announces. "Now I've given myself a sweet tooth. You want ice cream?"

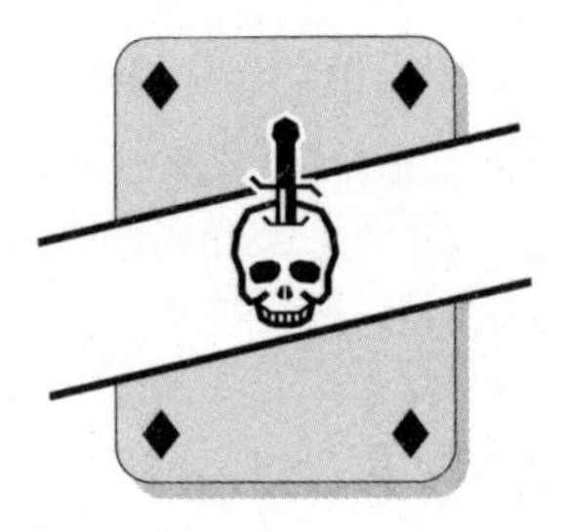

LOOSE ENDS

Agent Layne excitedly carves off another piece of his habanero chocolate chip ice cream, which sits as some proud abomination atop a warm slice of boysenberry pie. An additional dollop of dull pink bubblegum ice cream rests patiently nearby, waiting for its time to shine. It's a strange combination, but Layne made these bold choices assertively after proclaiming, "I've never had boysenberry pie before! Let's put *two* scoops on that!"

Now, he consumes this treat with innocent wonder as I watch in silence, my head swimming with so many thoughts that it's impossible for any particular one to make its way forward.

"You sure you don't want any?" Layne asks.

I shake my head in refusal. "I'm not hungry."

We're seated at a corner booth, tucked away by a window that looks onto the parking lot of this red-and-white-painted roadhouse diner. It's not too late in the evening yet, but it might as well be three in the morning because this place is clearly hurting for business. Save for a pair of long-haul truckers at the bar and a table of college kids looking drunk and weary across the dining room, we're the only ones here.

I'm vaguely aware that the sizzling, greasy food cooking nearby would smell amazing and decadent on any other day, but right now I'm too distracted to care. Agent Layne dives into the bubblegum ice cream next, fixing up his bite by swirling it through the melted purple boysenberry, then popping the whole thing into his mouth. He chews, then raises his eyebrows and nods approvingly.

"Good," Layne announces.

"You're so . . . odd," I say.

Agent Layne smiles. "Is it odd to live every day like it's your last?" he asks. "*You're* the odd one. You're like a cross between Morticia Addams and Cousin Itt."

"Oh please," I groan. "So you said yes to the day and ordered a boysenberry pie with chocolate and bubblegum ice cream? *Whoop-de-do!* Your inner child must be so pumped, but what's that gonna do for you when you burst into fucking flames for no goddamn reason? Or some wormhole decides to open up on your *face*?"

He considers this, taking another bite of his pie and chewing slowly. He swallows, but when he opens his mouth again he doesn't answer. Instead, he offers an observation of his own.

"First of all, it's *habanero* chocolate ice cream," Agent Layne states. "Secondly, for someone who says they don't care about anything, you've sure stuck around."

For the first time, I don't deny this accusation.

Layne scoops up another bite. He chews, taking his time, then swallows and makes his offer. "I can tell you everything I know—*everything*—and maybe together we can help a lot of people."

"The grand cosmic lie that we can *help* anything is a temporary balm on a festering wound of existence," I reply. "It's a way to pass the time while we decay, a magic trick. So yeah, maybe I got caught up in the adventure of it all, because it's nice to momentarily forget that everything we do is just a different flavor of suffering. Maybe I enjoyed a few moments of distraction from the brutal, suffocating truth that we're just electrified bags of meat with no other purpose than to fuck and die. I will finally admit that I care about something, but it's not *helping a lot of people*. It's burning Everett to the fucking ground."

Agent Layne's face is overwhelmed by an amused, tight-lipped grin, his shoulders bobbing in a moment of silent laughter. "Whatever works," he says, then consumes another enormous bite. "Here's the thing, though. Wouldn't you rather fuck and die and burn Everett to the ground while eating ice cream?"

Our waitress approaches, noticing that Layne is nearly finished with his dessert. "Can I get you two anything else?" she asks.

Agent Layne doesn't reply, just looks at me and waits for my response.

I hesitate, then reluctantly nod.

Layne turns back to the waitress. "You know what sounds good? Another scoop of ice cream for my friend here."

"Sure thing."

The waitress leaves as Agent Layne settles in, studying me.

"When I first took this job, nobody had any idea what the hell was going on," he explains. "I was on desk duty with the FBI, probably would've gotten fired soon, too. My life was a mess, but I started turning things around after the Low-Probability Event. They put me back in the field. Got lucky on a—"

"Wait," I interrupt. "After the Low-Probability Event, you *turned your life around*?"

"I did," he confirms, seemingly unaware of the vastly different paths that the hand of fate set us out on.

"Then you weren't in the thick of it," I retort. "You must feel pretty fortunate."

"My brother's face exploded," Agent Layne counters flatly. "I was sitting right next to him."

"Oh," I fumble.

Layne hesitates as some distant thought works its way through his mind. "Yeah" is all he can manage before straightening up a bit. "I drank a lot back then. Surviving a day like that really puts things in perspective. I *do* feel fortunate."

The waitress returns with a scoop of ice cream, placing the bowl in front of me. Layne takes his spoon and carves off a little piece for himself, but I'm not quite ready.

"Anyway, I got lucky on a tough case early on," Agent Layne continues. "Made a few connections and got transferred to a top position in the LPEC. Back then, there were about ten of us; now there's something like two hundred agents."

"What was this lucky case about?" I press.

"It was the first of those little holes we ever found," my companion explains. "I'd pulled some strings and gotten rehired at the Bureau. Beautiful day, sun was shining bright at a city park in Nashville, Tennessee. Folks walking their dogs, playing catch . . ." He trails off for a moment, a surge of emotion pulsing through him. "Kids on the playground," Layne finally continues. "Twenty-four people dropped dead at the exact same moment. Brain aneurisms. There's footage from doorcams across the street and I'll tell ya, it may have been quick and painless, but it's also one of the most horrific things I've ever seen."

I can't help imagining the bizarre and tragic scene, considering the whiplash of going from joyful summer fun to a cold blanket of death. A couple enjoying a picnic simply collapsing into their potato salad. A confused dog returning its thrown stick to find its master slumped awkwardly in the grass. Cries of playful excitement immediately snuffed out, leaving nothing behind but a chain clanging against a metal swing set.

"Everyone thought it was bioterrorism, you know? What are the chances two people could pop a spontaneous brain aneurism at the same time? Let alone twenty-four," Layne explains.

He seems oddly numb to his own story now, despite the brief emotional hiccup just moments earlier. Agent Layne's ability to compartmentalize these things is unlike anything I've ever seen.

"The Technical Hazards Response Unit goes in and does a sweep, but they can't find anything," he continues. "In fact, *nobody* can find anything. The whole case slows down."

I hadn't even noticed, but I'm so entranced by Agent Layne's story that I've taken my spoon and slipped it into the ice cream. I stop myself, pushing the bowl away.

"It's a few weeks later and we've still got no answers. Feels like this whole thing is just gonna fall through the cracks, but I can't get it out of my head. So I go to the park," says Agent Layne. "Nobody's allowed back in yet, which makes the place a little spooky, but there's something else that feels kinda different. You know what it is?"

I don't respond, waiting for him to continue.

"All that green grass had been overtaken by something new, a bed of clover covering the whole place," he reveals. "Nobody else was paying enough attention to notice, but I spotted it. Every single one of those clovers had four leaves."

"One out of every ten thousand clovers has four leaves," I interject. "Approximately."

"Looks like they're all at a park in the country music capital of the world," he replies. "Suddenly, it's not just one freak occurrence, it's two. Something sweet, something sour. Thanks to me, there's new life in the investigation and, lo and behold, we find one of those little reality tears near a storm drain down the street. That's when they moved me to LPEC and the whole game changed."

"So you're a *celebrity* in the world of unconstitutional government overreach?" I clarify.

"Nobody knows who I am," Agent Layne replies. "That's how this job works. People need time to heal after the Low-Probability Event; they can't know the wound is still open. The *economy* certainly doesn't need to know about that."

The initial formation of the LPEC was greeted with glorious applause, despite their carte blanche approach to what was, and still is, an abstract enemy. Basic expectations of privacy were rolled back in a way that made the Patriot Act look downright reasonable. Meanwhile, blind and belligerent nationalism shot through the roof.

But that initial surge quickly gave way to fear and frustration. The LPE was a new kind of problem, one that couldn't be bombed into submission with nightly drone strikes or curbed with the passage of new laws. The fear and anxiety here were intangible and mysterious, refusing to fit any particular sound-bite narrative.

It was a worldwide existential crisis.

"So every reality tear prompts a hard swerve in fate," I summarize. "Moments of extreme good luck and moments of extreme bad luck."

"We call them plot holes," Layne explains, chuckling to himself. "There's evidence each hole creates opposing sets of highly unlikely events like you're saying, but there's just as much evidence that it's totally random."

"What do *you* think?"

Layne considers this. "Well, opposing pairs implies the existence of an objective *good* and *bad,* which is a whole other can of worms. If you wanna talk about the potential existence of God we certainly can. In my experience, it amounts to more questions than answers."

I can still see that swirling dark portal in my mind, imagine its frothy surface as blue light surges across the churning edge.

"What's in the holes?" I ask. "That man in the trailer, he was reaching around inside."

Agent Layne smiles. "It's . . . complicated. None of them are big enough to fit your head through, but after we constructed a periscope, a few test subjects had a look."

"Test subjects?"

Layne seems amused by my apprehension. "I sure as hell wasn't gonna look through it first. Besides, they're paid well. We take care of 'em."

I furrow my brow, struggling to parse the unspoken complexities of what he's telling me.

"Everyone sees something different," Layne continues. "One subject said it was her childhood bedroom, another saw a circus. One guy claimed there was an orgy in there, although it took a while for him to actually admit it on the official forms."

"And you?" I ask.

"My high school shop class," he replies, then shrugs. "I mean . . . who knows? We tried recording it on video, but the transmissions are static. Audio is the same. We sent in a few rats and they suffocated, but if we give them an oxygen supply they usually live. They always come back a little off . . . Good?"

His final word comes out of nowhere, an abrupt fragment of question I'm not sure how to answer. For a brief moment I have no idea what Agent Layne's talking about, until I suddenly realize I've been mindlessly eating my ice cream.

I drop the spoon, a surge of embarrassment coursing through me. "Oh. No."

Agent Layne holds my gaze for a moment, struggling not to smirk. "Live a little," he finally suggests. "Living is all we've got."

I push the dish away. "So what happens to the holes?"

"We quarantine the area for a little while, then after a few months they start to shrink and disappear," he explains.

I sense a plume of sparks blooming in the vast dark space of my mind as renegade neurons reach out and grab for one another. This little sensation of excitement used to be a daily occurrence, connections constantly firing off in a euphoric search for order. It's been a while, though. As nice as it feels to work this muscle, I'm also painfully aware that I haven't been stretching.

"Historical inertia," I murmur, words falling involuntarily from my mouth as the phrase manifests in my brain.

Agent Layne pauses, recognizing this moment for what it is: genuine excitement and curiosity.

"In probability, we observe the frequency of variable outcomes," I continue, more and more lights in my skull flickering on. "The larger the sample group, the more accurate the results. The problem is, students would take this too far and start thinking about the real world like a giant lab, because what's a bigger sample group than the human population? It doesn't work like that, though. Life has too many variables. The Earth is not a sterile vacuum. We can make sense of it, but that takes time and effort and extreme attention to detail."

I suddenly catch myself, realizing I've fallen into one of my old lectures. My opinion on this point has fundamentally changed, because I now know there's no sense to be made. Existence is senseless.

"I mean . . ." I stammer, shaking my head to wipe the slate clean. "That's not the point. I'm sorry, it's been a while since I explained these things." I hesitate, planning to stop talking entirely, but I just can't do it. "Do you know what the butterfly effect is?"

Agent Layne shakes his head.

"Edward Lorenz, mathematician, talked about the power one small change can have as it cascades into others. A butterfly flapping its wings on one side of the world might disturb a plant, which then grows slightly shorter and isn't picked by someone passing by, and then their vase of flowers—which are different now—lasts longer than expected. Then they don't need to go out and buy new flowers, so they skip a car ride that would have caused a wreck, and now someone is still alive, and on and on and on, snowballing into larger events," I explain. "Eventually, the butterfly's flap becomes a tornado. It's the theory that small change creates massive impact."

"I mean . . . that's fascinating," Layne offers in a state of genuine awe. "I'm really enjoying this, but what's it got to do with the Low-Probability Event?"

"There's another theory that's a counter to the butterfly effect; it's called historical inertia," I say. "Essentially, historical inertia states that if the butterfly refuses to flap its wings, the tornado still happens, because a seagull flaps its wings instead. The same path is always created in a different way. Major events can never change."

I can tell Agent Layne's innate sense of wonder has been captured. His eyes are laser-focused on mine.

"According to historical inertia, if I went back in time and stopped Lee Harvey Oswald from shooting JFK, we'd return to the present and find everything was almost exactly the same. We'd open a newspaper and see someone else listed as the shooter just a few days later on some different stretch of road."

"I'm sorry," Layne blurts. "But I still don't see how this connects to us."

I mount my reply, then stop myself, realizing now that what I'm about to say is a massive leap. As a former mathematician, the very idea of the path I'm about to take feels strange and foreign in my throat, like an infection I can't help coughing out.

In my past life, it'd be impossible to form these words, but a lot has changed since then.

"What if fate is quantifiable and concrete?" I question aloud. "Not just a product of circumstance but a tangible, measurable *energy*."

"Luck," Agent Layne replies.

I nod. "When these holes arrive, they're plucking that energy like a string, rocking the pendulum back and forth and then, when the energy runs out, settling. It's no wonder they disappear. That's just historical inertia doing its thing and smoothing out the wrinkles."

Something about this connects with Layne. "Like ripples in what's *supposed* to happen," he offers.

"Sure," I confirm, unable to hide my excitement now as I watch this theory fall into place. It's a fucking *absurd* theory, but a theory nonetheless.

This is a system I can actually start to work with. It's logical in its own ridiculous way. It has meaning.

It suddenly occurs to me that I've finished my entire scoop of ice cream, the cold sweetness still dancing across my tastebuds in a way that's unexpected and indulgent and strangely fun. I wasn't paying attention as I wolfed down this dessert, but there's no question I enjoyed it.

"Which brings us to the Great Britannica," I finally continue. "This all started when you realized every person who died or was seriously injured during the LPE visited the casino. That's weird, sure, but you've also gotta consider the fact that there's *even more* people who visited the Great Britannica during that time who *didn't* die or suffer some grave misfortune. Suddenly, your data is not so exciting. But that's only because you're looking at the wrong variable. You're asking the wrong question."

"What question should I be asking?" Agent Layne asks.

"It's not *Did they visit the Great Britannica?*" I reply. "It's *Did they win big there?*"

"We already considered that. Eight million people is too many jackpots for one casino. Even the Great Britannica couldn't sustain it."

"But did you check it against each visitor's average yearly income?" I press. "The odds of a ten-cent slot pull turning into five hundred dollars are worse than ten bucks becoming half a million, so which one is the *big* win? How can you determine what wildly unlikely success means without considering bet *sizes*?"

Agent Layne's expression freezes, a wave of understanding washing over him as he connects the dots. "The pendulum swinging back," he says, more to himself than to me. Suddenly, curiosity overwhelms his face. "If you're right, then why not a big snap back into place for the losers? Along with the bad luck, why wasn't there also some kind of worldwide *lucky* day?"

"Maybe there was," I reply, the gravity of what I've just said causing an unexpected wave of sadness to course through me. There are implications about the human condition here that are much darker than any of my most nihilistic diatribes. "There aren't a lot of police reports about the day you get your promotion, hit every green light on the drive home, and sink a half-court shot with your eyes closed. Maybe someone found a thousand dollars in an envelope. Maybe someone made a new lifelong friend. Either way, most people remember the bad things and forget the good stuff. That's just how our brains work. A day holding just as much joy as the Low-Probability Event held tragedy could've already happened . . . we just didn't notice."

Agent Layne doesn't respond, and I don't fill in the empty space. Instead, the two of us let these feelings marinate.

There are billions and billions of paths for us on any given day, and we certainly remember the ones that lead to something like a brutal car crash. We think to ourselves, *Why me? How did I get so unlucky?* The problem is, we have absolutely no idea how many times we've missed one of the infinite tragic routes, ducking and dodging butterflies left and right. Every day, we never know the billions and billions and billions of car crashes we're *not* in.

I sit up a bit in my booth, clearing my throat. "Either way, Everett's found a way to harness this energy," I finally continue, struggling to fill in the blanks and make sense of this tangled web. "Maybe they've managed to keep one of those plot holes active."

"Maybe they know how to make new ones," Agent Layne interjects, already thinking ahead.

I nod. "Whatever it is, we're gonna find out."

BUTTERFLY HUNTING

Now that I'm an insider—a *consultant,* as Agent Layne says—I've found new momentum. Today, this onward push has manifested physically, Layne's rental car carrying us deep into the vast Nevada desert.

I asked Layne for all of LPEC's plot hole research data and he was happy to turn it over, blessing me with a disk drive that looks identical to the previous information trove from Everett.

What he didn't mention is that several of his LPEC research files have been deleted. Ironically, I only noticed his omission because of a statement that's been rattling around in my head since Agent Layne himself uttered it a few days back.

Sometimes you can learn more by the cards they don't *show.*

There are huge gaps in the drive's unseen naming conventions. Whoever encrypted these files was smart enough to keep me from making copies without Layne's personal USB key, but they still didn't manage to wipe the data spotless. There's been tampering.

I have no idea why Layne pulled this sneaky little omission, but for now I'm not interested in tugging the thread. This isn't the *whole pie* I was promised, but now that some real answers wait on the horizon, it's enough.

Unfortunately, there isn't information on the annual income of these visitors, but there's plenty of data on when their casino visits occurred. It took a while to sort through all the names and stories, but eventually I found the earliest guest who was later killed during the Low-Probability Event.

Donald Eastwick was a twenty-three-year-old Major League rookie when he booked a stay at the Great Britannica Hotel and Casino during the offseason. Fourteen years later, on May 23, Donald was clearing out brush on his property in Austin, Texas, when the man's young neighbors knocked a baseball into his yard and struck him in the back of the head. Donald tumbled into a wood chipper, first putting out his arm to stop the fall and then gradually getting sucked through as he struggled to free himself.

This particular baseball happened to be signed by an MLB rookie from years earlier: Donald Eastwick himself.

After uncovering this information, I got to work looking through Everett's Las Vegas real estate acquisitions, using the dates I'd already cataloged but narrowing it down to purchases made slightly before Donald's visit. From there, I did what any statistics and probability professor would do: I looked for outliers.

"Turn here," I announce suddenly, prompting Agent Layne to slow his vehicle to a crawl.

He glances around, surveying the endless expanse, nothing more than a single dirt road cutting through the sand.

"Turn where?" Layne asks, eventually stopping completely.

I point into the desert, miles and miles of untamed Nevada wilds awash with the early morning sun. It's wide-open on either side of us, flatlands pocked with cacti that gradually evolve into rolling ranges beyond.

There's absolutely nothing here, and that's exactly why it grabbed my attention.

Everett Vacation and Entertainment inexplicably purchased this land many years ago, a portion of desert so remote you'd require an off-road trek just to reach its border. Once there, you could drive for half an hour and hardly reach the other side. They've refused to develop the acreage in any way, hardly acknowledging its existence. Then again, why would they? We're two hours outside Las Vegas, far enough away that no tourist would ever feel the need to travel here, regardless of what Everett built.

Agent Layne eyes me. "How many times am I gonna have to tell you to put your seat belt on?" he questions.

I ignore the request, prompting a defeated sigh from the driver's seat.

"Good thing I got full coverage at the rental place," Agent Layne remarks, guiding us off the dirt road and into the great unknown.

It's slow going on the uneven ground, but that's alright with me. Without knowing what exactly we're looking for out here it's best to have confidence in our initial sweep.

Layne turns up his audiobook, an instructional guide to beginner's French, and we get to work. Soon enough, we're cruising back and forth across this massive, seemingly empty swath of land, combing the property in a simple zigzag pattern.

The sun creeps its way over the distant mountains, first creating long, endless shadows from every renegade cactus and then gradually shrinking these silhouettes as the day rolls onward. My eyes are peeled, searching for any sign of some strange hovering portal, an apparent tear in the fabric of reality just waiting to be discovered. Whatever Everett Vacation and Entertainment has at their disposal is likely much grander than the standard plot hole, but the previous visual cues are a great place to start when you have no idea what you're looking for.

Unfortunately, catharsis never comes.

Instead, I find myself greeted by more of the same. There's nothing out here but endless desert flats and a few rolling mounds that pock the landscape like random turtle shells of dirt and boulders.

There is *one* unusual moment during our search, however, a flash of excitement that courses through me when I catch sight of two dark vehicles perched atop the distant mountain range. They're barely visible and I only hone in on them thanks to a brief reflection of sunlight against some metallic detailing.

"There." I point.

Agent Layne follows my gesture, slowing our vehicle down to a crawl and then stopping completely. A knowing smile works its way across his face.

"Area Fifty-One," Layne informs me. "Sometimes they have security patrolling that ridge, but it's miles and miles away."

"Area Fifty-One is really out here?" I ask. "I thought Denver was just fucking with us."

Agent Layne shakes his head. "It's here. Down in the western valley. They've got some killer spy planes."

"You've *been*?" I exclaim, unable to help myself. Despite my commitment to indifference, more simmering fascination has popped its head out to have a look around.

"Didn't see any little green men, unfortunately," Layne admits. "I'll put in a word and see if they've noticed anything, but I doubt it. Those nerds have their hands full."

With that, Layne starts driving again. He turns up the volume, allowing a cascade of French words and phrases to narrate our fruitless journey. I can't help but feel like they're mocking me.

"Je vais souvent nager à la piscine en été," Agent Layne loudly repeats the sentence back to his car stereo.

Before my companion can get very far, I reach out and press pause, interrupting our journey for a second time. "Stop," I command.

Layne hits the brakes and brings us to a dusty halt.

"The only thing out here is dirt," I announce, frustration coloring my tone.

Agent Layne considers this, drumming his fingers on the steering wheel for a minute. Finally, he shrugs. "No problem. Let's just tell 'em we found something more exciting."

I glance over, not entirely sure what he's getting at.

"We don't know everything, but we've figured out enough," he continues. "I'm pretty good at getting information out of folks with a few well-placed threats."

I stare at him blankly. "Is that legal?"

Layne smiles, putting the car back in drive and cranking the wheel. We're now returning to the main road. "LPEC decides what's legal."

I can tell Agent Layne expects me to be joyful or relieved in this moment, thankful we can bend the rules to make things right. Instead, I feel deeply unnerved.

"You okay?" he questions.

"Nobody is okay," I reply.

Agent Layne glances over, then returns his focus to the path ahead. He reaches out and presses play.

"Je vais souvent nager à la piscine en été," the instructor says.

The massive plumes of flowers that rise before me are gorgeous, yes, but there's still something a little disturbing about seeing this lush display in such an unexpected place. If the Las Vegas skyline is mankind's defiance of nature, then the indoor garden at the Great Britannica is a monument to our knack for taming it.

From the shining marble floors below me to the glass ceilings some four stories up, the atrium is packed with beautiful flora, plucked from the dirt and planted here in strange, surreal arrangements. Some of the flowers exist in a familiar, semiwild state, filling the garden beds with their vibrant colors, but others have been arranged across huge wire meshes to create lifelike characters.

To my left is a giant smiling fox made of reddish-orange blooms, and to my right is a massive approximation of a white bird carrying crimson garlands in its mouth. These floral animals bob their heads from side to side with repeating animatronic movement, driven by a small motor tucked somewhere deep within.

"How's that?" someone calls out.

Denver White, clad in a navy suit and bolo tie, and sporting the same cowboy hat she'd worn before, offers an indifferent shrug. "How's what? The dog head? Looks good."

She turns her attention back to us. "The work never ends, huh? They build these things downstairs, then place them in a single afternoon."

"And you do this for every holiday?" Agent Layne asks.

"We find a new theme each month," Denver replies. "Sometimes it's a season, sometimes a holiday. This one is . . ."

She trails off a bit, then turns back to one of the Great Britannica gardeners who's carefully attaching a giant floral tail to the fox with a large machine.

"What's this one for?" Denver asks.

"Bawming the Thorn," the gardener replies.

Denver turns back to Layne, nodding in confirmation. "Bawming the Thorn," she repeats.

"Which is?" Layne asks.

"I have no fucking idea," the cowgirl says with a laugh. "It ain't from around here, that's for sure."

Usually the garden is bustling with hotel patrons, a showpiece sitting just past the lobby that lets every guest know they've arrived at a place of true luxury. However, changeover requires a portion of the casino to close for a few hours.

"We know about the property up north," Agent Layne says, diving in, "and we know what you've got up there."

Denver halts abruptly, now giving us her full attention. The woman doesn't seem frightened by this revelation, though. Instead, the faint curl of her lips suggests a touch of amusement.

"Oh yeah?" she retorts. "What is it you think I have up there?"

Layne just stares at the cowgirl for a moment, letting his words settle.

"Do you understand I can just shut this whole place down?" my companion finally says. "I can walk over to that lobby and tell them to stop checking people in. I can get your pit bosses and floor managers to turn off the machines and stop taking bets until we get this whole thing straightened out."

"Until we can get it straightened out, huh?" Denver muses, her skeptical smile now graduating to a full-on grin.

"Just under eight million people died on that day," Layne continues. "We have evidence directly connecting this establishment to the Low-Probability Event. If you work with us now, you might not get a needle in your arm. If you don't . . . well, who knows what could happen. That's a lot of grieving families looking to direct their anger somewhere."

Denver hesitates a beat, then breaks out in a fit of laughter. She can't help herself. "Did y'all forget I play poker, too?" she chides, eventually settling. "I can spot a bluff a mile away. If you found something out there, then why wait to shut us down? Why even have this conversation?"

Granted, this is only the second suspect interview I've been a part of, but I can't help feeling like things aren't going as planned.

From the corner of my eye I catch sight of Agent Layne, still deeply focused on his floundering intimidation. Layne seems blissfully unaware of how little we've accomplished, but it suddenly occurs to me there might be a reason for his blind confidence.

"I have cell phone records," Layne announces. "Based on the tower pings, we know you've been going to that plot of land on a regular schedule. We also have your text messages."

We do?

I try my best not to react, unsure if Agent Layne is still bending the truth as a means of intimidation, or if we've really crossed into a new paradigm. It's impossible to tell from his expression.

Denver seems impressed by Agent Layne's audacity, nodding along as she considers these words. "Last time I checked, it's not illegal for a company to keep tabs on the property they own."

Agent Layne doesn't answer.

"I might *seem* like one of them Blue Lives Matter girls, but if there's one thing I don't care for it's crooked cops rooting around in the affairs of an upstanding businesswoman who is just carving out an honest living," she continues. "You know, *don't tread on me* and all that bullshit."

"We're not cops," Agent Layne retorts.

Denver White takes a moment to eye us up and down, her judgment carrying an unexpected weight despite the fact that I don't give a fuck what she thinks. "Y'all sure act like it," she finally says.

Our confrontation reaches a standstill, a somber quiet falling over the three of us.

"Listen, you're just the gal who runs the Great Britannica," Agent Layne finally continues, trying one last angle. "We want Everett Vacation and Entertainment. If you help us out now, you still might get to keep a few crumbs of this very nice life you've built for yourself."

"Tempting," Denver sneers, "but I think I'll pass. I didn't get here by rolling over on the hand that feeds me just because a couple of dumb fucks tell me they found treasure in the desert. I know you think you're above the law, but guess what?"

Denver leans in close now, lowering her voice and reaching up to give her hat a little tip. "I am, too," she states with a wink. "I don't care what evidence you *think* you have, if you come in here and shut this place down then y'all better hope it's one hell of a smoking gun, because the lobbyist wing of EVE runs very, very deep. I believe they sign your paychecks."

The cowgirl straightens up. "Be seeing y'all," she says, turning to stroll away.

"Hey!" I yell, stopping Denver in her tracks.

The woman turns back curiously.

"You've had a good run, but you can't sustain this," I insist. "What happens when a swarm of some rare killer bee comes pouring out of these flowers? Or when a meteor lands on your poker room? If you don't stop, a lot of people will die, but I don't think you care about that. What I *do* think you care about is how much money it's gonna take to clean up."

For a moment, I think the cowgirl might break, that something I've said is going to pierce through her skull and take root in that greedy little brain.

Finally, she speaks. "Sugar, I have no idea what you're talking about," Denver says, then takes her leave.

"Okay then," Layne chirps, popping a stick of bubblegum in his mouth.

That's what I get for shooting my shot. Every time I give a fuck, the world comes right back over the top and shows me how little I matter.

"You wanna catch a show?" Agent Layne asks. "I hear the Eddie Michaels residency over at Caesar's is incredible. That's America's Elton John, you know."

"What was all that stuff about cell phone pings and text messages?" I counter, ignoring his question. "Is that real?"

The bubblegum chewing stops. Agent Layne nods.

"You're saying you can just go through people's cell phone records without a warrant?" I ask.

He shrugs. "It doesn't matter, there was nothing in the texts. These people make damn sure not to leave a trail." With that, he pops in his earbuds and starts up some unknown song. Layne turns and heads back toward the parking garage, bobbing his head as he goes. "Let's get back to the motel and regroup!" he calls over his shoulder.

I follow, fascinated by the way he takes these massive blunders in stride. Agent Layne is oddly unaffected by the world around him, unshaken by the highs and lows, and while part of me is jealous, the other part is a little frightened by it.

"Day party at Loch Luck, best wave pool in Vegas," a suited promoter announces, leaping from behind a *Dark Encounters*–themed slot machine and waving two passes at me.

I raise my hand to decline, but Agent Layne has already noticed.

He spins abruptly. “Pool party?” Layne questions, pulling out his earbuds.

“Oh—uh, yeah,” the promoter stammers. Layne is clearly not the market he’s been asked to target. The agent is handsome, but he’s also an older man.

“I’ll take ’em,” Layne says. “I’ve never been to one of these.”

The promoter retracts his passes awkwardly. “They’re for her,” he replies.

A startled chortle of laughter escapes me, but the fun of this moment is short-lived. Agent Layne opens his jacket and flashes his LPEC badge, a stern look on his face. “Give me the fucking passes.”

“Oh, sorry,” the promoter immediately mumbles, handing over two tickets before quickly moving on.

Layne glances back at me, raising his eyebrows mischievously, but I don’t reciprocate his joyful exuberance.

“Come on,” my companion demands. “Let’s regroup.”

I follow behind as Agent Layne makes his way toward the pool deck.

“We don’t have anything to swim in!” I call out, but Layne doesn’t listen.

Soon enough, the two of us are pushing into the hot afternoon sun, discovering a massive pool of turquoise water that weaves its way through a lush, tropical grove. An enormous waterfall spills continuously to the left, cascading into the shimmering lagoon below. To the right is a path that treks around either side of this immaculately crafted water feature.

A man greets us quickly, asking for the two passes that we promptly hand over. While most of the crowd is wandering around in this waist-deep pool, their drinks held precariously over the rippling surface, the rest of the partiers are simply grooving in their swimsuits at the edge.

Across the water is a large DJ booth, a man nodding enthusiastically behind his open laptop and a set of turntables. Thunderous house music emanates from his station, and from various speakers tucked under the ferns and man-made boulders. The rhythm is heavy and constant, hammering through my body with every booming kick drum.

My companion leads, heading around the edge and maneuvering us into a little cove where the crowd falls away. There's a relatively quiet bar over here, far from the central party zone.

Layne sidles up to the counter, then turns back to me. "What do you want? My treat," he says, no longer forced to yell over the pounding music.

"To escape the endless purgatory of this wretched mortal shell," I reply.

Agent Layne ignores my words and turns his attention back to the bartender. Soon enough, we're heading over to a round high-top table with two White Russians, one of them virgin.

The bartender was horrified, but he tried his best.

"I'm thinking we go over more property bought during your timeline," Layne announces as the two of us sit down. "You're definitely onto something."

"There's a lot of real estate to look over, and they're not all open pieces of land. We can't just drive out and kick open every door," I explain.

"We actually can. I'll get some agents on it," Layne counters. "Just make me a list of priority locations to start with. We'll get on it tomorrow morning with a whole team."

I hesitate, not quite sure if I want to dig into this right now and then finally plowing ahead. "What about protocol, or whatever? These people are evil fucks, but you can't just walk into hundreds of houses for no reason. Some of this property is high-density residential."

"LPEC has no protocol. So, I guess I can."

"No, I mean it's not *right*!" I exclaim.

Layne's expression immediately shifts to one of condescending amusement, as though I'm a puppy who just stumbled over its own front paws in a particularly adorable way. "Is the girl who doesn't care about anything actually coming to me with a moral stance? Is that what I'm hearing right now?"

"Fuck you," I snap, not the most eloquent response, but a good summary of how I'm feeling. "You can't just flash your badge at some kid handing out pool passes for minimum wage, either. Most people see that as a threat."

"A *threat*?" he laughs. "Oh God, that's rich. He'll be fine. The guy's got a story to tell his friends when he gets home."

"Don't you get it?" I snarl. "You're one of the biggest reasons why this world is so fucked-up." Despite all the arguing we've done, this seems to strike Agent Layne deeper than anything else I've said. He's genuinely stunned.

I let out a long sigh, then pull the straw from my White Russian. I take a massive gulp, swallowing a quarter of the milky beverage in a giant slurp. It's awful.

"You think you're so elevated with this new-lease-on-life, carpe-diem bullshit, but you're actually just like . . ." I falter in my proclamation, struggling to find the words. "You're the poster boy for privilege and toxic masculinity."

"I can't have toxic masculinity," he retorts. "I'm gay."

My eyes go wide. "Like *hell* you can't."

"You wouldn't understand." Agent Layne's tone is perfectly balanced between a serious response and something that's intentionally designed to piss me off.

"Fuck you, again," I say. "I'm bi."

Layne takes this in, raising his eyebrows and stirring his drink with the straw. It looks as though he's enjoying his own little private joke, declining to share it with me but finding amusement all the same.

"What?" I prod, fuming as my level of annoyance reaches its breaking point.

"Who *isn't* bi these days?" Layne finally sighs, gazing into his creamy beverage. When he looks back up our eyes meet, and he can now see that I'm deeply upset. I don't say a word, but my expression dares him to continue.

Agent Layne cracks a shit-eating grin. "All these supposed *bisexuals* are one of two things, Vera. Confused gays on their way over the bridge, or straight people looking for attention."

"I'm done!" I exclaim, slamming my hands on the table. I immediately stand, turning and marching away from Layne as a surge of venomous rage courses through my bloodstream.

It shouldn't hurt this bad anymore, certainly not like it did when my mother said something potently similar four years ago. Back then, the idea of nonexistence hit me like a truck, a fitting metaphor given the timing.

Of course, when Maria and Agent Layne made this claim they weren't speaking about some grand, cosmic *nothingness,* and I probably shouldn't interpret it that way. Unfortunately, it's hard for me not to.

Then again, in the existential sense they're both right: I don't exist, not *really.* I certainly don't matter when you consider the size of the universe and my place as an infinitely small speck of dust drifting somewhere within it. Maybe that's why these words cut me so deep, because even when I had my whole life laid out for me in perfect, linear steps, I'd still get those haunting nights lying in bed, considering how terrifyingly big everything was, and how little control I really had over any of it.

Or maybe I'm overthinking things.

Agent Layne is yelling behind me, his words unable to pierce the mighty thump of a bass drum that rolls out across the luxurious, palm tree–covered pool deck. I find myself weaving through a handful of barely clothed partiers, realizing just how bizarre I probably look sporting my heavy, jet-black pantsuit.

Something tickles my face and I wipe it away.

I round the lagoon, headed back the way I came, when another light touch against my cheek causes me to halt in confusion. I stop abruptly, now sensing a strange patter against my jacket. There's movement in my hair, tiny objects bouncing against its dark waves. One of the little falling pieces has gotten caught in my tangled mop, and I pull it out to inspect it.

"What the fuck?" I stammer, turning the object over in my hands.

The second I make sense of it, a startled gasp escapes my throat and utter horror shoots through my chest in a venomous surge. I'm staring at a tiny, edible horseshoe in dull pink. Along with blue unicorns and little pots of gold, it's one of the seven special marshmallows in every box of Lucky Crisp cereal.

I turn and look across the pool deck, seeing now that the partiers have stopped dancing as popped rice and colorful marshmallows rain down from above. Flamboyant bits of cereal float across the pool's surface, drifting in the water as swimmers curiously scoop them up.

A few partiers open their mouths and make eager attempts to catch the cereal as it falls, cheering playfully and high fiving their friends with every success.

It's fine. Everything's fine.

To quell any panic, I remind myself that these day parties have special machines to create similar effects, raining confetti from above or even dropping dollar bills to whip up the crowd. Unfortunately, it appears these Lucky Crisps are plummeting from much higher up than the pool deck, likely coming from an upper casino floor—maybe even the clouds above.

During the Low-Probability Event, an ultra-rare meteorological phenomenon occurred in which thousands of fish were swept into the sky and then rained down on the city of Chicago, so anything's possible.

I glance over at the DJ in his booth, desperately hunting for his reaction and then feeling my chest tighten even more when I realize he's equally confused. The house music cuts abruptly, shifting to an unexpected new track as our DJ struggles to untangle the ghost in his machine. The familiar swell of a gentle string section washes over us, a song I once found sweet and fun in its own silly way. Now, however, the tones fill me with nothing but dread.

"They call you Lady Luck," Frank Sinatra serenades, Old Blue Eyes crooning out the opening lines of "Luck Be a Lady" from the great beyond. "But there is room for doubt. At times you have a very unladylike way of running out."

It's only now that I notice the floating cereal is drifting with peculiar speed across the surface, gaining momentum as it swirls into a whirlpool. Swimmers fumble awkwardly in the waist-deep water, a few of them losing their footing and drunkenly stumbling under.

The young promoter's grating pitch lurches to the forefront of my mind, his words echoing in my skull. *Day party at Loch Luck, best wave pool in Vegas. State-of-the-art technology lets you feel the beat in the water.*

All this disparate information suddenly catches up to me in a single horrifying moment, my own past thrust forcefully into the present.

"Get out!" I scream, sprinting to the edge and waving at the confused swimmers.

The hail of pastel marshmallows and puffed rice continues tumbling down, but now something more pressing has caught the swimmers' attention. A few of them manage to reach the side, pulling themselves out, but the current is picking up quick. I can see now that three distinct sections of the pool have transformed into suction points, submerged pipes sucking in liquid with escalating pressure. Still, very few of the swimmers heed my cries, the unfolding scene just too strange and unexpected for them to react appropriately.

"Out of the pool!" I yell again, struggling to grab their attention over the music.

By now the force of the water has reached a point where only the strongest bodies can fight back against the current. There's a splash from one of the three central whirlpools, a swimmer tugged under by the mounting pressure as more cluster to take their place.

"You might forget your manners, you might refuse to stay," Frank sings, his velvety voice lilting in juxtaposition to the awkward splashing and shouting. "And so the best that I can do is pray."

The water's current halts abruptly as, somewhere below the surface, three bodies are sucked against their respective drains. It's surely a moment of utter horror for the poor souls at the bottom of the pool, but one of sweet relief for anyone struggling to get out. Those who were swimming against the tide have suddenly found their footing, sloshing through this giant cereal bowl as they desperately rush for the edge.

Hotel employees are hurrying back and forth, shouting into walkie-talkies as they scramble across the pool deck. Lifeguards have broken out their long metal poles with loops on the end, desperately helping as many folks as they can. Unfortunately, with five or six swimmers grabbing each pole, the majority of the lifeguards are simply yanked into the water.

I brace myself against a metal rung near a set of pool steps, reaching for a wide-eyed woman who's now just a few feet away from my open hand.

"Come on," I shout over a brief lull in the music. "I've got you!"

She's inches away from reaching my grasp when the current abruptly kicks back into gear, tugging even harder than before and with a distinct lurch. The woman is wrenched back with such force that she slips under the water, no longer able to slow herself by bracing her feet against the pool's slick bottom.

Now the screaming starts—not the confused, awkward cries of a disoriented crowd, but a cascade of unbridled shrieking that's so animalistic and guttural it hardly sounds human. Survivors are now sprinting toward the exit in terror.

The jolting current can only mean one thing: that the pressure has grown well beyond the limits of a human body acting as a plug.

The people who were held tight against the intake drains at the bottom of this pool are no longer relevant to the flow, not because they were able to free themselves, but because a large portion of their bones and flesh and blood has been sucked through a tube that's mere inches wide.

The song kicks back in with a confident rhythm and a blaring horn section.

Waterfalls spilling into the pool from their rocky, man-made ledges have turned a brilliant red, the overflow system spewing out utter carnage as it cycles back into the lagoon below. Gore blooms across the surface in frothy crimson foam. As the current escalates to an even mightier churn, body after body is sucked under the surface, the blood-to-water ratio flipping quickly. Intestines and long strips of flesh come slipping over the waterfall, splattering like marinara-covered pasta as it slithers off a plate.

I catch sight of the woman whose hand I almost grabbed, her head bobbing momentarily above the stark red water and our eyes meeting one last time. Her expression is not a frantic one, but instead a display of hopelessness and utter confusion. She appears baffled at the way this has all happened, still curious whether she's tripped into a nightmare, because going out this way makes absolutely no sense. It all seems less like a tragedy and more like a cruel, cruel joke.

I remember that feeling. Then I remember springing into action. I stand abruptly, turning in search of any concrete solution I can find. There must be an emergency pump shutoff.

Crash!

The sound of shattering glass causes me to spin around. A massive wheel has launched through the partition that separates the casino floor from this outdoor pool area, tumbling end over end with unexpected heft. It's giant, at least ten feet tall and three feet wide, with an alternating red-and-black pattern along the edge. There's also a single green space, mimicking a roulette wheel, and it's this portion of the edge that immediately mows down one of the panicked guests trying to leap out of the way.

To my right, a man stumbles over a chaise longue, his arms flailing like a comedic pratfall. The results are devastatingly unfunny, however. In the struggle to keep his drink from spilling, the man ends up face down in his own Bloody Mary, his head bouncing off the concrete with a sickening crack. His reusable metal straw is suddenly nowhere to be found. The man moves to climb back up, wobbling a bit as blood spills from the inside corner of his left eye, then moans and collapses again.

A growl pulls my attention to the left. Two tigers have sprung from the manufactured overgrowth, escapees from tonight's in-house magic show. They're slathered in dark paint for some reason, now appearing as two enormous black cats and leaving a trail of massive paw prints in their wake. I've never seen giant felines up close like this, and from my new vantage their majestic presence tips over the edge from awe-inspiring to terrifying—a pair of muscular, predatory behemoths. They let out rumbling snarls and spring into action.

One tiger bounds into the scattering crowd, leaping through the air and tackling a man to the ground. The other lashes out with its giant claws, swiping across someone's throat and triggering a crimson arc of arterial spray.

I turn to escape the mayhem, but my timing is unfortunate. A thump against my shoulder comes swift and sharp as one of the frantic escaping partiers collides with my body. I instinctively reach out to catch myself, but there's nothing to grab.

I'm sent tumbling into the frothing, bloody swimming pool.

The liquid causes my breath to catch and my senses to reach an even higher state of awareness, carnage and chlorine rushing up through my sinuses and down into my throat. I lash out instinctively, wildly grabbing for anything I can possibly find but coming up short.

The current is shockingly fast at this point, bodies being sucked through the nearby drain like slush through a straw. It pulls me immediately, tearing me away from the edge.

This movement is short-lived, however, as I suddenly feel a sharp tug against my shoulder and armpit. I'm hooked on something.

I do everything I can to cling tight against the object, using all of my strength to battle against the ferocious current that's fighting to drag me away. My head bobs in and out of the churning water, the force of the current nearly breaking my neck with every dunk. I can hear the music rolling on above me, the familiar song cutting erratically between sonic clarity and a haunting submerged tone.

Stick with me, baby, I'm the fellow you came in with. Luck, be a lady tonight!

For a moment it feels as though I'm slipping away, that my body is gradually untethering from whatever's holding me here, but seconds later I can feel myself pulled back the way I came. There's a brief rest, then another hard tug, and another.

Suddenly, a hand reaches through the current, wrapping around me and yanking me from the pool in a sputtering mess. I lie on the deck, gasping and coughing, utterly soaked in blood as Lucky Crisp cereal tumbles down and sticks to my cherry face. I can feel my chest heaving as I struggle for breath, then cough loudly as a spout of bloody pool water erupts from my lungs.

"I've got you," comes a familiar voice, a figure kneeling next to me and placing their hand on my shoulder.

I open my eyes to see Agent Layne, his suit covered in crimson froth but otherwise unharmed. One of the lifeguard's rescue poles, the tool that saved my life, lies on the ground next to him.

A handful of concerned helpers have gathered around us. They're worried about me, but I'm not ready to be fawned over just yet.

I sit up, refusing to wait. "We've gotta get more people," I blubber.

Agent Layne just shakes his head. “There’s nobody else,” he replies.

“We’ve gotta save them!” I cry out, trying again.

Agent Layne doesn’t budge. “There’s nobody else,” he repeats. It takes a moment for me to understand what he’s saying, but when I do a wave of nausea washes over me.

The giant wheel has come to rest at the edge of the pool. The tigers have already calmed down, quietly waiting on a distant boulder in the hopes they’ll be brought back to their enclosure. The cereal has stopped falling, and the music begins cutting out, eventually disappearing completely.

I lie back, exhausted.

Last time I was in this position, a fortunate survivor in the wreckage of some cosmic bad-luck tidal wave, I started running and I didn’t stop. Covered in other people’s blood, I did everything I could to move through the trauma and never look back. Now, however, lying against this pool deck as the chaos settles around me, I can’t run anywhere. I can barely catch my breath.

Instead, I close my eyes, existing in the moment as it stretches on and on.

♣ ♥ ♦ ♠

Back at the motel, I sit in my room for an exceptionally long time. I’m no stranger to gazing off into space, letting the world drift by while I remain in stasis. It’s comfortable here, like returning to a womb of quiet shadows and fluttering curtains. As close to *nothingness* as I’m courageous enough to get.

You could’ve just let go, I remind myself. *Would’ve been easy to get swept away.*

I catch sight of my reflection in the jet-black television screen that sits across from my motel bed, suddenly remembering that I’m still absolutely covered in dried blood. My hair is stringy and matted, the gore giving it a deep crimson shine, and my skin looks as though I’ve been dunked in a tank of wine and left out to crack and dry in the sun. The stark white blanket below me is in rough shape, slowly turning pink.

I want nothing more than to flop back onto this bed and sink into its overwhelming blandness. I yearn to disappear into every crack and mark and imperfection in the ceiling above, a brand-new canvas to explore for hours, days, weeks, or longer.

I won't answer when the curiosity finally gets to Agent Layne and he comes over to check on me, knocking softly on the yellow door of my room. When he pushes inside and lets the overhead light wash over the quiet darkness, I won't be here. All he'll find is the pink, smudged outline of my frame, dried blood on cheap bedding with absolutely nothing in between.

I close my eyes and start leaning back, but as these instructions flicker within the electrical current of my brain, something bizarre happens. I don't move.

My eyes open again, staring at myself in the warped television reflection. One could see this moment as a grand internal struggle, a war waged entirely within my own psyche as apathy and hope battle it out like gargantuan monsters from the deep, but it's really not that complicated. This moment isn't as magnificent as one might think.

It all comes down to a simple choice. I can lie back in the bed, or I can clean off this blood. Nothing more, nothing less.

I put my hands on my knees, my whole body aching and sore as I struggle to push myself upward. The second I do this, however, I remember the decaying cat who lies sprawled out in the overgrown grass of my backyard, rotting in the sun. I remember the fact that every step toward caring about something is also a step toward having it ripped away. I remember that perseverance is just masochism.

It's not enough to stop me, though.

I try again, only this time I somehow manage to stand on two wobbly legs. It's only now that I realize how exhausted I really am, whatever adrenaline I'd been carrying around over the last few hours finally slipping away to reveal the frail, shattered body underneath.

I stagger toward the bathroom, catching myself against the wall as I go and leaving a bloody smudge.

I strip off my clothing and start the shower, not even waiting for the water to heat up as I step inside and let the fresh, clean liquid envelop me. I stand like this, gazing upward with my eyes closed, the water's sharp chill gradually transforming into a warm embrace.

I don't move much, just enjoy the spray against my skin.

After an hour or so, I shut off the faucet and step out to dry off. It's only then that I notice a distinct sound coming from the other room. Agent Layne shares this wall with me, and through the paper-thin motel insulation I can hear him laughing at something on TV.

HUNGRY

Denver's ranch is fittingly enormous, a sprawling expanse of brilliant green lawn amidst an ocean of golden sand. It looks like a golf course, or maybe a vineyard, but before I can decide between the two I realize that her property actually features *both* of these accommodations.

The house itself is luxurious, but it's not the mansion you might expect. Compared to what Denver White could afford, it's downright modest, but I suppose that's the whole point. A cozy rambler dropped into the middle of all this land calls to mind a simple life out West, like Denver herself is setting up a homestead and working it with her own two hands.

The only thing she's working when I find her, however, is an outdoor grill and the remote to her patio television set.

"Thanks for coming," she calls out, nodding as she catches sight of Agent Layne and me crossing the backyard toward her. She gestures to the pair of security guards who escorted us in, prompting the men in dark suits to hang back.

Agent Layne and I arrive at an open-air kitchen where Denver is waiting for us. This area is separate from the house, equipped with four sandstone posts that hold up a small roof. A large flatscreen television is mounted above the wood-fired pizza oven.

Onscreen, a cage fight is violently playing out, the crowd cheering as two shirtless men pummel each other in the middle of a chain-link octagon. It feels surreal to hear this rowdy—but ultimately joyful and excited—cheering from the crowd after what happened no more than twenty-four hours ago, to recognize that the whole world took a great and terrible pause and then decided to keep going.

There will be new billboards and plenty of prayers and even a few charities popping up, but the deeper feeling that permeates everything has hardly moved an inch.

Historical inertia.

Denver's eyes keep darting back to the fight playing out next to her, then over to the grill where a sizzling burger awaits its final form. She's predictably distracted, despite the fact that sixty-nine people were churned to a grisly pulp in her highly pressurized wave pool. Four were crushed under a massive prize wheel. Three were mauled to death by tigers. One was killed by a straw.

"Turn the fucking TV off," I command, stepping up to Denver.

Her eyes dart over to Agent Layne and me, holding our gaze for a moment. She's not upset or offended, just a little shocked. Finally, she takes the remote and shuts off her television set.

I suppose some things *do* change, in their own small ways.

"Y'all don't like MMA?" she questions.

I ignore this statement, motioning instead toward her grill. "Your burger is burning."

"Aw shit," Denver groans, suddenly aware of the same charred scent that's been flooding my nostrils. She rushes over and grabs a spatula, awkwardly separating her jet-black burger from the grill rungs as dripping oil and meat scraps produce a quick burst of flame. She grabs a trash bin with her other hand and pulls it over, then tosses in the crispy patty with a hollow thud.

"I wasn't actually hungry," she admits.

My eyes dance across the fixin's so diligently laid out across the outdoor bar: ripe tomatoes; crispy lettuce; plump, golden buns; and some kind of fancy, pungent cheese.

Denver motions for a maid I didn't notice before, a woman who stands patiently nearby. "Throw all this away," she calls out.

The maid immediately hurries over and starts scooping leftover food into the same trash bin.

Denver turns back to Layne and me. "Y'all want something to drink?"

"We're good—"

"Chocolate milk," blurts Agent Layne, his words spilling over mine.

"Goddamn it," I sigh in frustration.

Denver sends off her maid with Layne's order. When she turns back to face us she's smiling, but there's an intensity behind her expression that makes it feel more like a mask than a genuine display of emotion. It almost looks like she's struggling to hold back tears.

"Y'all caught me in a bit of a bind," Denver finally says. "Here to rub it in?"

"A *bit of a bind*? That's an understatement," I counter.

"You're right, we lost a lot of money over this."

"Seventy-seven people *died* in your casino," I snap.

Denver seems confused by my distinction. "Yeah. That's a lot of settlements."

"And criminal liability," Agent Layne interjects.

"Well, let's not get carried away," Denver retorts. "Those settlements are just to cover our bases, of course. As our lawyers can tell you, the real party at fault here is Nevada Pools and Aquatics. Despicable folks over there, always cutting corners."

Agent Layne and I exchange glances, immediately recognizing where this is headed.

"We're here to make the same offer as before," Layne continues. "You didn't listen then; maybe you will now."

Denver chuckles. "An offer to turn myself over like a *criminal degenerate* and give up decades' worth of trade secrets? I don't think so. We're doing just fine, thank you very much."

"Are you?" Layne presses. "Everett Vacation and Entertainment has dominated the international news cycle for the last twenty-four hours, and something tells me that's not gonna stop anytime soon. These lawsuits will drag on and on."

"Not to mention the criminal prosecution," I chime in.

Layne nods. "I could pull your gaming license right now and you'd be done for good."

"Then why haven't you?" Denver asks smugly.

There are two reasons for this, neither of which I say out loud.

One, whatever's causing these events has no guarantee of stopping if we simply close down casino operations. In fact, halting the Great Britannica in its tracks might only serve to make our investigation even more convoluted.

The other answer is much more sinister, a harsh reality that Denver has been dangling over us since day one.

The cowgirl grins knowingly. "I told you last time. If y'all come for me then you better have some damn good evidence, something the folks signing *both* our checks can't deny. Finding an empty piece of land out in the desert isn't going to cut it."

"An empty piece of land and sixty-nine bodies' worth of ground meat in a giant swimming pool," I retort.

Denver shakes her head and rolls her eyes. "Here's the thing folks like y'all don't understand: at a certain point, the world's attention moves on. Nothing *really* changes. Sure, we might take a hit to our bottom line for a few years, but eventually everything just returns to the same old pecking order as before."

Nothing matters.

My heart sinks, pierced to the very core. I'm trying my best to stay strong and put up a fight, but I'm still wrestling with the cosmic truth behind these words. Deep down, I know she's right.

"Y'all remember that elevator collapse about ten years ago? A bunch of folks crammed into a lift at one of the casinos right here on the Strip. They were *well* below the weight limit, but, I'll be damned, once those poor suckers reached the sixteenth floor the cable snapped and every safety feature failed. Do you realize how *difficult* it is to have a *modern elevator* actually fall down a shaft? Outside a cartoon, you'd have to be running a pretty inept safety crew to see that happen."

The maid returns with Agent Layne's drink, handing over chocolate milk in a tall, frosty glass.

"Twelve people died, including four precious little kids," Denver continues. "It was a gruesome, *gruesome* scene, and there were photo leaks. Of course, the stock plummeted. Late-night television had their say and on and on. Everyone working at the casino was worried they'd be bankrupt within a month. Y'all remember this?"

I nod, and so does Agent Layne. This story was everywhere, headline news for weeks as authorities uncovered the grand incompetence that led to such a tragic accident.

Denver just stares at us, taking her time.

Finally, she asks a devastatingly simple question. "What casino was it?"

We stand in awkward silence for a moment. I'm confused at first, but Denver's point slowly dawns on me.

"Nobody remembers," she finally says, a twinkle in her eye. "That crashing stock is worth forty times what it was back then. I should know, I bought the dip."

Denver takes the remote and turns the TV back on, fight announcers barking an enthusiastic play-by-play of the latest knockout. Their words seem oddly fitting as I reel from what the cowgirl just said.

"Eight million people died on May 23," Denver sighs, her eyes glued to the TV. "Now here we are, four years later, and the world is still just . . . cruising along. What's seventy-seven more?"

Agent Layne, however, seems unimpressed. My companion reaches out and grabs the remote from Denver's hand. He shuts off the television and then hurls the remote across her yard. It lands in a bush.

Layne takes a long sip from his chocolate milk.

"Y'all really tryin' to get in a scrap or something?" Denver asks. "Should we pull on some gloves and get in the octagon?"

"I might not remember what casino it was," Layne says, "but I *do* remember it was the head of casino management who took the fall."

I decide not to mention that a whopping 35 percent of all CEOs who are fired after a disaster return to some kind of executive position within two years.

"I have the full support of Everett Vacation and Entertainment," Denver recites, a little too fast.

"Well, I have emails that say otherwise," Layne replies. "Your inner circle might be careful about what they write down, but your bosses aren't."

Denver doesn't have a response to this, her poker face slipping entirely to reveal a brief expression of utter terror. We've stumbled upon a painful thought that isn't new, but rather a deep wound that's been festering for days now.

Clearly, it was a mistake from the beginning to threaten this organization as a whole; all we have to do is threaten the interests of *one* powerful CEO who doesn't want to lose.

"They're cutting you loose next week, but that's only the beginning," Layne continues, his voice taking on an unexpectedly menacing tone as it reveals something else just below the surface. "You're about to be the fall girl."

Denver just stares at us, struggling to synthesize what Layne's telling her. To be fair, I'm not sure where *I* stand in all this, either. Agent Layne has, yet again, pulled out a generous helping of information I'd been totally unaware of until this very moment. I no longer have any doubt about the truth of these claims when Layne makes them. He probably *does* have emails from executives at Everett, and Denver makes sense as the next one on their chopping block. Of course, I want to punish these people for what they did, and what they continue to do, but every revelation of hacked emails and monitored texts puts a bad taste in my mouth.

For a brief moment, I consider speaking up about it, but I hold back. Maybe Agent Layne's approach is the right one. Maybe getting our hands dirty is the only way to fight back against these people who've made a fortune playing in the mud.

"Y'all don't have shit," Denver finally says, her voice wavering ever so slightly.

"We do," Layne asserts. "The weight of a whole multibillion-dollar conglomerate is about to roll over on top of you, and there's only one force mighty enough to stop it."

"What's that?" Denver questions.

Agent Layne smiles. "Why, it's the United States government, of course."

Suddenly, it all clicks into place. I now realize with sinking horror what's about to happen, but before I can formulate an interjection, Agent Layne makes the leap.

"If you help us right now, we'll grant you and your top staff full immunity," Layne states bluntly. "This offer is only going to happen once, so think before you speak."

Blinding anger flashes across my vision. "I'm sorry, what?" I shout. "No!"

Agent Layne snaps his head toward me, returning fire with equal intensity. "Yes!" he booms in a powerful, one-word command.

"You can't just let them get away with this," I cry. "She's the biggest cog in the fucking machine right now, and you're telling me you're just—"

"Vera!" Layne shouts, cutting me off as his anger grows even more. "This isn't your fucking case!"

"I don't care whose case it is," I yell, not holding back. I realize now tears are welling up, threatening to spill over despite my best efforts to keep them at bay. *Sad* is certainly not the emotion I'm feeling, but whatever sensation it is has got me pressurized like a boiling kettle. "We can take them all down! That's what you said when you brought me here! We're partners on this!"

Exasperated, Agent Layne reaches into his jacket pocket and rips out his badge, thrusting it in my face. "Get in the fucking car right now!" he screams, completely unhinged, his cheeks red and his eyes bulging out of their sockets. "Get in the car or I'll fucking arrest you!"

The outburst is so intense, so heightened compared to the rest of our already heated confrontation, that I halt in my tracks. We've obviously had our differences, but for the first time it feels like I'm talking to a wholly different person. Something deep inside Layne is finally peeking its head out to say hello.

Not knowing what else to do, I turn around and start crossing the lawn, heading for the car. Behind me, I can hear Agent Layne's voice soften as he returns to his negotiations with Denver. A deal is being brokered, the kind of bullshit backroom handshake that used to drive me mad again and again as I struggled to uncover the truth. It's a familiar moment across boardrooms and police stations and senators' vacation homes in the Hamptons.

Of course, back in those days I wasn't seeing the *actual* handshakes go down, just the breathtakingly unjust results that paraded across the nightly news.

I open the passenger-side door of Layne's car and collapse into my seat, watching as my companion and Denver chat with ever-lessening intensity.

A little toy showgirl with an enlarged bobblehead sits on Agent Layne's dashboard, likely picked up at some gas station since our arrival. This bobbing figure stares blankly from her fixed position on the dash, a reminder that Agent Layne's habit of "saying yes to life" is likely fruitful in many ways, but certainly not in matters of taste.

Across the yard, Denver actually laughs and begins nodding along. They end with a handshake, my first real nefarious backroom deal caught in the wild.

I feel like a seething child right now, forced into a time-out while adults take care of some "real-world" problems. It's not a comfortable place for me to be, but it also forces me to confront another nagging question that lingers in the back of my mind.

Why should I care?

This time I have an answer: if everything's already fucked, the least we can do is take down as many scumbags as possible on our way to oblivion.

Agent Layne and Denver eventually part ways, my companion now marching toward me through the grass. When Layne arrives, he yanks open the door and flops into the driver's seat, staring straight ahead for a moment and then turning to face me.

"She's showing us everything," he announces.

I can't help the tug of excitement deep within, then disappointment for allowing a slight break in my anger. Fortunately, it quickly comes roaring back.

"And you're giving her full immunity?" I snarl. "Fuck you."

"Her and her whole team," Layne clarifies, not a shred of guilt to be found.

"Then who the hell is gonna answer for all this?" I scream, completely losing my cool. "Who is gonna *pay for this*?!"

Even Agent Layne is a little shocked by my outburst, pulling back for a moment as his eyes widen.

I find myself hunched over, tangled hair covering my face and my breathing heavy like I'm some kind of ferocious, feral creature.

Layne allows me a moment to stew in this caustic state, then cautiously pushes onward with a calm, quiet statement. "I thought you didn't care," he offers softly. In the past, this line of questioning has been nothing more than a wry joke, a jab at the expense of my lukewarm nihilism, but this time it arrives with utter sincerity.

"I thought so, too" is all I can think to say in return.

What I'm not telling him is that the seed of hope within me has started growing, only now it's mutating and changing in strange, terrifying ways. Taking care of a stray cat is an easy way to get your heart broken, but that kind of compassion is not the only path. My interest in burning the whole thing down has transformed from a silly little goblin into a hulking beast.

"Vera," Agent Layne says, snapping me out of my unexpected daze, "I'm sorry. It's the only way."

"Sure," I mutter in return, far from convincing.

"You're looking for order," Agent Layne reminds me. "*This* is order. This is how it works out here in the real world."

Exhausted, I submit my resignation from this argument with a single word. "Okay."

Layne furrows his brow. "Really? That's it?"

"I don't think you should give them immunity," I say, "but if that's what it takes, that's what it takes. I don't care."

But I do care.

Layne buckles in, then starts the car. He glances over at me. "For the *last time,* put on your goddamn seat belt," he demands.

I ignore him, gazing silently out the window.

♣ ♥ ♦ ♠

Stepping from the black SUV, I immediately recognize this street—not in some distant memory, but from the pages and pages of home titles and commercial deeds I've been obsessively scouring.

Las Vegas has recently seen a boom in residential development, huge swaths of desert bought up and transformed into spacious tract housing, brilliant green lawns and white picket fences lining peaceful streets.

It made sense for Everett Vacation and Entertainment to invest in these projects, so the paperwork never really struck me as odd. Now that I'm here, however, something definitely feels off.

Our small group took two vehicles, all black SUVs that cruise through the night like sharks in dark water. Now that we've arrived, they seem to fade into the shadows, parked away from the streetlights on a quiet suburban cul-de-sac.

It wouldn't matter if we *did* seem suspicious, however, because there's nobody around to notice us. Driving up, there was plenty of movement and life within this little slice of suburban heaven. Dining room lights shined out into the evening as we made our way past, neighbors taking their dogs for a final walk and teenagers shooting a few more hoops in their driveways before the gloaming faded.

Turning onto this particular street, however, reveals something unusual. Although these lawns are mowed, and a few automatic lights have blinked on for the night, nobody actually seems to *live* here.

I peek into a few windows, hunting for the slightest bit of movement or the dancing glow of a flickering television set.

Nothing. Nobody actually resides on this dead-end street.

"Y'all follow," Denver calls out, motioning to Agent Layne and me.

There are eight of us in total, if you include the two drivers waiting patiently behind in their respective vehicles. Three armed security guards fill out the group, rifles by their sides.

Our motley crew stands on the pavement before a large, modern home, gazing curiously up at the inconspicuous building that could easily feature a father and son tossing baseballs in the front yard. Light emanates from within, the warm glow of what appears to be a few scattered lamps.

Denver leads us up the driveway toward the unassuming two-story structure.

We stop on the front porch, hesitating a moment before heading inside. "I've gotta warn y'all, it's a lot to take in on your first rodeo," Denver states, preparing us for the big reveal. "When I first saw it, I was . . . well . . ."

She's briefly at a loss for words, an unusual sight for this typically boisterous woman. I can tell being here makes her deeply uncomfortable.

"Feel free to come outside and get some air if you need it," she eventually continues.

The mysterious circumstances of this evening's forum are now just too bizarre for me to ignore. "I thought we were meeting with your *Luck Department Head,*" I say in frustration, letting my skepticism ooze through the final three words.

In all my research of basic casino practices, this is certainly not a position I've heard of.

"He's right inside," Denver informs me, then checks her watch, a gaudy gold timepiece lashed across her wrist. "Mark will be here for another eight hours. After that, his shift ends and he'll eat like a prized pig. These boys get so goddamn hungry. Y'all have never seen anything like it." With that, Denver gestures toward the door. "After you," she says with a knowing grin.

From the corner of my eye I catch Agent Layne's right arm reposition itself, dropping a little lower and resting near the holster on his belt. The idea that Denver could simply be waiting for the right moment to kill us in cold blood is not lost on either of us, but she seems a little too thrilled about the prospect of legal immunity right now.

I had pushed for Layne to bring a few more agents, to let LPEC know what's going on out here. Agent Layne refused, claiming it was part of Denver's deal.

"Besides," he said. "More consultants and low-level agents involved means more mess to clean up. The mess is the worst part."

Whatever that means.

Layne cautiously reaches out for the doorknob, turning it with a soft click and then making his way inside.

I follow behind, finding myself in the dimly lit foyer of this modern tract home. A staircase is on the left, and a kitchen lies beyond. The right opens up into the living room, a large communal space with cheap vinyl flooring designed to look like hardwood.

The walls in this section, absolutely covered in intricate, rootlike designs, immediately grab my attention. It's a breathtakingly complex web of scrawled, intersecting lines in black pen. The maze of markings has started to creep its way out into the foyer, each thin stroke crawling around the corner once it's run out of room in the initial chamber.

There seems to be no furniture in this house, save for the sparse arrangement of freestanding lamps.

I glance back at Denver, hoping for some kind of explanation, but she just nods toward the living room, motioning us onward. My heart pounds within my chest. I step deeper into the home, the space to my right revealed even more as I creep forward.

"Oh my God," I gasp, jumping instinctively when my gaze arrives on a figure standing motionless at the center of the room.

I recognize him immediately. Before me is the thin man I watched devouring mountains of food at the closed Great Britannica buffet. He's just as gaunt and pale as ever, positioned at the dead center of this lamplit space with his mouth hanging open and his eyes rolled back so far, only the faintest sliver of iris is visible. Veins run along the bottom of each optical globe, quickly disappearing into stark white. His face is so stretched and contorted that I'm surprised his jaw isn't broken—or maybe it is—looking as though it's popped off the hinge like an anaconda ready to swallow. The man is clad in a dark suit, a strange black scarf slung over his shoulder.

My eyes drift across the scarf. It's sturdy and thick, somehow glistening under the dim light. I focus on its strange appearance, then let out a startled cry when it scuttles back over the man.

It's not a scarf.

"What the fuck is that?" I gasp.

Denver laughs. "That's a tougher question than you might think. Why don't *y'all* tell me?"

I creep along the edge of the room, keeping my distance from the inordinately still man, his eyes rolled back and drool pooling at the edge of his open maw. As I come around the side I get a much better view, my gaze adjusting to the dim light and revealing a long black centipede attached to the back of his neck.

The creature is thick, about three inches in diameter, and

approximately two feet long. Its head features a large, four-pronged mandible, each point driven deep into the host's flesh to create a tight grip. Along the centipede's form, hundreds of sharp little legs click and scratch awkwardly.

I glance across the room at Agent Layne, who is equally horrified by this inexplicable scene, then over at Denver.

"Is that some kind of insect?" I ask.

Denver answers my question with one of her own. "Is it? What do you see?"

Again, I lock eyes with Agent Layne, only now my companion seems vaguely confused. "I see a long metal rectangle with wires and gears and blades," Layne says. "It's a machine."

"*What?*" I scoff, now the confused one.

I focus harder on the squirming, wriggling centipede, struggling to make sense of Layne's patently wrong observation.

"There's little glowing lights along the side," Layne continues. "They're blinking red."

A quiet chuckle starts building within Denver, growing until she can't help letting out a wild cackle of laughter. "Y'all really see that shit on the back of his neck?" Denver jokes. "A little machine is original; I'll give you that."

"What do *you* see?" I question.

Denver steps to the side a bit, gazing over the thin man's shoulder. "Same thing I always see, some little varmint weasel-lookin' bugger. Hair is all bristly and gray."

I glance back and forth between my two companions. I can't tell if they're being serious or not, and wonder if this is some kind of poorly timed joke.

"You're *seeing* something else?" I clarify. "Is that what you're telling me?"

Agent Layne's eyes light up with sudden understanding. "Just like the inside of a plot hole."

Connections begin to form in my mind, clues falling into place as my subconscious frantically organizes this information. Despite my best efforts to give up on our chaotic world, I still can't help striving to make sense of the vast unknown.

"Is it true?" I ask Denver. "Did he come from inside one of those holes?"

"Why don't you ask him?" she offers. "He's standing right there."

I cautiously step around to the front of the emaciated man, close enough to notice the subtle quiver of his violently rolled-back eyes.

"Where did you come from?" I ask.

There's a moment of hesitation, then suddenly the stiff body quakes ever so slightly. From deep within the man's throat I can hear a strange, painful gurgle, like something hidden in his stomach has reached up and wrapped its claws around his vocal cords. The man's eyes are shaking even harder now, then his whole face, but just as suddenly, his body resets.

He's frozen in place again, but a strange, guttural voice creaks out, somehow forming words despite the man's jaw remaining slack and his tongue flopped to the side. It sounds like air is pulling into his lungs, rather than expelling forth, and his vocalization has a strange rasp that bubbles and churns like five distinct speakers all talking over one another at various speeds.

"The space between lines," the thin man says, his words sending a chill down my spine.

I glance past him, taking in the enormous web of complex markings that has been sketched across these walls. It's only now I notice dozens of felt-tipped pens scattered around the room, capless and dried up.

"Those lines?" I question. "What are they?"

The thin man smiles suddenly, his mouth pulling tight in an awkward grin. He holds like this for a few seconds before dropping back into the previous slack-jawed expression.

"Timelines," he says flatly.

Denver speaks up from across the room. "Sometimes he'll just grab a pen and start charting paths across the wall. They all do it."

"*They all?*" I ask.

"Ten-hour shifts," Denver replies. "Like I said, Mark here has eight hours to go. After that, we'll pull that thing off of his neck and transfer it to another Luck Department Head so the guy can get some rest. Fuckin' heroes. You wouldn't believe the toll it takes on their bodies. Mark was *at least* a deuce and a half when he started, now he's skin and bones. Couldn't eat enough if he tried."

"Have *you* worn it?" I ask.

Denver snorts loudly. "Hell no!"

I consider this. "Do they tell you what it's like?"

She shakes her head. "Nobody remembers once they pop it off, but that thing will yap at you if you want. Go ahead and give it a shot."

I turn my attention back to the thin man. "What's it like where you come from?"

The thin man smiles again, his expression holding for another three seconds of a terrifyingly exaggerated grin and then dropping. "Empty," he offers in the creaking, throaty wheeze. "There is a line for every shifted moment that has been, and for every shifted moment that will be. I am what cannot be, the void that seeps between worlds."

"I've talked to it for hours," Denver jumps in. There's a hearty dose of excitement in her tone, but it makes perfect sense. After suppressing the truth for so long, Denver's finally able to speak with someone else about this discovery. "Pretty darn fascinating, to be honest. Turns out bringing something impossible into existence rustles up events that are very, very unlikely," she explains. "You can let it run wild, or you can put that sucker on the back of your neck and pluck the strings of fate like you're strumming a guitar."

The existential implications of this are already giving me a headache, but my quest for order and understanding plows onward. It's not lost on me that this could be the key to everything, a master code that explains away all the bullshit and chaos and finally offers the one thing I've always been hoping for: a reason.

Denver has said as much, and while her words are not quite the ones I'd choose, her hypothesis is intriguing: What if the space inside those plot holes really was *nothing*?

People throw around that word a lot, but in the grand cosmic sense it's almost always misused. If someone glances into an "empty" box, they might report there's nothing inside, but in reality there's plenty to fill the space. The most obvious would be all the oxygen molecules floating around, but there's also dust and light and energy.

True nothingness is almost impossible for the human mind to comprehend. It's found in the sterile vacuum of mathematics, but rarely elsewhere. Maybe that's why I enjoy statistics so much.

Most folks agree our universe started with the big bang, that all matter and energy—every molecule and atom and quark—started as one tiny speck and then burst wide open to create the world we live in. Light and heat and even time itself were compressed into this teeny little ball before the colossal explosion that kicked things off, but the real question is this: What surrounded that singular point?

Try to imagine that pure nothingness. No matter, no energy, not even time.

It's difficult to even *conceptualize* how we might experience this kind of space, whether our brains are up to the task or they'd simply collapse under their own weight. We are not discussing a location where time has stopped, but one where time does not exist. It is not a realm of eternal darkness, but a realm with *no* color or shade *at all.*

When confronted with something like that, it's not a stretch to assume our minds would just do the best job they could to fill in the blanks. Maybe our brains would protect us from the oppressive cosmic magnitude of true nothingness by making it look like a machine, or a small mammal, or a writhing black centipede.

I step even closer to the thin man now, my fascination growing. I cut right to the heart of it. "Why are you here?"

"I'm not," he replies in his strange, backward rattle.

If my theory is correct, then I suppose that's true. Nothingness doesn't exist, so it's never in any particular space. It's the *lack* of space.

It's still difficult to wrap my head around, but I suppose that's the point. True nothingness rarely interacts with our daily lives—how could it?—and now that it's been thrust into our reality, it's no wonder things are going haywire.

"We crafted a few massive winners and a steady stream of small losers," Denver says. "It was a perfect system. Just pay some folks a healthy wage to set that thing on their neck and control the flow of fate each day."

I can't help shaking my head in amazement, words spilling quietly from my lips as the pieces fall into place. "Perfectly legal games that are technically in the player's favor, but the house still wins."

"Far as I can tell, after all those years stretching the strings of fate, everything up and snapped back into place," Denver continues, a hefty emotional weight brewing in her voice now. "The small-time losers who passed through our doors over the years probably found a ladybug or caught a bus they should've missed. Nobody really notices the little things. The big winners, though . . ."

"Seven million, nine hundred and fifty-four thousand big winners," I remind her, my eyes still glued to the thin man but my mental canvas flooded with horrific images of that terrible day in May.

I see all that good luck returning like a boomerang to even the score with astronomical vengeance, a primate with a typewriter in downtown Chicago taking back what's owed. Never in a million years could a reasonable set of circumstances lead to that occurrence, but that's exactly the point.

"Fate had a lot to say," Denver adds.

I now see why the previous plot holes managed to reseal

themselves, yet whatever we've stumbled upon is getting worse over time. This little centipede—this brain-breaking piece of nothing—is not allowing the tear to mend. It's refusing to let historical inertia run its course and correct all the mangled timeline tangents. This *thing* is a blight on our reality, a festering wound that must be healed.

Fortunately, now that I've reached a basic level of understanding, where we go from here seems obvious.

"We need to pull that thing off of his neck and destroy it," I announce.

Denver lets out a hearty laugh behind me. "Better be quick about it. Did a slow changeover last month and had to buy a new house because the last place got struck by lightning four times. Y'all think it's wild when he's channeling fate into big wins at a slot machine across town? Just wait until you see what happens when there's no river to guide it."

"We'll be quick then," I reply, exchanging glances with Agent Layne.

"We tried destroying it already, tried to go legit a few times, actually," Denver says. "Burned it, shot it, smashed it. No dice."

I shoot her a skeptical look. "*You* did that? Denver White, in all her moral fortitude, decided to go legit?"

She hesitates, feigning confusion. "What?"

I hold her gaze.

Finally, she breaks. "*Alrrright,*" Denver sighs. "A small faction of renegade employees tried to go legit."

"And?"

"They're no longer with the company."

Agent Layne finally chimes in with a bark. "That wasn't the deal! The deal was that you tell us what's going on *and* you help us end it."

I'd love to pile on and yell at Denver, too, but unfortunately what she's saying actually tracks. Kinda.

"We can't destroy something if it's not here," I announce. "There's nothing *to* destroy."

I watch their attention wander past me, lingering over my shoulder as they struggle to understand the basic laws of this distinctly lawless incursion. Layne seems deeply fascinated, his natural desire for novelty kicked into overdrive by our otherworldly encounter. Denver, on the other hand, looks exhausted, frustrated, and ready to head home.

"We might not be able to destroy it," I continue, "but maybe we can return it. All we have to do is push this thing through a plot hole."

"And then what?" Denver interjects. "Pray it works? Y'all can't just get rid of it and cross your fingers hopin' that little varmint doesn't scamper back out. What if things keep getting worse and now we're suddenly out of options?"

She's right.

A wave of disappointment washes over me. I begin to pace, a habit I used to have while thinking hard in front of my class. My mind is racing, back in my analytical professor mode.

"If there was a hole big enough, then someone could carry it through," I state, already shaking my head as the words tumble from my mouth. I know this isn't possible, I'm just talking to myself and working through every idea as it comes. "They could make sure it got to the right place, or bring it back out if we're on the wrong track."

Denver awkwardly clears her throat, drawing the attention of Layne and me. "We've got one that's big enough, but you don't wanna go in there, sugar. Trust me."

I narrow my eyes in confusion. "You've tried?"

"The hole where we initially found this thing has been fattening up for years," she explains. "We sent in an employee, but that only messed with the focus of our Luck Department Head across town. It was like ripples in a pond."

"And what happened to the employee?" I ask.

Denver pauses awkwardly. "He's, uh, dead," she finally replies. "Suffocated. We pulled him back out, but it was too late. We cut our losses and haven't tried since."

Now, it's Agent Layne's turn to interject. "I don't think suffocation's gonna be a problem this time."

NUMBER STATION

The truck sitting quietly in our parking lot is large and white, its boxy frame reminiscent of a vehicle that might deliver bread or crates of milk. It's free of any Low-Probability Event Commission logos or insignias, built to fly under the radar.

I've seen this kind of truck on the road before and thought nothing of it. Little did I know what could've been hidden within.

The driver who dropped it off is long gone, disappearing into the night at Layne's insistence. Now, it's just the two of us standing at the far end of an empty parking lot, gazing at a closed roll-up door that Agent Layne has swiftly unlocked with a four-digit code on a tucked-away keypad.

He glances back at me, then over my shoulder to see if anyone happens to be wandering behind us at this late hour. Nobody else is here, but he's still cautious.

Agent Layne pulls up on the door handle, hoisting it just enough for me to slip beneath. At least, that's the intent, but as the back of the truck cracks open I find myself briefly halting in shock. This is not at all the interior I was expecting. The chamber is not dark and sweltering in the desert heat, but cooled to perfection and featuring a pale white light that emanates outward with a haunting glow.

I slide under the roll-up door, followed shortly after by Agent Layne as he shuts it behind us.

The entirety of this cargo area has been meticulously crafted, having more in common with a science lab than the cargo hold of a standard moving truck. The walls, floor, and ceiling are stark white and shiny. For the impressive size of this mobile room, there's surprisingly little in here, but what I *do* find is breathtaking.

Hanging in a transparent case is what appears to be a space suit, a puffy one-piece uniform with boots and gloves that would cover a human body from head to toe. This suit is slightly more fitted than astronaut gear, with much less bulk to contend with, but it's otherwise very similar. Where the wearer's head should go sits a large circle, and hanging next to it is a bulbous, clear-visored helmet. An LPEC badge is affixed to the uniform's chest, resting right above the heart.

There is a hose hanging next to the suit, coiled perfectly and fastened to the wall. The front end is disconnected, and I assume it attaches to the back of the outfit. The hose then snakes down and plugs into a rectangular device that's approximately the size and shape of a rolling karaoke machine.

A small assortment of boxes line the back wall, likely hard-shell travel cases for this equipment when the time comes.

Layne and I stand here for a moment, taking in the strange majesty of it all.

"So, you've been waiting to go inside one of these plot holes for . . . a while," I reflect.

"LPEC knew it might happen sooner or later, so we prepared," he informs me. "There's a fairly large waiting list of volunteers. People who've trained for this without actually knowing what they trained for."

I can't help scoffing. "You *can't* train for this."

From the corner of my eye I can see Agent Layne shoot me a glance: plenty on his mind but the words held back. There's plenty on my own mind, too.

Thrusting myself back into the real world has been a difficult task, and while some of this journey has been horrific and draining,

I'd be lying if I denied the few moments of light that've snuck in through the cracks. I'm evolving through all this, moving forward instead of just staring into the abyss for hours on end.

But now that I'm here, on the precipice of finding real answers to the questions I once considered futile, I feel like all those years spent gazing into the vast, endless nothing of my living room ceiling were the best preparation that anyone could ask for. My circumstances have been driving me toward this moment for a very long time.

Inertia.

"I want to go," I announce.

Layne takes a deep breath and lets it out. "I figured you'd say that," he replies. "If you want the job, it's yours. You may not have a badge, but we've been working this together."

His words are meant to be reassuring, but they strike a nerve. Yes, I've been along for this horrific roller-coaster ride of governmental overreach, but the more time I spend on it, the more disenchanted I am.

Searching through the phone records of hapless Everett employees is a massive ethical violation that I've gone along with in service of a greater good, but it's getting harder for me to ignore these indiscretions. Making a deal with Denver will never sit right with me, either, yet I've already helped myself to the fruits of that offense. I now know more than I ever could've dreamed, but I'm left feeling deeply conflicted about how we got here.

When you start caring again, *really* caring, the implications are larger than you might think.

"What are you going to do if this works?" I question. "You'll know what caused the Low-Probability Event and the plot holes will probably stop happening. LPEC can close up shop."

Agent Layne just chuckles to himself. "There's always gonna be something," he replies.

I hesitate. "So you're just gonna keep doing whatever you want?"

Layne turns to me, smugly raising an eyebrow. "I'll keep

making sure people are safe. They're lucky someone's out here doing whatever it takes, and I'm not just talking about me. I'm talking about you, too."

Again, I feel a slight clench at the pit of my stomach. "Don't you think it might be better if there was a *little* bit of oversight?" I say. "I mean, I get it, these are desperate times, but when the emergency bells stop ringing it might be good to pull back on the throttle."

Agent Layne's grin only widens. "Sounds like this really matters to you."

He's testing me.

"I don't know" is all I can offer in return.

"So what do you want from me?" he asks, running through the scenario aloud. "You want me to do the talk-show circuit? Write a book? Should I load up a hard drive with everything LPEC knows and release it into the public domain?"

I consider this. "Actually, yes."

Agent Layne laughs. "You're a funny kid."

"I have your files," I retort. "*I* could do it."

The second I say this something changes in the room, a chill falling over Agent Layne as his laughter fades away. The typically confident man seems strangely distracted, as though I've just reminded him that he left the oven on.

"I know you could," Layne finally replies, then strolls toward the suit and immediately changes the subject. "This hose has two functions," he explains. "It's a source of oxygen, but the main purpose is to pull you back if you hit the abort button. It's extremely durable." He walks around the suit, admiring the handiwork. "If this hose *does* happen to get severed, you have a backup tank of air that will last you an hour."

He's trying to move on, but I'm not prepared to let him.

"I have your files, but I don't have all of them," I state. "You deleted nearly half the LPEC video logs. I could tell by the metadata."

Layne sighs, growing frustrated with me in a strangely heavy way. "Don't say that."

"Why not?"

He hesitates. "Because some of us have the stomach for this job and some of us don't. Because I need you focused. Because we're a team."

The intensity behind Agent Layne's eyes is elevated to such a point that, finally, I decide to drop it. Still, his cryptic words hang over my head.

Because some of us have the stomach for this job.

"Like Agent Martin and Agent Peters in *Dark Encounters,*" he adds. "I've got your back, you've got mine. Besides—" He laughs. "You can't copy those files without my USB key."

I just stare at him blankly, then finally nod in confirmation. I've made a deal with the devil, pledged my allegiance to something I'm not entirely happy about for the sake of the greater good.

To Layne's credit, he's not wrong. If this works, many lives will be saved, potentially thousands, or millions, or . . . I'd rather not think about how astronomically unlikely it is for an extinction event–sized meteor to strike Earth, because who knows what unspeakable rarities an ever-expanding plot hole could bring.

But does that really nullify the needless abuse of power along the way? Was all that unjust action necessary?

No more than a week ago, I would've said it didn't matter, but a little momentum and a solid goal will change you. It's time I finally admitted the truth that refuses to die, shambling around my mind like a zombie.

I do care.

The faint rumble of engines gradually alerts us to the presence of two other vehicles in the parking lot. We've been expecting them.

Layne opens the roll-up door just enough for us to slip back under, revealing that Denver White and her posse have arrived. Two black SUVs are parked haphazardly beside us. It's the same crew from before, featuring the cowgirl herself along with a handful of armed guards and two drivers.

We're about to undertake a journey into the unknown that could potentially change everything humankind understands about reality itself, but Denver's attention is clearly elsewhere. "My lawyers are very happy," she announces, smiling wide as she approaches. "Y'all know how to strike a fuckin' *deal.*"

Denver's expression of delight has not grown any less sickening. The amount of death that hangs over this woman would weigh down the conscience of any other soul, but she's completely unfazed.

"Vera is going in," Layne announces.

Denver glances over at me with a look of shocked amusement on her face. "Well, would you look at that? I guess that's the good thing about believing in nothing. You've got nothing to lose."

She's not wrong, but she's still annoying.

"Let's get this show on the road," I say. I turn and head for our truck, but Agent Layne stops me.

"Actually, I was thinking about riding with Denver," he carefully states. "We've still got a few more details to work out."

The look on my face says more than words ever could, so Layne pulls me aside even more and lowers his voice. "We'll be able to keep an eye on 'em this way," he insists.

I glance back at Denver, who catches me and tips her cowboy hat in my direction.

"Fine," I reply. I force a smile as we return to the group.

Denver goes with Agent Layne, while one of the armed guards directs me to the back seat of the second SUV. He opens the door as I approach, motioning for me to get in.

I follow the man's lead, then abruptly stop and gasp. Sitting in the back seat is a new centipede host, a rail-thin woman with the wriggling black creature attached to the back of her neck. She's just as gaunt as the previous man was, her mouth hanging open like a silent, slack-jawed groan that never ends. On the middle seat is a small cage made of metal and glass, which I assume will host the centipede once it's removed from the back of her neck.

The woman doesn't acknowledge me, just stares straight ahead as the parasitic organism crawls around her shoulders.

"Ready?" my driver asks.

I nod. "Let's go."

♣ ♥ ♦ ♠

The first time Agent Layne and I trekked out to this massive plot of empty desert, I'd been shocked by just how barren my surroundings were. Now, in the dead of night, this sensation is only amplified. It feels like another world.

Gazing out the windows on either side reveals nothing but endless darkness, a black abyss covering the landscape like a blanket. Our headlights—and those of the vehicles before us—can only hope to slice through the veil so much.

I lean my head against the glass, looking upward.

"It's been a long time since I wanted to look at the stars. Now they're missing," I offer to no one in particular, but the driver is willing to respond.

"Weather got weird," he says. "Clouds rolling in."

For the first part of our journey I could glance over my shoulder and see the brilliant lights of Las Vegas fading behind, but over time a cresting hill has risen up and swallowed the cityscape whole, leaving nothing in its wake.

Next to me, the centipede is calm and subdued, lying across the shoulders of its host. I've been trying to ignore this expression of nothingness that my mind has grafted an arthropod over, but it's difficult not to examine.

"What does it look like for you?" I ask the driver, my eyes still glued to the eldritch creature next to me.

"A plant," he says in return. "Dark green. Covered in crawling vines."

"*A plant,*" I repeat back, fascinated. "Do you have any past trauma falling into a patch of poison ivy or something?"

The driver chuckles. "Nope."

I don't recall any nightmarish personal encounters with centipedes, either.

The driver glances in his rearview mirror, taking note of my thoughtful expression. "Want my advice after working here for half a decade?" he asks. "Don't try making sense of it. You won't find meaning in nothingness."

I nod along, not quite sure I agree just yet.

Through the window, something catches my eye, a flicker of light dancing across what I can only assume is the distant ridge. I inspect the darkness, straining to see and then finally identifying the muted headlights of other vehicles on the mountains that run parallel to us.

"Those yours?" I ask, nodding toward the hill.

The driver shakes his head. "Military security," he explains. "Area Fifty-One is over that range."

Layne mentioned this on our previous trip, but the fact had already slipped my mind. Area 51 is known for its association with flying saucers and government conspiracies, so it's tempting to connect these wild rumors with our current adventure, explain everything away in a brilliant eureka moment. My driver is correct, though: there's no making sense of this. Certainly not that easily.

"You're a statistics expert, right?" the driver asks. "What are the chances there's aliens out there in the universe?"

"In the *whole* universe?" I muse, clarifying the boundaries of our hypothesizing. "It's actually very, very likely that there's some kind of life out there. We'll probably never encounter it, and even if we did, it might be nothing more than some kind of bacteria."

My driver pauses to consider this, then moves on to his follow-up question.

"What about aliens here on Earth?" he asks. "You know, little green men with big black eyes?"

"Extremely unlikely," I reply, the typically comforting phrase suddenly giving me pause.

There's a faint rumble as our SUV turns off the main drag, trudging over the raw desert now. We're getting close.

My eyes can't help focusing on the vehicle before us, the rumbling truck where Agent Layne and Denver sit perched in the cab. In tense moments like this, silence seems to permeate everything, spilling through cracks and filling the empty spaces, but with those two yappers on board I'm guessing that vehicle is anything but quiet.

The ache I feel over this is comically juvenile, a strange sense of jealousy I haven't had in a very long time. There are certainly terrible deals being made, things I'd admittedly rather not be a part of, but still . . . *shouldn't I be there?*

Regardless of the framing, Layne and I were partners in this, two investigators from vastly different backgrounds who suddenly found themselves knee-deep in the supernatural, and now I've been relegated to the SUV with the centipede-neck lady.

As far as I know, this never happened on *Dark Encounters*. Agent Martin never stepped aside to make a deal with the shadowy government figures they were trying to take down.

But I have to accept the difference between this moment and a popular '90s television show. In real life there are no clean endings, especially not when it comes to overpowered ruthless governmental bodies with a monopoly on violence.

At least, that's what *part* of my brain is telling me. The other part is shrieking that I might as well burn it all down.

Get out of the car right now. Walk back through the desert. Fly home. Find the gun.

Specks of dust start dancing and swirling in the headlights, alerting us that our off-road trek has somehow gotten even more treacherous. The driver slows to a crawl, but as he leans forward and regards the dark sky above, I suddenly realize his expression is not one of caution, but of awe and wonder.

These flakes of dust and sand are not churning up from the tires, but falling from above. They're pouring down even harder now, a cascade of brilliant particles lilting through the desert air, but the longer I stare at them, the more I realize my initial read had been slightly off. These tiny drifting shards aren't the tan hues of sand. In fact, they're brilliantly colorful.

I roll down the window and stick my hand out, allowing a few of the flakes to land on my skin for clearer observation. This isn't sand and dust, it's rainbow confetti.

A digital chime suddenly rings out over the car stereo, prompting me to jump as my driver presses a button on the dash. The next thing I know, Denver's voice is crackling through the SUV. Somehow, she retains phone service out here, likely connecting through some private Everett cell tower.

"Things have been getting stranger near the opening. The longer we take to get through this shit, the more squirrely it's gonna get," Denver says, her drawl wafting through the speakers. "Y'all don't take your foot off the pedal."

"Yes, ma'am," replies the driver.

The rocking, shuddering journey of our off-road convoy was already cause for concern, but adding a cascade of falling confetti to the scene is a recipe for disaster. Then again, if we're already in fate's crosshairs then there's not much we can do about it. It would certainly be unlikely for a bolt from an airplane wing to hurtle down through the atmosphere and crack my skull wide open, but that hasn't happened yet.

For now, all we have is falling paper.

I lean forward between the seats, raising my voice so Denver can hear me over the sounds of the bouncing, trembling vehicle. "Isn't there a road to your site?" I ask, staying focused.

"Nope, too easy to spot from a drone or a satellite," Denver replies. "We'll make the drive tonight, but most employees hike in."

No wonder we couldn't find the place. Everett Vacation and

Entertainment has done everything in their power to cover their tracks and make this acreage seem like nothing more than a vast, empty plot of land. The fact that there's no security guards out here to patrol things is a form of security in itself.

"Where exactly is this portal of yours?" I press. "Because we—"

The thought is cut short by an abrupt loss of power, all three vehicles plunging into darkness. Suddenly the only sound is the crunch of rugged terrain below, my driver fighting to control the SUV as our power steering deteriorates. We roll to a stop, silence falling over the pitch-black void.

"What the hell just happened?" I ask.

"I think the battery died," my driver suggests.

"All three cars had their battery die in unison?" I scoff, then realize what I'm saying. "Sounds about right."

Doors begin to open and slam closed as my companions climb from their vehicles, struggling to regroup. I fumble around in the darkness a bit, eventually finding the handle and pulling it back. I'm quick to jump out, relieving myself of proximity to the strange host and her writhing parasite.

"Somebody fix these fucking cars!" Denver shouts, pacing back and forth in the confetti in frustration and anger.

Unable to see much through the darkness and the falling paper, I only know she's pacing because I can hear the rustle of her boots through the ever-thickening scraps.

One by one, flashlights turn on and illuminate our surroundings, yellow light slicing through the darkness of this surreal rainbow landscape in wide cones. Flecks of color drift and dance through the beams, settling to create a vibrant ground cover that's already a few inches thick.

I have my doubts about getting these vehicles started again, and even if we do, I question whether they'll be capable of pulling out from the confetti drifts that have swiftly built around them. On flat asphalt this might be possible, but out here on rugged terrain it'll be difficult to find a spot where the vehicles don't already have a tire placed awkwardly in some dirt hollow.

Gazing into the darkness, I can't help wondering how far this uncanny event stretches. Is it raining confetti for miles?

"Where's the plot hole?" I yell, speaking to Denver but willing to settle for anyone who will listen. "Are we close enough to hike?"

"I have no goddamn idea!" Denver shouts, her irritation growing. "We can't find the place without GPS coordinates, and those are plugged into the cars!"

"What about putting the location into your phone?" I barrel onward. "You have service out here, right?"

"Sure, sure," Denver affirms, her mind clearly elsewhere.

The guards are already hard at work on various tasks, rushing through the angular shafts of light that crisscross our scene. Meanwhile, Agent Layne has thrown open the rolling door on the back of his cargo truck, intensely focused on the task at hand. "A little help here?" he calls over, then hurries back to the hanging suit. Layne begins unhooking various cables and unscrewing a few massive bolts as he prepares the apparatus for walking transport.

"I've gotta get the coordinates," I yell.

Now it's Denver's turn to interject. "That's not your job," she barks. "They know where they're going, sugar. Stay calm and we'll get these batteries sorted out."

Agent Layne stops what he's doing, glancing over and locking eyes with me. He hesitates a moment, then nods as though he's reading my mind.

Fuck these guys. We'll do it ourselves.

I break off to get the information we need, tromping over to my vehicle and quickly discovering that the driver is nowhere to be found. "Hey!" I call out, struggling to be heard above the chaos. "Can anyone tell me where we're actually headed?"

Nobody pays much attention. My eyes work their way across

the hectic scene, hunting for the man who'd previously sat behind our wheel. He doesn't seem to be part of either group: not the folks lifting a crate from the back of the truck, nor the ones popping car hoods as Denver angrily snarls out her desperate impromptu plan.

I make my way to the other side of the SUV, and it's here that I finally discover my driver wrapping the thin woman in a blanket. She's shivering hard in the back seat of the car, her jaw no longer hanging open and her eyes thankfully returned to their normal state.

My driver closes the door, determined to keep the thin woman as warm and comfortable as possible. At his feet is the glass-and-metal cage, the massive, squirming centipede now held within.

"Oh!" I exclaim. "Isn't that dangerous?"

"She's too tired to walk," he explains. "If you're hiking, you'll have to do it without her."

There's a loud rattle as the centipede throws itself against the cage interior.

"Can I . . . put it on?" I ask.

"Did you take down thirty thousand buffet calories this morning?" he sighs. "Nobody's trekking anywhere with this thing attached to their neck."

I accept this and press onward. "What are the coordinates for our destination?" I ask. "Do you remember?"

"It's in the car's GPS," the driver replies. "I think the first one is thirty-seven north. The other one is a hundred something west."

I appreciate his valiant recall effort, but without the exact latitude and longitude we might as well start searching back on the Strip.

Bang!

Utter shock rips through me as my senses pique and my muscles clench tight. The pop is so abrupt and deafening that I actually feel like I'm choking on my own breath as it pulls back into my throat. I duck behind the SUV.

That was a gunshot.

I press myself against the side of the vehicle, expecting my driver to do the same. Instead, the man draws a weapon of his own, lifting his flashlight and placing his handgun against the barrel in a distinctly rehearsed manner.

"Everyone alright?" someone calls out. "Who was that?"

My ears are still ringing, so I'm guessing whoever fired the shot was nearby.

"I think it was over here," I yell.

My driver scans the confetti-covered desert before us, searching for any sign of movement. It's a tall order, given the oppressive darkness and the sheets of plummeting paper, but the two of us quickly spot a disturbance. It looks as though someone was dragged off in a long, mostly straight line, their eventual resting place obscured by our surreal weather conditions.

"Over here!" my driver shouts.

Nearby, another concerned question rises above the others. "Anyone seen Davidson?"

Nobody announces themselves in return, no voice to quell the fears that bubble up within our group as any feeling of security crumbles. There was a certain arrogance to our arrival, a sense that the cavalry was finally here to save the world, but that confidence has dissolved almost instantly.

A hurried roll call reveals that not just one, but three members of our group are missing.

Three members of our group are missing.

Panic surges as my gaze sharpens even more, darting across the confetti mounds for any sign of movement. I now catch sight of another unexpected trail, a path the size of a human dragged roughly through the slush of vivid hues and cutting to the dirt below. In this particular track, a mash of footprints tramp in and out of the groove, as though something was pulling its victim.

A sudden presence to my right causes my heart to skip a beat, but the familiar face of Agent Layne provides immediate remedy.

A large crate sits next to him, waist-high and square, with a long handle protruding from the top. On the base of the crate are two large wheels, like you might find on a rolling dolly. Fortunately, they're plump enough to pull this box across rough terrain.

"I've got the suit and the generator," Layne states, his face tense. "You ready?"

"Ready for *what*?" I cry. "We don't even know where it is!"

"You wanna stay here and get picked off one by one?" Layne counters.

I glance over at one of the vehicles, its hood popped as one of the guards frantically works to get our convoy back on track. It's a mess.

However, taking off into the darkness sounded much better before folks started disappearing.

There is *another* option, of course, one that doesn't even occur to a guy like Agent Layne, but has already managed to shuffle—moaning and gnashing its teeth—from the dark recesses of my already panicked brain. You hear a lot about *fight or flight,* but there's a third choice that's often overlooked.

I could always freeze and do absolutely nothing, let the hand of fate sort us out. I could always give up.

Glancing back over my shoulder, I spot the thin woman tucked away in the SUV, staring off into space. Her energy has been sucked dry, drained from her frame like the poor victim of some twisted existential vampire, but while there's a certain discomfort in this, she's also very lucky.

As chaos and disorder continue to rage outside the vehicle, she has found herself utterly disconnected. There's no fear in her eyes, nor concern about what to do next. She's too exhausted for any of that, barely existing.

"Hey," Agent Layne blurts, tugging my attention back into focus. "Grab the cage and let's go."

I glance down, suddenly remembering the writhing centipede

locked away at my feet, a physical manifestation of that nonexistence I so desperately crave. Looking at the box—and the disgusting creature within—it's difficult to parse what I find so alluring about it.

Regardless, the pull is still there, burrowing even deeper within me.

"Y'all quiet down!" A familiar voice suddenly cuts through the scene, Denver's southern drawl rising above the rest. "Listen!"

What's left of our crew immediately settles as a hush falls across this darkened landscape of tumbling confetti. Even Agent Layne and I stop, training our ears to the colorful panorama that surrounds us.

The stillness seems to permeate everything, and in this unnatural quiet I can actually hear the sound of paper circles tenderly settling across one another. It sounds like snow.

"I don't hear anyone," I whisper to Agent Layne, but the man puts his hand up to stop me. Layne's weapon is at the ready, held tight against his flashlight as it carefully sweeps the darkness.

The faintest unexpected gurgle causes my breath to catch, snapping my head to the left as Agent Layne's illuminated beam follows suit. This area is empty, save for a thick, angular Joshua tree that stands before us in the quiet.

The sound was brief, but it felt distinctly organic, the hollow rattle of some eldritch larynx.

"Anything over there?" Denver finally calls out from her spot near the truck, dismissing the silence. "Y'all better not be afraid to put a bullet between someone's eyes."

Layne flashes his light at the cowgirl, and my gaze follows his beam. Agent Layne's intent is nothing more than an offer of his attention, to illuminate the speaker in a nonverbal expression of *loud and clear,* but what he reveals is so much more.

Denver stands by the side of the truck, a semiautomatic rifle by her side and her signature white cowboy hat placed atop her head. Confetti has started pooling along the brim. The woman's expression is one of frustration bordering on anger.

However, it's not Denver that draws my attention. Snaking around from behind the truck is a long, glistening tendril, the pale noodle lifting high and then rearing up behind her in a predatory curl. The appendage is freakishly skinny for how nimble and powerful it is, with no problem holding itself up despite being the thickness of a garden hose. From what I can see, it already measures more than ten feet in length, and I can only assume even more of whatever this tendril connects to remains tucked out of sight.

It reminds me of a video I once saw of a deep-sea worm, the creature's physical might seeming profoundly at odds with its awkward length.

At the end of the tentacle is a three-pronged barb, the hooks held open and a single, needlelike spine protruding from the middle.

I can't even process a verbal warning. In the split second it takes to recognize what's happening, Denver is only vaguely tipped off by my expression of shock.

"Ma'am!" one of the guards manages to call out, but it's too late.

The pale noodle whips forward and strikes Denver in the back with a distinct thump, prompting her eyes to widen in an expression of shock and confusion. Strangely, she doesn't turn around, nor cry out in pain.

Guns immediately blast away, their flashes sporadically illuminating crouched, abstract figures creeping around the other vehicles.

Of course, the tendril is much too thin for any bullets to strike its slender musculature, and the surprise of popping weapons only provokes it to pull taut and yank Denver backward. Her hat flies off in a scatter of confetti.

Now the cowgirl is tumbling away through the mounds of rainbow paper, unable to fight back as she's dragged by some unseen figure.

"Come on!" Agent Layne bellows, suddenly forcing me to act.

I reach down and grab the centipede cage, then follow my companion as the two of us take off into the desert. Gunfire fills the air behind us, a chorus of deafening bangs accompanied by shrieks and purrs. The vocalizations are otherworldly. It sounds like marbles rattling their way down a host of writhing bamboo shoots, but every so often it mutates into a choir of melodic chirps that ring out like they're being strangled from the bent necks of enormous, fantastical birds.

I refuse to look back. Instead, I stay focused on the darkness ahead.

Don't stop running.

I've told myself that before, and as my feet slam hard against the desert below, my mind leaps back to my first experience with the madness that occurs when fate snaps back into place. Instead of dashing through confetti and sand, I feel as though I'm sprinting down the streets of Chicago on that horrific, awful day.

Don't stop running.

I remember the way the diner smelled when I returned for my friends, the typical scent of grease and coffee now blended with the iron tang of fresh blood. I remember the seasick feeling I got in that mirror-covered department store, the illuminated walls spinning past me like a giant roulette wheel. I remember the sound of Elvis's "Good Luck Charm" blasting from every radio in the city, flooding the streets and painting the scene with a brush that might be darkly comic if it weren't so horrific.

Every radio was playing that song but one . . .

Suddenly, I recall the numbers ringing out from an overturned truck as I hid against it, meaningless digits seared into the depths of my subconscious brain.

Thirty-seven. Eighteen. Thirty-two.

One hundred and fifteen. Thirty-six. Fifty-two.

Thirty-seven. Eighteen. Thirty-two.

One hundred and fifteen. Thirty-six. Fifty-two.

My pace begins to slow, the hard work of my brain slowly overtaking the physicality of my body.

Agent Layne, who is somehow pulling ahead despite the massive crate he's wheeling along, catches sight of me.

"Let's go!" he commands through the falling confetti. "It's too dangerous to stop!"

That's probably true, but right now my focus has been gathered up and tied in a knot. These numbers have always stuck with me. Knowing the Low-Probability Event, the unlikely idea of these digits returning has always lurked in the back of my mind.

Now the answer is right in front of me.

I recall the muddled response my driver gave as he struggled to remember our destination's longitude and latitude.

Thirty-seven was the best he could offer. Then *a hundred something.*

I stop running. "Wait," I cry out, my breathing heavy. "We need Denver's phone."

"Who the fuck are we gonna call?" Agent Layne retorts, fear and confusion battling for space behind his eyes. "LPEC? I'm already here."

"We're not calling anyone, we need her GPS," I reply. "I know where the plot hole is."

HEADS AND TAILS

It's not long before the sonic bombardment of gunshots and shrieks tapers off, giving way to the oppressive silence that came before it and will stand long after we're gone. We're all guests out here in the wild, passing through like we own the place and quickly discovering that nature has other ideas.

There's evidence whatever attacked our convoy is not entirely *natural*—mostly the fact I've never seen a slithering, whipping appendage like that on Animal Planet—but if that's true, then *what is it?*

My wildest guess is that something escaped from a government lab. Whether Area 51 holds real-deal extraterrestrials, or just some frightening biological chimeras crafted here on Earth, is another question.

Agent Layne has turned off his flashlight, plunging us into darkness as we creep along the edge of our marooned convoy. Our eyes have adjusted to the night. It also helps that the clouds have parted just enough to let in a little moonlight. What was once a blizzard of paper scraps has settled into a light flurry, increasing visibility but making the whole scene even more difficult to existentially parse. Now that things have calmed a bit, the stark reality of our situation feels even more absurd.

Agent Layne and I eventually reach the side where Denver was yanked into the darkness, and despite the newly fallen confetti, there's still an obvious path where the woman was dragged.

We slip deeper into the black abyss, our eyes scanning various lumps and shadows, dark shapes that gradually reveal themselves as standing cacti or Joshua trees.

My heart is slamming hard, adrenaline igniting my senses and forcing me into a state of high alert. Despite my nihilistic disposition and flirtations with a literal death wish, this body of mine isn't going down without a fight.

Agent Layne grips his handgun and sweeps the barrel from side to side, eyes darting like those of a man who's been bingeing *Dark Encounters*.

Fortunately, there are two new factors working in our favor, and while this mission to find Denver's phone might seem like a lost cause on the surface, there are legitimate reasons to—

I cut this thought short, refusing to finish it. I'll push onward, but I refuse to *hope*.

Regardless, it helps not to be flashing a high-powered light beam in the middle of this darkened landscape, giving away our location to any strange creature that might be lurking within a ten-mile radius.

The next advantage is a little macabre, but I can't help the thought that anything currently devouring a fresh kill might be distracted for a while.

Agent Layne abruptly puts his hand up, stopping me in my tracks. The two of us stand in complete silence as he points to a slight divot in the topography before us, a natural trench positioned among three or four large boulders.

It's here we leave Layne's rolling crate and my handheld cage, the unearthly creature still curled quietly within. If this were a real animal that I'd been tasked with safely transporting, then I'd probably balk at the thought of leaving it behind to become some jackrabbit's snack, but there's no *real* animal in this box. There's absolutely nothing inside it at all.

Agent Layne, who claims to see the centipede as a humming mechanical device, certainly isn't worried.

My hands now free, I find a large, sharp rock, picking it up and gripping the jagged stone tight. Based on what I've witnessed already, there's little this makeshift weapon will accomplish against whatever monster lurks in the shadows, but I'm making do with what I've got.

We creep a little closer to the boulders with soft, patient steps.

A slow, rattling chortle rings out through the darkness, softer than the first we heard, but more than enough to stop us in our tracks. This strange noise is accompanied by a horrible squishing sound, a soggy, fleshy chew that's difficult to place.

Layne and I round the ditch, keeping our distance as we move to the side that will provide a better view and then freezing in astonishment at what we've found. Two figures are huddled in the darkness, one lying flat on its back and the other crouching over it. These ambiguous shapes are no more than thirty feet away.

Abruptly, the slurping halts.

"Shoot it," I hiss.

Agent Layne doesn't pull the trigger, however, his innate fascination with novel experiences clearly fogging his survival instincts.

"Which one?" Layne murmurs back.

The crouching figure slowly stands, transforming from a hunched ball into an unexpectedly humanoid shape. When the silhouette reaches full attention, Agent Layne pops on his flashlight and bathes it in a brilliant spot of illumination.

A pale being with a bulbous head stands before us, slender and nude, but with no discernible genitalia. Its head is unusually large, nodding awkwardly atop a skinny neck as it bobbles slowly toward the light. Its eyes are massive and black, two almond-shaped forms attached to the head in a wide-set frame. Scraps of rainbow confetti are still stuck to the creature's giant cranium.

This is, from the looks of it, the species so often described in alien abductions and close encounters, a genuine extraterrestrial life-form that's so unexpected it sucks the air from my lungs. I'm overwhelmed with shock, frozen in place as the entity wobbles toward us.

What are the chances?

As bizarre as this life-form is, and as dangerous as the circumstances are, I somehow find its approach distinctly nonthreatening. There's a unique stumble in its walk, like that of a toddler struggling with their first steps.

It's almost silly, in a way.

The creature holds up its hand in a peaceful gesture, waving with its four long fingers as a soft coo rattles from its throat. This is the same vocalization we'd heard earlier, only this time the cadence is distinctly welcoming—*cute,* even.

It's not until I notice a disfigured body laid out on the ground behind our new friend that panic sets in.

"Hey—hey, Layne!" I stammer, then repeat my previous command with significantly more gusto. "Shoot it!"

Still, my companion doesn't react, hypnotized by his own fascination.

A real-life alien.

The humanoid figure begins to shift, the lower half of its face splitting open in a vertical maw that runs all the way down to its neck. It's only now that I realize the broad black eyes atop the creature's head are not eyes at all, but distinct inky markings against the entity's gray skin. Real eyes are attached to the sides of its neck, beady little nubs flickering open to reveal themselves.

A slender, hoselike appendage begins to slither out of what appears to be the entity's true mouth, emerging from the vertical slit that runs all the way down its throat. It lashes violently in the air.

The adorable alien presentation is a ruse, clearly, a display of bodily familiarity that's swiftly dismissed at the moment it realizes we're not buying it. What I once considered the head is actually a giant snout, and this is made even more apparent when the thing falls forward onto all fours.

"Shoot it!" I scream.

The creature leaps forward as Agent Layne pulls the trigger, bullets erupting from the chamber in a series of brilliant flashes and deafening bangs. The moment is quick and frighteningly reflexive, as though Layne's trigger finger would've remained static unless otherwise coaxed into action by the sudden movement.

The creature is galloping on its knuckles. Its long tendril whips forward, traveling so fast I can barely see it, and strikes Layne in the shoulder. This attack is perfectly timed with Layne's third shot, our aggressor's slender appendage hitting him with a thump just as a bullet rips through its chest, tugging the tendril out again.

The alien staggers back in alarm. It tries altering course to dodge the bullets, showing off an impressive display of dexterity in the process, but Layne isn't taking any chances.

Agent Layne empties his clip, and although only half the rounds seem to find their target, the last strike is enough to drop the creature into a drift of confetti with a hefty thud.

The bangs stop, transitioning into the quiet clicking of Layne's trigger finger.

"Hot damn," he groans, voice slurring as he clutches his left shoulder. "Ow!"

Layne's arm is hanging limp at his side, while half of his face has stiffened into a permanent frown. It appears the tentacle has delivered some kind of paralytic venom.

"Am I okay?" he wonders aloud.

Before I get the chance to reply, animalistic shrieks and rattles begin to fill the night air.

No time.

I spring into action, bounding through the paper shreds toward Denver. A wave of nausea washes over me as I finally bear witness to her evolving form, barely recognizing the woman if not for her familiar attire. The cowgirl's body is strangely rigid, huge portions of her skin mutated into a translucent plastic shell. Within this warped casing is a vague approximation of Denver's body, but portions of meat and bone have started to melt. Large sections of her face are gone, the flesh dissolved across her neck and chest to reveal a semiliquefied rib cage and a completely missing right arm. The only thing left of this lost appendage is the clear casing that once served as Denver's skin, already starting to crack and deflate now that the viscera has been sucked out.

I'm immediately reminded of arachnid feeding habits, the way they capture their prey and dissolve its insides, eventually sucking it dry like a smoothie.

"Oh fuck," I groan, faltering slightly.

Denver's only remaining eye darts around to find me, her face still frozen in the same expression of abrupt shock. It's only then that I notice her heart is still beating within her translucent chest and half-melted rib cage, hammering like a hummingbird thanks to some visceral cocktail of traumatic shock and unfathomable pain.

"*Oh fuck,*" I repeat, a second wave of nausea washing over me as I struggle not to vomit.

"Come on!" Layne yells, now the one egging things along as he desperately reloads his gun. His voice is a little slurred, but things don't seem to be getting any worse.

Fortunately, that barb was only inside Layne for a split second, and it's possible he's only received a portion of the paralytic dose.

Across the desert, the shrill braying draws even closer.

I dive immediately into Denver's pocket, quickly finding and extracting her phone. I turn it around and hover the screen above what's left of Denver's face, praying it unlocks.

"You got it?" Agent Layne calls over.

"Hold on!" I shout, checking to discover that Denver's facial recognition has been, not surprisingly, rejected.

I turn my attention to the woman below me, looking Denver dead in her frantically darting eye. "What's your password?" I demand.

Denver's gaze immediately locks onto mine with visceral intensity, but her jaw doesn't budge an inch. Whatever poison has flooded her veins is far from releasing its grip, and I can only hope it includes an anesthetic.

I try again, holding the phone above her face for a second pass and struggling not to succumb to the utter dread that has overwhelmed my thoughts. Even now, a little voice is reminding me how easy it would be to give up and lie down next to her.

I check the phone again. No dice.

Buying us a final morsel of time, Agent Layne hurls his flashlight as far as he can. Footsteps gallop past us through the confetti, but this diversion won't last.

"What's taking so long?" Layne hisses, no longer safe to shout as the creatures enter our proximity.

In one final attempt, I grab Denver by the side of the head and tilt it perfectly upright, a straight shot of her melted visage from the phone's camera above. This movement causes a sickening crack as the shell around her neck breaks, yellow-and-red carnage spilling out like a dropped smoothie on a hot day. Denver's eye rolls back in an expression that could either be mind-numbing pain or sweet relief, her pumping heart finally seizing up in a sputtering arrythmia.

I flip the phone around, already prepared for a wave of devastation but slapped with the emotional whiplash of sublime gratitude. The device is unlocked.

"I got it!" I whisper with a little too much excitement, springing to my feet.

Agent Layne and I scurry out of the ditch, rushing back to our crate and cage under the cover of darkness. The squeals and chirps behind us paint a vivid picture as the rest of the creatures discover the half-finished meal we've left for them, immediately diving in.

I can't help thinking I did Denver a favor by snapping her neck.

Once we've put some distance between us and the creatures, I plug a memorable set of latitude and longitude coordinates into Denver's mapping software, instantly pinging off the private Everett cell towers.

37°18'32" N
115°36'52" W

Sure enough, this input prompts a tiny pin to drop—of all the places on Earth—into the middle of the Nevada desert no more than two miles away.

♣ ♥ ♦ ♠

Our journey across the desert alternates long stretches of nothingness with punctuations of outlandish novelty. Every so often, a song or some inexplicable noise will pierce the relative quiet of the open landscape, echoing across the sand—little bubbles of chaos spring up as fate rocks violently on its axis.

At various points we're treated to snippets of "Good Luck, Babe!" by Chappell Roan, "Take A Chance On Me" by ABBA, and "Lucky" by Radiohead, the last of which I recognize because Annie used to listen to it constantly, and this fact gives its arrival even more cosmic heft. These clips ring out from random locations in the darkness. Sometimes the music is joined by other sounds, like a cacophony of pig squeals, or what seems to be an air traffic control broadcast in German.

During "Lucky" our path is blocked by a handful of massive, hulking creatures lumbering through the haze of falling confetti. It's arresting at first, but my anxiety settles when I realize the herd of gentle elephants seems unfazed by our presence.

A few minutes later, headlights appear, bobbing violently as some distant vehicle struggles over the rough desert terrain. Flames roar from every window as the car bumbles along. The vehicle slows as it crosses our path, then stops, revealing an old Volkswagen Beetle with a red base coat and big black spots of paint. The flaming ladybug illuminates the scene for several yards in every direction, and as we trudge by it I can make out four bodies within the roiling blaze. The heat has already melted their flesh away, giving them the appearance of a skeletal family on some hell-bound road trip.

We pass a full living room set with a circular rug, a couch, a coffee table, and a standing lamp that has somehow been electrified. A flayed corpse sits upright on the couch, still glistening, while a single pair of shoes rest side by side on the table.

At one point, a bright red drone buzzes past us. It's no larger than a pie box. A handwritten sign hangs from the device, the words AS LUCK WOULD HAVE IT scrawled across rectangular posterboard in fat black lines. Somehow, the drone maintains its balance with a pair of severed human hands attached to either side of its body, their fingers spread open like bat wings.

The most important thing we see, however, is a hump looming in the darkness. The bulge is about the size of a large, one-story rambler, a mass of boulders and dirt that has been covered by a faint dusting of confetti. Out here, the rainbow paper is spread much lighter, our trek leading to the very edge of whatever strange weather force created this bizarre phenomenon.

It's hard to believe Agent Layne and I didn't notice a mound like this the first time we were trekking around, but then again why would we? The desert is relatively flat, but at the base of these rolling hills the humps become commonplace, an expected part of the landscape.

Denver's phone finally runs out of battery as we make our approach, but we no longer need it. The closer we get, the more apparent the features of this landmass become. I can now see the sharp curve of its slope and the gathering of cacti around its base. More important, however, is the faint source of light emanating from the mound's right side.

Agent Layne is limping slightly, but his mobility remains steady as we trudge onward, making our way around this hump to find a large crack in the knoll.

The opening is unnaturally straight despite its position between two massive boulders. It's some kind of industrial sliding door, likely hidden away and disguised to look like sandstone, but easy to spot now that it's frozen ajar.

I step toward the opening, but Layne reaches out to stop me, nodding toward a figure that rests slumped against this mysterious entrance. It's a guard, his legs splayed wide and his arms by his sides. He's wearing a nondescript work uniform, navy blue in color, with short sleeves that reveal his bloated arms and fingers. His face is plump and red, eyes swollen shut and a sickly crust built up between the slits.

There's no confetti on the security officer, suggesting he hasn't been here long.

"Looks like an allergic reaction," Layne suggests.

I take note of the bruising around his neck and the still-burning cigarette that rests in the dirt next to him. I try imagining the circumstances that led him to this deeply unfortunate position, considering that he might've forgotten his own pack of cigarettes at home. They could've been fresh out of his brand at the liquor store, the one on the corner just before the turn off the main road. I wonder which coworker might've let this poor soul borrow a cig, and which slight variation in ingredients led to this disaster.

"A lot of bad luck out here," Agent Layne says, his speech clearer now but his face still paralyzed right down the middle. "Goddamn, am I ready for some of the good stuff."

The caged centipede squirms, rattling the handle held tight in my hand.

Layne and I continue onward, cautiously making our way through the hidden entrance to find ourselves within a spacious industrial chamber. The floor is smooth cement, and the walls are ribbed metal like the sides of a shipping container. Steel beams frame either side of the area and run across the ceiling. I'm no architect, but I get the feeling this structure was built before the mound was ever here, then dirt was trucked in and dumped on top of it. According to the data, there are no movable plot holes, so if you wanted to keep one a secret, your only option would be to hide your find wherever it landed.

A handful of maimed and mutilated bodies are strewn about

this facility, each one offering its own outlandish tale of misfortune.

To my immediate left is a former guard, her face obliterated by a bullet wound. The wall behind her is painted with a crimson stain that spreads out like a comic book exclamation bubble, framing the place where her head used to be. Her body is slouched on the floor under this flashy red halo.

Across from the woman is another guard crumpled next to a large metal desk, blood glistening on the corner and pooling around the back of his cracked skull. A banana peel rests nearby, something I might otherwise take as coincidence if not for the fact that I'm deeply and personally aware of fate's dark sense of humor.

A gun is gripped tight in the dead man's hand, and from his final resting place I can trace how he accidently shot his companion midfall. There's also a pack of cigarettes on his desk—a likely double homicide.

At another desk it appears someone has been electrocuted, their clothes singed off and their skin charred black. In places the dermis is cracked to reveal bright red layers of flesh underneath, cooked like a sausage from within until the casing finally split. This shocking death was likely abrupt, sudden enough to scare someone who might stagger backward and slip on a banana peel.

The corpses spread out in a horrifying chain reaction, a Rube Goldberg machine of carnage. Somehow, a staff member managed to wrap an extension cord around the large industrial ceiling fan spinning overhead, the cable tangling around his neck and yanking him up like a terrible marionette. He's still spinning, the ghoulishly rigid state of his corpse showcased by the endless circular movement.

As the corpse swings around again a small object flies from his jacket pocket, finally lining up with some old hole in the fabric and making its escape. It hits the ground with a soft ping, then rolls toward Layne and me, circling once before falling directly at our feet.

Heads.

I bend down and pick it up, already knowing what's going to be on the other side. The answer, of course, is the most absurd and unlikely thing I could possibly imagine, a trillion-to-one shot.

I turn the penny over to find a faded gold star sticker. Despite knowing it was coming, it's hard not to stare. I hold the coin in my hand for a long time, gazing down at the little copper circle as memories of Annie come flooding back.

I feel her squeezing my hand on the morning of May 23, a simple gesture of reassurance. It's the last thing she did before I left and chased after my mother, the last connection we ever had.

"What is it?" Layne asks.

"Nothing," I finally reply, slipping the penny into my pocket.

We step farther into the room, shocked by just how much blood there is. The gore is splattered generously, and the scene has been recently disturbed because something has tracked through the red liquid and stamped it everywhere.

The footprints are immediately recognizable: horseshoes.

"Whoa!" Agent Layne cries out, lifting his weapon and stepping back as a large steed casually saunters around the corner.

The horse loudly snorts and shakes his head, showing off a glorious mane. He's light brown and muscular, unexpectedly relaxed given the bizarre circumstances we've found him in. He's equipped with leather reins that hang down around his face, and a saddle rests tight against his back. Green fabric is wrapped around the horse, displaying a massive *7* in bold white font and the name *Last Chance* written below.

Layne and I watch as the massive creature trots past us. Last Chance pays no mind, clopping through the half-opened metal doors and disappearing into the night.

"What's next, a fucking leprechaun?" I murmur.

From the corner of my eye, I spot Layne's half-faced expression shift to one of childlike excitement. "Wait, you really think there might be a leprechaun?"

I let out a defeated sigh. "There's a difference between unlikely and impossible," I remind him, then continue onward.

However, my confident expression falters the second he can no longer see it.

Please don't let there be a leprechaun.

Soon enough, we've arrived at another large metal door, similar in size and construction to the one that initially guided us inside. I press a black button to the right, some hidden mechanism eliciting a loud clang as the double doors glide slowly apart and reveal a dancing blue light within.

The room is a little smaller than the last, perfectly square and featuring a one-foot-high platform at the center. Hovering above this platform is an enormous swirling plot hole, this tear in reality approximately ten feet in diameter.

The portal's rim is a dazzling blue, with surges of energy coursing through it like the hot coals of a turquoise flame. The inner rim is a thick and oily black, the same as I saw back at the trailer park, but as the hole widens this texture dissipates and becomes semitranslucent.

The body of the portal appears to be empty, at first, showing off nothing more than the wall that rests behind it, but as my eyes dance across the shifting image I realize it's an illusion. It's an approximation of what I *think* rests behind the ring, my mind filling in the blanks the best it can. Entering the room, I wasn't aware of two surge protectors that sit humming against the back wall. Therefore, I couldn't see them through the center of this glaring plot hole. Once I move to the side and spot them, however, my brain places these machines within the fluid display.

I'd love to experiment more, but every passing second is another moment for the strings of fate to snap back into place and cause yet another disaster. We need to hurry.

Agent Layne is already hard at work unboxing his crate and preparing the generator with honed efficiency, despite just one working hand. He nods toward the protective suit and I spring into action, pulling on my gear and preparing for a journey into the great unknown—into nothing.

I'm aware these final moments of anticipation should probably terrify me, but for some reason fear is the last thing on my mind. I've had time to mentally prepare, of course, but that doesn't quite explain the unexpected emotions as I cinch my boots and lock them to the pant leg, creating an airtight seal.

While it hasn't been said outright, the odds of me never returning from this plunge into the infinite are substantial, and that's fine. This was never a mission I was looking to come back from, just a final desperate search for meaning before returning to the great nothing. You'd think a certain loneliness might accompany this knowledge, a natural, stomach-churning dread in the face of oblivion, but that feeling never comes. Instead, the ache that washes over me is one of bittersweet comfort.

I'm reminded of road trips with my mother when I was younger, jaunts up to Door County to visit distant family elders. There were no other kids my age, and certainly no toys to play with, just quiet houses where time seemed to stretch on and on. I could stomach an hour or two in this purgatory, but eventually I'd be desperate to return to my friends and my things and my own bedroom after days away.

There was such a powerful sense of relief when we finally loaded back into the car and started our journey home. At a certain point on those return drives I'd start recognizing landmarks, distinct clusters of trees or a specific bend in the road. Suddenly, counting down the minutes didn't seem so hopeless after all.

As I carefully latch the round, windowed helmet onto my airtight suit, this is the feeling that greets me. I'm going home, returning to a place I've foolishly ventured away from for far too long. My time with Agent Layne over the last few weeks has shown me there are still nuggets of adventure and fascination and joy to be mined from the hard, cold stone of life, but I'm not sure it's enough to tip the scales. Not for me, anyway.

There are four loud bangs to my left. I turn to discover Agent Layne has used a powerful, pressurized drill to drive metal stakes through the feet of his generator, sealing it to the cement floor below. He pulls two levers, and soon enough the device is roaring to life, filling my suit with oxygen and immediately clearing the fog away from my visor.

Layne shows me a button to trigger my air reserve, then helps with my gloves. The second they're sealed into place my suit feels completely different, fully disconnected from the outside world.

"Can you hear me?" Layne asks, his voice filtered through tiny speakers in my helmet.

"Sure can," I reply, offering a thumbs-up.

Layne pats my shoulder, then nods and steps back.

Before me, the portal looms vast and mysterious, beckoning me into oblivion. I pick up the cage, sensing the massive black centipede as it squirms inside, then walk straight into the void.

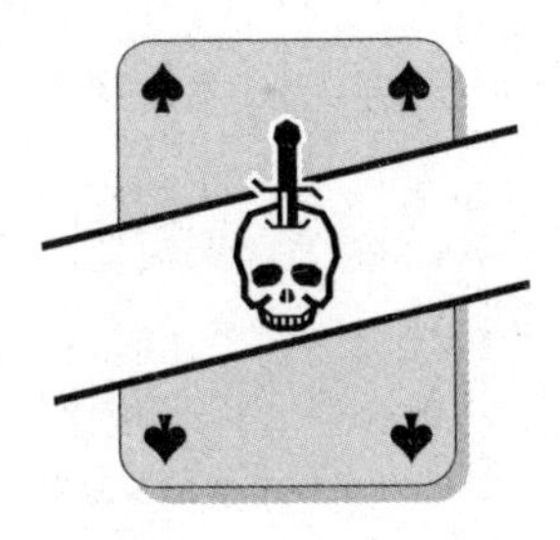

OBLIVION

Visually, the change is quick, like walking through a thin stream of water. The instant shift from one state to the next is curiously anticlimactic, none of the swirling visual effects you might find in a blockbuster science-fiction film, no sparks of magical energy pulsing around me as I'm yanked into the vortex. One second, I'm outside the portal—the next, I'm in.

The temperature shift comes slower, thanks to my suit, but I *do* notice an odd balance in the air around me. There's no chill or warmth, but a complete absence of either.

The darkness is oppressive, a vast black space with no perceivable boundaries. I reach up and place my own hand on the rounded curve of my helmet, pressing against the glass to make sure I'm still here.

I now notice how heavy my breathing is against the inside of my mask, the breezy excitement I'd previously displayed quickly melting away now that I'm neck-deep in the unknown. Maybe I'm not as comfortable standing within this endless nothing as I'd initially thought.

This isn't the home I imagined it would be.

I tighten my grip on the centipede's cage, perceiving its weight in my hand but fully aware there's no tangible heft to the creature itself. Could this be far enough? Can I drop the package right here and turn back around?

Is this all it takes to save the world?

It's certainly possible, but in that case we could've just pushed the cage through a smaller plot hole and let the chips fall where they may. I'm here to drop off a package, but the more understanding I can glean, the better. The last thing we want is for this little slice of *nothing* to crawl back out again.

I reach out my arm and step forward, greeted by more empty space. I take another step, then another.

A flat surface registers against my open palm, the glove pushing back against my skin as a startled breath escapes my throat. I spread my hand, letting it drift a bit lower and then exploring the space to my right and left. There's a wall here.

Eventually, my fingers arrive at a small protrusion, no more than an inch long and resting about waist height. I take a moment to explore the shape of this strange imperfection, struggling to understand its form through the clumsy bulk of my gloves until, suddenly, I realize what I've discovered.

I flip on the light switch, my eyes adjusting to yet another monumental shift as the room around me manifests with glaring brilliance. I blink a few times, struggling to focus as my pupils shrink and restrict the warm glow cascading from above.

The space that had seemed so endless in the darkness is actually quite small, a cramped room featuring dark green walls with a light gray floral design swirling across them. It's wallpaper, and it's oddly familiar.

Before me hangs a mirror, within which the reflection of an utterly confused woman stares back from the rounded visor of her space suit. I catch my own gaze, hardly recognizing myself and then offering an unexpected smile.

Turning slowly, I assess the tight quarters and discover yet another odd sight: a toilet.

I'm in a restroom.

I've been here before, although the details of a why or when still elude me.

Behind me, the wall undulates with the same strange energy as the portal's opposite side, cosmic blue vitality coursing along its circular rim. I can't see back through it, my eyes choosing instead to fill in an approximation of the bathroom's wallpaper.

To my right is a wooden door. I stare down at the brass knob before me, briefly halted by the mundane nature of this new setting. It's surreal in just how *ordinary* it feels, and the sense that I've been here before only looms larger with every passing second. Even my hesitation feels strange, like this moment is the final iteration of some bizarre cosmic dress rehearsal that's been repeating forever and ever.

I reach down and grab the knob, twisting slowly and pulling the door open. A new wave of sensations wash over me, and within a fraction of a second I know exactly where I am. While there's supposedly no oxygen within this portal, a lack of atmosphere doesn't stop the potent scent of sizzling, greasy potatoes and freshly brewed coffee. I can hear the faint sound of some early '90s pop-rock ballad drifting down from speakers hidden somewhere above, loud enough for me to recognize the hook but not remember the lyrics.

This is the diner where I had brunch on the day my mother died; the day of the Low-Probability Event.

I've found myself in a short hallway, not nearly as dark as the restroom but still tucked away from the brilliant daylight glow of the main dining area. From here, I can only make out a sliver of the central room, and what few tables are visible are completely empty. I creep forward, my breathing amplified by the dome of my helmet and vibrating through my skull. The dining area is slowly revealed, utterly devoid of patrons until a specific table causes my muscles to clench in shock.

Sitting quietly is a familiar collection of long-lost friends, the same group who joined me on that terrible day. None of them are speaking, the arrangement frozen in place as they gaze stoically at one another.

One figure, however, is already looking in my direction, apparently knowing I'd come strolling around the corner at any moment: my mother.

Maria Norrie is smiling warmly. "There she is!" Mom cheers, prompting the rest of the table to turn their heads and greet me with loving grins of their own.

It's impossible to avoid the wave of emotion that crashes into me as these memorable faces manifest across my field of vision, the bittersweet nostalgia pumping into my heart with such force that it wells up in my eyes as salty tears.

Still, there's something uncanny about them, more than just the stiff expressions. It's hard to tell *exactly* what tickles this deep, primal warning within me, but the subconscious portion of my brain that evolved to know the difference between a stick and a snake has been activated.

Most of the folks who sit at this table are dead, after all.

My attention wanders over to Annie, briefly appreciating her adoration before noticing the faintest twitch of her right eye. For a split second her iris shoots off to the side and then darts back into place, a flicker that happens so fast it exists as more of a memory than a present observation. Fortunately, it's enough to quell any romantic longings that might've bubbled up.

I tear my focus away, addressing my mother. "What are you doing here?" I ask, the words feeling awkward and juvenile as they stumble through my lips.

I don't know what else to ask.

Weren't you crushed by a truck the day it started raining fish?

Mom tilts her head ever so slightly in a *bless your little heart* moment, her body language gently implying that I should already know the answer to this one.

"Waiting for you," she says tenderly. "I'm very, very proud of you, sweetheart. You've finally done it."

"Done what?" I question.

"You don't exist," she replies, beaming with joy.

I can't help scoffing. "You told me the exact same thing the last time we were here."

My mother closes her eyes, taking some time to bask in the moment. "Well, I was right."

This is what finally causes my emotions to spill over, the tears no longer just welling up but running down my cheeks.

Unspoken words from age-old family drama are rising from the deep, a subconscious part of my inner voice that refuses to sit back any longer and has clawed its way to the surface. They tumble out of me in a torrent of fire and lava, but I'm far from a blubbering mess. In fact, I'm unusually centered in this moment of release.

"You were *wrong,*" I counter. "I was happy then, Mom. Everything felt like it fucking *mattered,* and every day was new and exciting and important. I was in love."

I call her *Mom* in this exchange, even though, deep down, I know this isn't really my mother.

"You were in *love*?" She laughs, her smile briefly taking on the wryness of a smirk before shifting back again. "With that woman you met in college?"

"With Annie," I reply.

"A phase," Mom retorts. "An important phase, probably a fun one, but still just a phase. Nothing but dust."

"We were together a long time," I firmly counter. "I just didn't tell you."

My mother hesitates, slightly annoyed. It feels as though she wasn't expecting me to fight back this much, didn't think I'd offer retaliations to the bold statements she's parading out.

"Do you realize how long *time* is?" Maria asks. "You weren't together a long time. You've never done *anything* a long time, Vera."

"I spent my whole life trying to help people," I say. "My *whole life.*"

My mother rolls her eyes, a series of facial tics and movements that are unmistakably her own. For a brief moment, I find myself questioning my initial skepticism of our interaction, wondering if somehow the real Maria Norrie has been resurrected in flesh and blood.

"Are you saving the world now?" Mom asks, her voice dripping with sarcasm.

"I . . . am," I fumble, not sure how else to respond.

Maria's expression straightens out again. "What world? There are billions and billions and billions of worlds, Vera. For every timeline where you save the world, there's another one where you destroy it. They fall apart like tissue paper because there's nothing holding them together, no *real* substance. Remember when you tried baking that pie with all your favorite foods?"

I do remember that shining moment of childhood ignorance, and while I look back on the day fondly, it was certainly a learning experience. Turns out a ranch dressing, cherry, and Oreo cookie pie isn't as delicious as each individual flavor might lead you to believe.

Unless, of course, you're someone like Agent Layne, but that's a whole other issue.

"It was a mess," I admit.

"*Everything's* a mess," Maria continues. "Every moment of clarity cancels the next one out, every epiphany just leads to another question. It's static. It's chaos. It's noise. Too many things spilling into one another to create a sickening, painful, exhausting soup called life. Reality is ridiculous, and the only thing that makes any sense is the nothingness between worlds."

My gaze keeps drifting back to Annie. Despite knowing this isn't really her, the approximation of my ex-fiancée is difficult to ignore.

"Sometimes it makes sense," I counter.

"When?" Mom demands to know. "Name a time when there wasn't a pebble in your shoe. Tell me a moment when you actually felt like everything was as it should be."

I don't have an answer for her, and the two of us fall into a brief silence.

"You left the numbers for me," I finally state. "You wanted me to come here."

I'm speaking to my mother, but by now I'm fully sensing the dichotomy between her physical form and some larger, cosmic thing. Who *exactly* lies behind this mask remains a mystery, however. Am I talking to myself, or does the physical manifestation of nothingness have a sentience of its own? Am I speaking to God? Or the devil? To be honest, breaking down this encounter with religious implications seems downright quaint, surprisingly arrogant in its own little way.

"Historical inertia," Mom replies. "Fate was always bringing you here."

This statement hits me like a punch to the gut, a terrifying thought I'd certainly waxed philosophically about but that sounds so different slipping from her lips. As many times as I'd made the proclamation that *nothing matters,* it still felt like there was a counterpoint lurking deep within me, safely tucked away as a violent storm raged around it.

Whether I could admit it out loud, the faintest shred of meaning—of hope—always stuck around through even my darkest moments.

"So, I was right?" I ask, my voice cracking as Maria's words finally hit their mark and sink into my aching, exhausted heart like brutal talons. "Nothing matters?"

"Nothing matters," she repeats. "Just an endless circus of celebration and trauma. Rinse and repeat."

The tears are pouring from my eyes now, years of emotional weight finally surging forth as the dam cracks, then erupts in a cascade of grief. The self-control I've been so desperate to maintain has completely washed away, leaving me bare and exposed to this onslaught of feelings and thoughts and aches.

I begin to shake, trembling so hard I'm forced to turn away and place my hands on my knees in an effort to keep from falling over. The first frantic thought that comes ripping through my mind is that my space suit has malfunctioned and I'm running out of air, but through my blind terror I'm somehow able to grasp the hidden truth that I'm having a panic attack.

Fuck.

The grinding, searing misery is too potent for my physical body to reckon with any longer. I open my mouth and let out an unbridled shriek, the sound reverberating through my skull and building within the suit speakers like an endless feedback loop. When I finish, I take a deep breath and then scream again, and again, each time feeling like the whole of my tired soul is being vomited up and expelled from my mortal frame.

I somehow find the coherence to focus on various objects around me. I spot a fork lying on a nearby table, then accept its presence and make a proclamation out loud.

"That's a fork," I state, then move to another object. "That's a napkin. That's a chair."

But while my effort is valiant, and this technique is usually useful during normal panic attacks, this particular situation is different. Despite my own words, that is *not* a fork, nor a napkin, nor a chair.

There's nothing here but a vast, endless void, along with my reeling mind's best attempts to fill it.

Unless, of course, the very concept of nothingness has a *personality*. Is it possible this strange approximation of my mother really *is* a separate force outside my spiraling brain, some sentience that exists beyond our understanding of matter and energy?

Suffice to say, none of these thoughts help me calm down.

In a moment of desperation, I reach up and start clawing at my helmet, struggling to break the seal and tear it off my head. There are multiple safety latches, but my gloved fingers somehow manage to make their way across the first clasp and unlock it.

I move to the second latch, but my mother's voice calls out to stop me.

"Vera Norrie!" she shouts, using the same tone I heard as a child when my behavior got out of line. "Come on!"

I hesitate. I'm still sizzling with raw emotion, but the familiar cadence of my mother's voice somehow yanks me back from the edge.

"If you take that off, you'll die," Mom continues. "We wouldn't want that."

When I glance back up to address her I find the diner has completely fallen away, along with the table of friends.

Instead, Maria and I stand in an enormous white room, the walls starkly painted and extending up to massive vaulted ceilings. The floor is constructed with beautiful tan wood, and there are two benches in the middle of the large chamber. It has the distinct feeling of an empty art gallery.

A portal still swirls behind me, the same place it hovered when I arrived, only lacking the trappings of a restaurant. The hose of my space suit snakes toward it, winding across the ground and then eventually disappearing into the luminous, swirling pool.

"I'm sorry if having your friends around made things too emotional," Mom apologizes. "Let's slow it down. We can't have you hurting yourself now, can we?"

"Just tell me why I'm here," I demand, my eyes red and swollen.

"Because I have something for you," she explains. "A gift."

Somehow, a small, round table has appeared before my mother. Upon this waist-high furniture sits a simple glass-and-metal cage, a massive black centipede coiled within. The insect is restless, its many legs tapping against the glass as it arches back to explore its surroundings.

I glance down, making sure my own cage is still there and glad to find it resting at my feet.

"Take them both with you," my mother suggests.

"Why the hell would I do that?"

Mom tilts her head to the side again, eyeing me with a well-worn expression of amusement. "Because *not* existing is so much cleaner, isn't it? It's so simple."

I consider this, taking a moment to find my footing.

"If you can't slow chaos down, then you might as well speed it up," Mom continues.

Despite all the hardship and trauma that weigh upon my mind, the analytical part of me is impossible to quell. I can't help this craving for order.

Maybe it's not order I'm looking for, though, and maybe that's been the problem this whole time. *Order* and *purpose* are often considered synonymous, but there's a subtle difference between the two. Finding order in this chaotic world has turned out to be a fool's errand, but *purpose* might still have a chance.

"You want me to take it, though," I suddenly blurt. "That means you have intent. If there's intent, then all this chaos amounts to *something.* I might not know what that something is, but I *feel* it. I feel it when I think about Annie, or you, or Agent Layne. You're right—there are billions and billions of stories that are much larger than my own, and that makes me feel very, very small. But it also makes me feel very, very unique. The fact I even exist in the first place is the most astronomically low-probability event there is. I'm not gonna waste that because nothingness is easier."

I leave the caged centipede at my feet, turning around and stepping confidently back toward the swirling portal.

"There's only grief out there," my mother calls. "A carousel of misery."

I keep walking.

"Wait!" she screams, so loud that it finally stops me in my tracks. "Let me *show* you what existence brings."

The overhead lights abruptly dim. To my right, the dancing lights of a projected film begin to swirl across the massive museum wall.

I know I should just keep walking, but I'm captivated by the strange, colorful images. It's not often you find yourself in the presence of something so cosmically powerful, and I have no doubt ignoring this presentation would haunt me until the day I die. The secrets of the universe are hovering just beyond my reach, tempting me with glimpses beyond the veil.

As I gaze up at the screen, however, the video feels oddly pedestrian. A group of disheveled men are shown sitting around a poker table. They're seated in a dim, dirty cardroom with low ceilings and sickly yellow walls. The tables around them are empty. It's not security footage, but it's certainly not cinematic, either. The film is grainy and old, and the words the men exchange are barely audible thanks to a strange, wobbling drone that washes over everything.

The sound is slightly nauseating, and it gives the visuals a potent sense of unease and foreboding.

At the poker table, a man with long dark hair and a shaggy beard suddenly throws his cards down, erupting from his seat and clapping his hands together in a burst of excitement. He accidently rams his elbow into the player next to him, quickly apologizing before returning to his celebration.

The body language of this brief interaction is all I need to recognize that the man is completely plastered, dangerously close to toppling over as his arms flail wildly. His grin is crooked and a little *too* confident, regardless of how much good luck he's just stumbled into.

The celebration continues until, suddenly, it doesn't. The bearded man stares down at a set of cards laid out on the green felt table before him, an opposing player showing off their hand with cool, laid-back poise.

The drunk man freezes, then starts yelling. He grabs the edge of the poker table and tries flipping it, hoisting it far enough to spill some chips before two security guards appear out of nowhere and grab him by either arm. They drag the player away, kicking and screaming.

The camera changes to another view, hanging above a gravel parking lot and looking down upon three beat-up cars sitting in the morning light. The lot is grimy, dumpsters overflowing and shattered glass covering one of the empty parking spaces like unfortunate tinsel.

The bearded man staggers through this scene, howling eccentrically and punching himself in the side of the head before arriving at one of the derelict vehicles. He pulls a ring of keys from his pocket, taking quite a while to find the one he's looking for and even longer to insert it into the driver's side door of a blue sedan parked haphazardly across two spaces. The man misses a few times, but finally hits his target and yanks the door open.

I expect the worst, ready to watch as this belligerent drunk pulls out and weaves onto the road in a liquored-up stupor. Instead, he just sits there. From this angle, the back of his head is visible, a silhouetted mass just resting in place for what seems like forever. He doesn't even start the car.

"What the hell is this?" I finally ask, turning back to my mother.

"Strings pulling," Maria explains over the sickening drone, then nods back at the projection, directing my gaze.

I return to the flickering scene, discovering that the bearded man has since emerged from his vehicle. He's pacing around the parking lot, talking solemnly into his cell phone.

The camera's perspective shifts a third time, apparently skipping ahead. The projection now offers a view from the rear middle seat of someone's truck interior, a passenger and a driver positioned up front as city streets roll past.

For the first time, I can hear what's being said, the voices of these two men suddenly cutting through the wobbling, otherworldly tone that overwhelms my body.

"Put on your seat belt," the driver demands, his voice echoing strangely off of the blank gallery walls.

The bearded man ignores him from his place in the passenger seat, prompting the driver to hit the brakes.

"Put on your fucking seat belt, Jonah," the driver repeats. "*You* called *me* to pick your drunk ass up."

There's something familiar about that name.

The disheveled passenger lets out a long, disappointed groan, finally obeying the command and connecting the strap to his waist. The truck starts moving again.

"How much did you lose?" the driver asks.

"You don't understand," the bearded man sighs, avoiding the question as he cradles his head in his hands.

The second I hear his voice, an icy chill surges through me. Even in this drunken state, I know that voice.

"That was the worst bad beat of all *tiiime*," the bearded man continues, rolling his head back on his neck and letting the word *time* spill out of him in a long, frustrated moan. "Royal flush over straight flush, *twice*. How is that even possible?"

This downtrodden gambler is the same clean-cut partner who's been working by my side for days, the guy who somehow found a new lease on life on the same fateful day my existence fell apart.

It's Agent Layne.

"I have no idea," the driver counters, rain now pattering gently against the windshield. "I don't know what any of that means."

"I—I lost with a straight flush," Layne stammers. "Do you have any idea how *impossible* that is?"

"I do not."

"What!" Agent Layne snaps, frustrated and shouting now. "Pops taught us to play at the same time, Ben. How do you not remember any of this stuff?"

"I've got more important things to think about," the driver, who I now assume is Agent Layne's brother, sighs.

"No way! You've gotta pass that shit on! Your kids need a dad who—"

"What do you know about being a dad?" Ben suddenly explodes, his face red and his eyes wide. "Your fucking daughter won't even talk to you!"

The vehicle falls into silence.

Now, the only sound is the softly tapping rain, but this reprieve doesn't last long. Ben leans forward, staring at the base of his front windshield as small silver objects begin to pile up.

"Are those . . . fish?" he questions.

Before Layne can respond, there's an earsplitting bang and simultaneous crash, a massive salmon bursting through the glass and striking the driver's face. I jump in alarm, staggering back from the projection.

Blood paints the truck's cab, splattered across the driver's side and spilling gratuitously from the space where his missing face once rested. Ben slumps awkwardly, rocked by the enormous fish that's now stuck halfway through his windshield. There's nothing left of his expression but a tangle of broken glass and shredded crimson meat.

Agent Layne is staring at his brother in shock and abject horror.

I remember that feeling very well.

Seconds later, Layne is screaming, but the sound of his gut-wrenching howls are drowned out by the roar of the truck beneath him. Through the smashed windshield I can see the world zipping past at an alarming rate, the driver's heavy foot pressed hard against his gas pedal.

Realizing what's happening, Layne reaches out and yanks the wheel, desperately trying to avoid another vehicle but creating a whole new mess of problems. There's a hard lurch as the truck bounces over the curb and suddenly a solid brick wall is looming fast.

A hollow metallic crunch rings out, the truck slamming hard into the building and finally coming to rest. A static car horn fills the gallery, followed shortly by the frantic screeching of a woman in agony.

It's the sound of my own voice.

The projection comes to an end, disappearing as this horrible chorus of car horn and human wailing cuts short and leaves me to wallow in silence. The lights of the gallery return to their full glow, but they're flickering now, cutting in and out with moments of intermittent darkness.

Mom's voice rattles through the speakers of my suit. "Random paths crossing and uncrossing," she groans. "Fleeting moments of novelty cast adrift across an ocean of pain and tragedy. Who are you trying to save by leaving these gifts behind? Your new friend?"

I turn back to my mother, discovering her appearance has been dramatically altered. Her eyes have rolled back into her head and her mouth hangs ajar in that frightening, inhuman way. She looks just like the thin man, taking on his features as her manifestation taps into the endless current of the abyss.

The centipede cages have moved, sitting right in front of me now. They rest side by side as mischievous little nuggets of oblivion squirm within.

"A chaotic existence is a *cruel* existence," Mom says, her slack jaw hanging wide but her voice still crackling through the speakers. "Your *only friend* made me this way. He cut me in half. Is that the world you want to save? Is that fair?"

"I don't know," I fumble.

"Is that fair?" my mother repeats. "Answer me."

"No," I admit.

"Reality is cruel. The void is relief," Mom states, her words striking a chord at the pit of my stomach.

I immediately push back on this, feeling myself sinking a little too deep in the existential quicksand. "You're—you're not real," I stammer.

"Maybe not," she counters, her jaw agape as the words fill my skull, "but you're not, either. Your mother said the same thing—that you don't exist, that your love doesn't exist—she agrees with me, Vera. Deep down, everyone knows the truth."

I'm running on instinct now, struggling to keep the weight of grief and darkness and sorrow from seeping into every corner of my mind.

"Would you like to see?" my mother asks, her hanging jaw snapping up into a frightening, alien grin.

With every flicker of darkness I begin to glimpse past the boundaries of this room, the gallery walls disappearing in a haphazard smattering of split-second reveals. Instead of shadows, I bear witness to an endless rolling panorama of dark hills and jagged crags, a landscape unlike anything I've ever seen. Beyond the peaks is an infinite cascade of cosmic dust, swirling in impossible patterns and unfathomable hues.

Enormous creatures sway in the distance, miles wide and churning strangely like gibbering towers of black flesh. They dot the panorama in bizarre, unexplainable shapes, rocking from side to side and disappearing into the void above.

This celestial expanse is both awe-inspiring and terrifying, a world beyond the edge of existence. It lies somewhere outside time and space, rejecting any mortal understanding, and as I gaze past this curtain I find myself achingly thankful for the blissful ignorance I've maintained until now.

My brain has protected me from an onslaught of existential knowledge, working overtime as it translates pure *nothing* into the eerie *something* of a scuttling centipede and my own dead mother. Now, my mind is growing weary, allowing this deeper layer to pour through the cracks like a flood of sticky tar.

But along with the looming dread, another feeling begins seeping into my bones. Relief. After all this searching for order, I've finally witnessed the beautiful cleanliness of zero.

"The world deserves some relief from all this pain," my mother announces.

A surge of emotion pulses through me, compelling me forward. I stand above the cages.

Nothingness is so close, the glorious offering of an entire timeline slowly ground to dust. A clean ending for me. A clean ending for everyone. It wouldn't be painless, unfortunately, just more and more unlikely chaos until all reality is nothing more than a finely blended pulp of matter and energy. Eventually, that haze would flatten out. The portal would widen, and the void would consume everything. Creation, along with all its sickness and decay, would cease.

I open my hands, ready to pick up the centipede enclosures and bring them back with me, then hesitate.

"Release yourself," my mother groans. "Sentience is nothing but a theater for grief."

Across the flickering gallery walls, new projections begin to appear. They sputter into existence over every surface, dancing back and forth between vivid suburban imagery and some unfathomable cosmic landscape. Each displays a different setting from my life, drawing on every corner of my memory. I see my second-grade classroom. I see the pizza place I once drove five hours to meet a guy at when I was sixteen years old. I see a barn, a hotel lobby, a bowling alley.

Locations keep appearing in a seemingly endless parade, and every one of them stabs into my heart with some terrible new knife. This assortment of spaces from my life is not random. Instead, it's the greatest hits of where the wheel of fate doled out something cruel and cold, not because of something I did, but simply because that was how the cards fell.

My first memory of that second-grade classroom is getting accused of stealing Ryan Thatcher's turtle eraser when I absolutely did *not* do it. The guy I drove to meet at the pizza place stood me up. The barn is where my cousin pushed me off of a hay bale and I landed on a nail, permanently scarring my left hand. The hotel lobby is where I found out my friend's mom had just died of liver failure, and I don't even remember why I hate that bowling alley, but the vibes are *terrible*.

"Existence is built for cruelty," my mother tells me. "For misunderstanding. For sickness."

My eyes drift down to the projection of my own trash-covered living room.

"For loneliness," she adds.

From this angle I can see everything: the garbage and filth piled high, the long yellow grass crawling up outside the French doors, a pallet of unopened cat food.

This last detail, however, gives me pause. The destructive feelings that've been growing within me are suddenly rocked by an unexpected blow. A reminder of my brief time with Kat the cat should feel terrible and tragic, but for some reason it doesn't. In retrospect, those few days of hope amid an ocean of sorrow were fulfilling in a way I haven't realized until this very moment. Yes, Kat died, but the time we spent together mattered.

I smile, actually laughing to myself at the fact that all these connections to other humans didn't seem to faze me, but thoughts of that silly little cat have cut me right to the bone, snapping me out of this ever-darkening spiral.

"Where's Kat?" I ask.

"Dead," Maria replies flatly.

"Yeah . . . but you can show me *anything*," I press. "Why isn't she here?"

Wisdom from Agent Layne suddenly comes parading through my mind, banging drums and blasting trumpets—sounding the alarm.

Sometimes you can learn more from the cards they don't *show.*

I glance from place to place, noticing the very important thing that's been stripped away from each of these visions. They should be teeming with people, a far cry from the lonely, liminal spaces on display.

These locations still fill me with unease, but that's not everything they represent, not by a long shot. The people who filled them were complex and difficult and, yes, sometimes terrible, but not always. There were other moments in the classroom, like when I made my first best friend, or in the hotel lobby, where I came back and stayed for a birthday trip.

There was the time Kat, as skittish as she was, actually curled up on my lap and let me pet her for a while.

I also remember my time with Agent Layne, remember the terror of dipping my toes back into a bruised and battered world. At first, our mission felt like the excruciating personal exorcism of some horrible demon, unpleasant from beginning to end and fueled by nothing but my desire for justice, which was ultimately a cover for burning revenge.

It's been exhausting, and just as painful as I expected, but along with the aches came moments of clarity and, yes, even happiness. I suppose it's difficult to have any adventure and not find oneself the least bit entertained.

I step back, my heart slamming in my chest. "A lot of people were hurt on May 23. I can't make this decision for everyone else."

My mother's frightening grin drops again, her expression returning to the hanging jaw as her rolled-back eyes gaze onward. "Do them this favor," Mom commands through the speakers in my suit. "You're giving them mercy. Once the universe is in shreds, they won't even remember the pain."

"They won't remember the love, either," I counter.

There's something inside me that wants to keep going, that finally accepts the bittersweet taste of existence in all its macabre and magnificent glory.

"Layne was gonna drive home drunk, but he made the right choice to call his brother for a ride," I state. "My mother would be alive if he'd driven himself, and yeah, that's a little hard to understand. Good choices cause harm, too, and bad choices can turn into something beautiful. Maybe it's my fault. Maybe you'd have been standing somewhere else if we didn't have our fight that day. Maybe it's the waiter's fault for being slow to take our order. Maybe it's the architect who put a brick wall there instead of a nice garden. Existence is chaos and there are no answers. Even in statistics, you're often just hedging your bets . . ."

I trail off for a moment, shocked by what I'm about to say.

"But maybe that doesn't matter. Maybe the battle isn't actually between chaos and order, because let's face it, chaos already won.

From the second the big bang kicked things into gear, chaos has been taking victory laps. As tangled and strange and fucked-up as all this is, maybe just *existing* is enough, because the *real* battle—the one we've all been fighting from day one without even knowing it—is between existence and . . . whatever you are."

"I'm nothing," my mother replies. "Just like you."

"No," I retort bluntly. "If there's one thing I'm finally certain of, it's this: I do exist."

"You're a tiny grain of sand on an endless beach," my mother groans, her voice echoing through my skull. "Your voice is meaningless against the crashing waves."

"If my voice is meaningless, then why'd you ask me here?" I counter.

Mom is silent.

"If all this little voice of mine gets to do is tell oblivion to fuck right off, then that's enough for me," I announce.

With that, I leave the centipede cages and turn abruptly.

I march back through the portal.

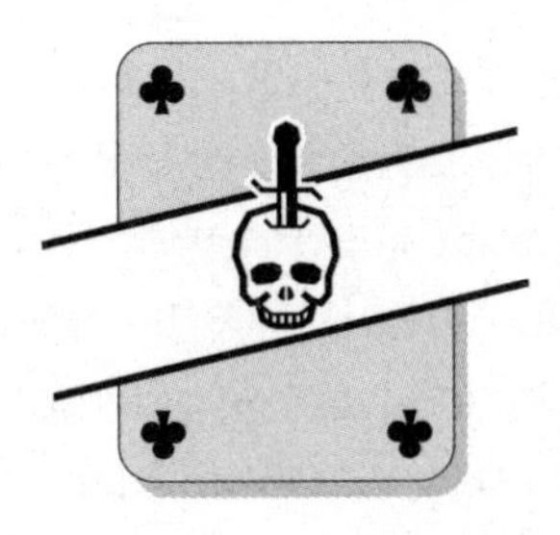

POKER FACE

Agent Layne springs to his feet as I step through the plot hole, an expression of relief overwhelming him. He's been sitting on the generator, his eyes glued to the swirling tear in reality for any sign of life.

After all this time, he's likely grown curious about where I've been and what I've seen, but he gets the gist by glancing down at my hand and noting that the cage, and the nothingness within it, is gone.

I unlatch my helmet. There's a sharp hiss as I take it off, then a loud clatter when I haphazardly toss it to the side.

"You did it," he gushes, unable to keep the grin from creeping its way across half his face. The other side is still numb, but little by little his smile is returning.

Unfortunately, all I can see when I stare back at this clean-shaven man is an image of what he looked like all those years ago. On the morning of the Low-Probability Event, his hair was long and his beard was coarse and scraggly. He likely stank of booze and sweat.

The void could've made all that up, of course, but for some reason I can feel the truth deep down in my bones. Now that my memory is jogged, I recall him driving past Annie and me on our morning walk. I can see him standing below that poker room sign in my mind's eye.

He killed my mother.

This potent, blunt statement stays locked in the forefront of my consciousness until Layne's expression begins to soften, transforming from elation to concern. "What's wrong?" he asks.

I realize now that I'm at a very important crossroads, standing on the precipice of one tiny decision that's certain to cascade into another, and another, and another, growing like a snowball in whatever direction I send it off in.

Fate had bad plans for Layne's good choice, a perfect example of life's grand absurdity, but what can you do? I step toward him, weary and exhausted as he opens his arms. The two of us hug, using what's left of each other's strength to avoid collapsing.

"What did you see in there?" Layne asks, his face cast in the shimmering blue light of the plot hole.

It only now occurs to me that Agent Layne is probably just as ignorant of our bizarre connection as I was. By the time anyone got out of that crashed truck, I was long gone.

"Nothing," I reply, which is technically the truth.

My companion hesitates, thinking about this for a moment. "Just endless nothing?" he asks.

We release and I offer a nod of confirmation. Behind us, the portal has already shrunk to half its size, rapidly breaking down as fate starts repairing itself. The open equation is finally closed, a massive off-kilter loop of chance no longer pushing things further and further out of balance. The wound is healing.

Layne and I watch in awe as the plot hole gradually winds down, making sure no cosmic centipedes crawl back through, and then breathe sighs of relief as, half an hour later, the whole thing disappears in one final sizzle of turquoise energy.

♣ ♥ ♦ ♠

Morning light has started shining through the cracked doors of the hidden bunker, casting the remaining carnage in a strangely beautiful glow. This is the endless dichotomy of existence, I suppose, moments of visceral horror and divine beauty happening all at once to create an impossibly unique thing called life.

The guards remain dead and mangled, our victory having no effect on their tragic state, but outside it appears the confetti has stopped falling and the skies have cleared.

In an existential sense, order has not been fully restored. Order will never be restored. Stability, on the other hand, is washing across the land like some kind of karmic baptism, easing the scales of fate that had been rocking so violently for so long.

Tucked away in the corner of this bunker is a single emergency vehicle under a black tarp, an off-road SUV that should have no trouble handling desert terrain. Hopefully, the workers here take enough care to turn its battery over from time to time—just in case.

"Thank God," Agent Layne groans as he climbs into the back seat of the SUV. "This mess is gonna take so long to clean up. We'll have to contact the military, the FBI. Fuck. So many loose ends."

"You're taking the back seat?" I ask. "You always drive."

Layne nods, struggling to remove his jacket while his paralyzed arm gets in the way. When he finally pulls it off, the man bunches up this fabric to create a pillow. He climbs into the vehicle and lies across the back row, head resting right behind the driver's seat. "I know," Layne replies. "This arm isn't gonna let that happen, though. Take the lead, Vera. You've earned it."

His statement is designed to make me feel some kind of heroic pride, but for some reason that emotion doesn't come.

If there's one thing I notice, it's patterns, but I also notice when patterns break. Discerning meaning from repetition is where the real challenge is, and right now I'm at a loss. It makes sense for Layne to give me driving duty thanks to his dead arm, but why lie in the back like that? Is his wound worse than I initially thought? Could be. It's from a fucking *extraterrestrial life-form,* after all.

Is Layne about to die?

"Are you okay?" I ask, standing by the open door as Agent Layne sprawls out across the back. "I think we should get you to a hospital."

I know exactly what he's going to say, can already hear the words in a stern cascade as he explains the importance of discretion within the LPEC. He swears up and down that he's not a cop, that *we* are not cops, but his tight-lipped, thin-blue-line mentality says otherwise. We saved the day, sure, but we kicked in a lot of doors to get here.

Layne's right about one thing: there's plenty to clean up. Finding a doctor will just mean another headache.

"Yeah, let's head for the hospital," Layne says.

"What?" I blurt, thrown for a loop by his response.

"Get me to the hospital," he presses. "Once I'm in cell phone range, I'll call the rest of the LPEC for cleanup."

Fuck, it must be way worse than it looks.

I take careful note of Agent Layne's features, concerned he might be melting away like Denver, but it appears this half paralysis is the extent of his trauma from that strange barbed tendril.

Still, something's off about my companion's expression, a graveness on his face that might be hidden if he still had control over the whole thing. Layne's behavior is often a mystery to me, utterly bizarre in a way that is both charming and a little unsettling, but suddenly that charming veneer has slipped.

His notoriously effective poker face isn't working—quite literally. He's giving it his best shot, but I know something's wrong.

"Alright," I finally reply. "Let's get out of here."

I sprint back to the main entrance, hunting for a panel or a lever that might help fully open the sliding metal doors. They're stuck just wide enough for a human to slip through, but a vehicle would prove impossible.

Fortunately, I find and press a button that prompts a clang to ring out through the hollow facility, the doors groaning as they open wide and let in even more of that radiant morning light. The sun is just cresting the distant mountains, giving the confetti-covered desert a surreal, picturesque quality that sure makes a girl glad she decided to save the world.

I hesitate, taking it all in, then return to the SUV. I climb into the driver's seat and buckle up.

Soon enough we've emerged into the fresh light of a glorious Nevada sunrise. We rumble along in silence for a bit, just appreciating this moment of relative normalcy after the mayhem we just experienced. It feels especially quiet without one of Layne's bizarre music choices or his language lessons ringing in my ears.

Slowly, the creeping weight of regret starts pushing down on me, filling the massive void in our conversation as I'm finally left alone with my thoughts. Reaching the finish line is a blessing, but I'm still having trouble ignoring the things Agent Layne did to get here. The things *we* did to get here.

It's too much.

"You should turn everything over to the press," I say, oppressive guilt finally pushing me over the edge. "It's the least we can do."

Layne hesitates, his pause drawing out longer and longer, and with every passing second I brace myself for his inevitable rejection. I've thrown out this wild idea before, and the rebuttal was firm enough that I feel foolish bringing it up again. I *have* to bring it up, though, because regardless of our current victory, this specter will hang over me for a very long time.

Unless I do something about it.

As the quiet drags on, I consider what would happen if I decided to leak it myself—although there's no question the most important files were redacted long before arriving on my laptop.

Finally, Agent Layne breaks his silence. "Yeah, I think you're right," he replies. "We should turn everything over."

I glance in the rearview mirror, hoping to make eye contact with Layne and then remembering he's laid out flat. Instead of the man's face, I catch a glimpse of his good arm slipping behind his back, gently tugging at something. Layne pulls forth an object and quickly brings it up to his chest, moving so swiftly I can barely tell it's his gun. It is, though. He's now holding the weapon directly behind my seat, perfectly positioned so I can't see it.

I'm so relaxed around Agent Layne that I almost come out swinging with a "What's with the gun?" joke, but I manage to bite my tongue.

What are you even thinking? Layne is your friend.

It's true—in fact, right now he's my *only* friend. We've grown together through triumph and tragedy, and there's a powerful bond that comes along with that.

Friendship isn't what drives Agent Layne, though.

This is a man on a mission, a man wholly devoted to the cause for better or worse. A man who bends the rules when he has to and isn't afraid to tie up loose ends.

Tears start welling up in my eyes, my body accepting the truth before my mind fully can.

"Vera, I'm—I'm really sorry," Layne stammers, finally breaking the silence. "You're a good kid. It usually doesn't take so long for me to do something like this, but . . ." He trails off for a moment.

I see his body shift a bit, feel the gentle push of something hard against the back of my seat.

Outside, the desert landscape is just as rocky and treacherous as ever, but the confetti has disappeared. My path is now lined with renegade cacti and a few massive boulders—a beautiful place to kick off, at least.

I consider playing dumb, but at this point we both know the game is over. I've served my purpose and served it well, but after everything I've seen there's no way the LPEC will just let me move on. Pinky promising I'll keep my mouth shut isn't gonna cut it.

"You don't have to do this," I suddenly blubber. My words are coming out tangled and strange, desperation at their core. "I can work other cases for you. You'd be losing a valuable resource."

"Or a huge liability," Layne counters, his voice wavering. The man is tearing up. "Fuck. It's really never been this hard with a consultant. I want you to know that."

A consultant. I remember him using this specific phrase before, recalling the pained expression on Agent Goodwin's face when he heard it. I didn't understand at the time, but it's clear now that "consultants" are expendable by design. One and done.

"Yeah, that makes me feel *way* better," I retort, my voice cracking.

Layne sighs loudly, pushing his weapon even harder against the back of my seat. He's ready to take the leap, ready to finish the hard part and get on with filing his next report. "I'm sorry."

"Wait!" I blurt. "There's one more thing you should know. One more thing I really *can* help you with."

Agent Layne is growing restless. I can tell he hates drawing it out, and I believe him when he says this is the toughest execution of his career.

I press the gas a little harder, quietly picking up speed.

"The portal is closed," Layne counters gruffly, annoyance finally seeping into his tone. "Our deal with Everett is signed and delivered. There's nothing left for you to teach me, professor."

The statistics on car accidents are clear. People not wearing their seat belts in a crash are thirty times more likely to be ejected from the vehicle, and 77 percent of all people thrown from the vehicle will die.

For years, the prevailing data suggested it was safer to sit in the back seat, but as time goes on and safety features are added, this has shifted. Without airbags to stop the occupant from shooting through the windshield, a passenger in the rear seat with no belt is in deep trouble.

I've finally found a bet I'm willing to take.

"It's actually something *you* taught me," I reply.

I slam my foot down on the gas, yanking the wheel to the right and careening toward a handful of boulders that are much larger and sturdier than this SUV. A gunshot rings out, but my sudden jerk was enough to pull Layne's one good arm to the side. I hear his weapon clatter under the seat.

"Always buckle up!"

My runway is short, but it's enough. Despite the rough terrain, our SUV has no problem launching like a rocket in five seconds flat. When it all clicks into place, Layne barely has time to find his safety belt, let alone grab his weapon off the floor.

The SUV slams hard into the largest of the boulders, a head-on collision at what must be sixty miles an hour. Fortunately, the seat belt I'd been so keen to ignore these last four years has done its job today.

My body snaps forward and then abruptly halts, but the belt across my chest locks so swiftly that the whole experience feels like a singular moment. The pain is instant and overwhelming, so powerful that my whole field of vision turns brilliant white.

I can feel the air in the cab shift as something hurtles past me, blasting through the front windshield in an eruption of glass.

Then silence.

It takes a while for me to realize the stark white vista is not actually a visualization of my own blinding pain, but the sudden inflation of an airbag that is now pressed against my face.

I clumsily search for my buckle as the bag deflates, struggling to undo the perfectly crafted safety regulation prison that's sprung up around me. It takes a while to find what I'm looking for, but eventually my fumbling hand wraps itself around a little flat square. I press the button, relieving the tension of my strap and immediately collapsing against the door.

I stumble out of the SUV, a dull ache radiating across my body. It's particularly focused on my chest, where the belt so efficiently held me in place, and I notice now that every breath causes this pain to surge. My head is throbbing and my ears are ringing, but I'm alive.

I turn back to the wreckage, discovering that most of the hood has collapsed in on itself while the back of the vehicle remains completely unharmed. This creates the strange appearance of an SUV that has simply disappeared into the side of a large boulder. A mess of glass and blood offers hints of something far more destructive, however, and the tangled body slumped on what's left of the front third of our vehicle is a dead giveaway.

I step a little closer, eyes blurring in and out of focus.

Agent Layne's head has been obliterated, split open like a watermelon after slamming against the rock, his neck bent so far back that the rest of his body is essentially using his skull as a pillow, propped up in a muddle of contorted limbs. Steam rises from the car's hood, passing through the remains of Agent Layne like a ghost leaving his body.

I'm furious with him, horrified at what he tried to do, but I also can't help the sadness and grief that grip me.

I stand here, staring at the corpse. It's not often one gets to see a dead body like this, surrounded by nothing but meditative stillness and quiet. The peculiar splay of Layne's arms and legs reminds me of something, and at first I'm not entirely sure what it is.

The macabre circumstances eventually jog my memory, however.

Layne is the second friend I've tried to make since the Low-Probability Event and they've both ended up the same way, lying dead in a ragdoll pose while I solemnly look on, not quite shocked, but disappointed. A man and a cat. Ashes to ashes, dust to dust.

Something feels different this time, however. I no longer have the urge to run away, nor do I feel like wallowing forever in a state of despondent stillness. I choose a third option.

I might just save the world for a second time.

STRANGE ATTRACTORS

I spring from the rideshare before it can fully stop, thanking my driver as casually as I can despite the circumstances. Time is always limited, but this truth is not always so visceral and present.

I march upstairs to the motel's second-floor landing, where our rooms are located, and pull out the key I pilfered from Agent Layne's jacket pocket.

When I searched his body I discovered two things: this plastic card and something much, much more important. Layne's keyring is small, featuring no more than two house keys, the rental car fob he'd recently attached, and a dainty plastic key chain designed to look like a miniature deck of Bicycle playing cards.

When I tugged at the end of this plastic rectangle, however, the true nature of his key chain was revealed. It's a USB thumb drive. Not only is this a physical key chain, it's a *digital* key chain containing all of Layne's passwords. Should Layne ever have misplaced his keys, it wouldn't matter much to the random person who found them. Even if they *did* happen to discover the hidden port within the tiny plastic cards, they'd need Layne's laptop to apply the passwords.

Now, I've got both.

I slip into Agent Layne's motel room, closing the door behind me and pausing to take in the incongruous collection of artifacts on display. The guy sure loved his kitsch, as evidenced by the tiki mugs that line his desk and the Las Vegas snow globe on his nightstand. There's also a banjo case leaning against the wall, the price tag still on it, and some kind of balance-based workout equipment stacked neatly in the corner. The fire-spinning gear remains unopened.

Layne really *was* out to appreciate every bit of life he could, just not the lives of other people.

I immediately get to work, pulling his bag from the closet and extracting his laptop. Part of me wants to open it up and start diving in here and now, but I have no idea if or when I should expect a mob of LPEC agents to kick down the door and shoot me dead.

Instead, I take his laptop, headphones, and charger under my arm, then hurry outside. I head down the stairs and around to the back of the motel, returning to the same secluded parking lot where we met Denver and her cronies just hours earlier.

Behind the far dumpster there's a small brick enclosure with a fair amount of shade, and it's still early enough that the full-on Nevada heat hasn't quite reared its ugly head. This little corner of the lot is tucked away enough for me to avoid detection, but it also allows me access to the motel's Wi-Fi network.

From here, I've also got a great view of any suspicious vehicles that might pull up.

I sit with my back against the brick wall, taking a good while to position myself thanks to the terrible ache that comes with slamming into a boulder at sixty miles an hour. When I finally settle in, I open up Agent Layne's laptop, which immediately prompts me to enter a password if I'd like to continue.

Username: *Jonah Layne*.

I insert the USB key chain, followed by the hard drive he gifted me in another port.

The password prompt disappears, revealing a particularly clean desktop with minimal folders tucked away in the upper right corner. One of them is a stone oven cooking master class, and Layne's background is a promotional photo for a zydeco band. Based on the sticks in his hand, it appears Layne is the drummer.

Well aware that the files I'm looking for are probably squirrelled away in some hidden folder, I cross-reference using the drive I already have access to. I do a computer-wide search for the missing file names—the cards he didn't show—and immediately hit my target. Soon enough, a long list of images, videos, audio files, and text documents appears on my screen, the selections that were initially missing now freely accessible. There are thousands upon thousands of files, more information than I know what to do with.

I knew Agent Layne was holding out on me, but I assumed this meant something like *half* of LPECs data was out of my reach. Now, it appears I was only privy to the tip of a very large iceberg.

Not quite sure where to start, I click on a random video file. It's labeled simply, offering a date and a catalog number, followed by the name *Alice Friedman*. The video fills my screen and begins to play. The footage is crisp and high-quality, but the camera is static and a timecode runs across the bottom of the window. It looks like something you'd see played during someone's trial, a star witness's video deposition.

Onscreen, a woman sits quietly at a table in a nondescript room. Her face is smiling, but there's something about her expression that seems vaguely coerced, like she's trying her best to be social at a party full of deeply exhausting people. The woman's shoulder-length blond hair is a little greasy, and she's not wearing any makeup.

Her left hand has been placed within a small metal box, which sits upon the table and has numerous wires sprouting from the back of it. They snake along in a mess of color. Half of these wires split away and disappear off camera, while another bundle connects to an ancient computer monitor.

The monitor displays a mostly black screen with a green digital border. There are several rows of numbers, alike in hue and ranging from one to fifty-two.

Resting near the woman's right hand is a fresh stack of what appear to be standard playing cards.

"Can you state your name and date of birth?" someone asks from off camera, a voice I immediately recognize as Agent Layne's.

"Alice Friedman. April thirteenth, 1984."

"You've signed all your intake forms I see," Agent Layne continues. "That's good. I just need you to verbally acknowledge that you've volunteered for this project of your own free will, without any coercion. Do you agree with that statement?"

The woman hesitates, then nods.

"Sorry, Mrs. Friedman, you'll have to say it out loud," Layne explains.

The woman briefly smiles. "I agree," she confirms, then quickly shifts to an expression of practical concern. "When am I getting paid for this?"

"Right when you walk out that door."

The woman regards him with both skepticism and exhaustion, the look of someone who's gotten used to being fucked over. "Cash?"

"We'll give you the cash and drop you off exactly where we picked you up," Layne promises.

The woman hesitates again, then finally agrees. "Okay."

"Can you confirm that you reside within one mile of Allengrove Park in Nashville, Tennessee?" Agent Layne questions.

"Sometimes," the woman replies, then shifts in her seat. "Most of the time."

"And would you consider yourself a lucky person?" Layne asks.

The woman pauses, taking a deep breath as she gives this some serious thought. The expression on her face slowly begins to falter, gradually worn down by the tide of memories that push and pull across her mind. I watch as her lips start trembling. She begins to cry.

The camera picks up a faint *skirt* sound as someone pushes back their chair and rounds the table. Moments later, Layne appears on camera, kneeling down and putting his arms around the woman in a gesture of comfort.

In the video, Agent Layne has already evolved into the clean-cut investigator I once called my friend. The man holds his subject for a long while, gently offering words of encouragement.

"It's gonna be okay, we're gonna help you out," he says. "It's gonna be fine."

Eventually, the woman calms down and Agent Layne returns to his feet. He strolls back to his original position behind the camera.

"This isn't part of the script, but I just wanna remind you that you'll get paid either way," Layne offers. "Fifty dollars no matter what, one thousand dollars for each ace. Plus, you get to come back if you're one of the lucky ones."

"Or unlucky?" the woman asks.

This time, it's Agent Layne's turn to hesitate. Finally, he clears his throat and asks his question again. "Would you consider yourself a lucky person?"

The woman's lips curl into a terrible, heartbreaking frown as she shakes her head, but this time she pushes through the feelings and manages an answer. "No."

"Alright, let's get started," Agent Layne replies, getting down to business. "Your first test is digital. Are you ready to proceed?"

The woman wipes her eyes with her free hand, the one that's not stuck within the metal box. She nods. "I'm ready."

Out of fifty-two numbers displayed on the lab's old computer monitor, four suddenly shift from green to white. Four others turn red. A digital box begins to dance from number to number, swiftly at first and then gradually slowing as it drifts across the fifty-two options. Meanwhile, the computer crackles and hums as it runs its calculation.

The woman's eyes are closed and her teeth are gritted. Every muscle of her body is pulled taut, preparing for something awful.

The digital box finally stops moving, resting around one of the green numbers.

"Standard result!" Agent Layne announces happily, immediately prompting the woman to let out a sigh of relief. "Fourteen."

Alice can't help the smile that breaks across her face, clearly thrilled by these results despite the fact that it appears she didn't win.

"Moving on," Agent Layne continues. "The second and final test of today is analog. The deck before you has been shuffled by one of our technicians, but you're free to cut it anywhere you'd like. You can also choose to *not* cut the deck."

Alice considers this, then very carefully cuts the cards with her free hand. She moves slowly and deliberately, as though she's handling a dangerous wild animal.

"Very good," Layne offers. "Aces are winners, deuces are losers. Please take the top card off of the deck and show it to the camera."

Alice's body language has tightened again, and I don't blame her. As I watch this scene unfold from my shady spot behind the dumpster in a Las Vegas parking lot, it feels as though I'm right there with her.

Alice turns her card toward the camera, displaying a two of clubs. She pauses for a moment, her eyes locked on Layne's.

"What?" she worries. Within a fraction of a second, Alice goes from grave concern to horrible understanding.

A shriek of pain explodes with such abrupt sonic force that I jump in alarm, almost dropping the laptop. The test subject is screaming frantically, struggling to pull her hand from the little metal box and toppling her chair in the process. The table must be bolted to the floor, because it refuses to budge despite Alice's desperate tugs.

"No, no, no," she's begging, tears streaming down her cheeks.

I close the video, sick to my stomach, then continue my hunt through the rest of the folder. There are more Alice Friedman files. Many more. Simmering with anxiety, I click another video. This is dated six months after the previous one.

Layne's computer screen fills with a nearly identical shot, the same room with the same metal box and the same old computer monitor sitting next to it. This time, however, Alice isn't around when the video begins.

A woman shuffles in. Only a portion of her frame is visible thanks to the camera's limited POV, but even from this angle I can see her body language is awkward and stiff.

"How we doing today, Alice?" Agent Layne asks in an upbeat tone. "You feeling lucky?"

Alice mumbles something, the words slurred and inaudible.

"Good, good," Agent Layne replies. "Big day, huh? Last chance for the top prize."

As Alice sits down I can't help noticing her right hand, an observation that prompts me to gasp in shock and hit pause. All four fingers are missing, severed close to the joint and leaving nothing but stubs in their place. Only her thumb remains.

Having witnessed more than enough, I close the video. I take the entire folder and compress it into a single file, then open up Agent Layne's email.

Suddenly, I stop, my fingers freezing in place above the keys. I didn't really notice how hard I've been trembling, but as I catch the potent quiver running through my hands there's no denying the gravity of the moment. If I take off now and let the dust settle around these bizarre events, the odds of my survival could rise significantly. LPEC will be after me regardless, but the resources they put behind the hunt will certainly change if I release this trove of sensitive information.

If they can figure out who did it, I'll probably be the most wanted woman in America.

As the former youngest statistics and probability professor in U Chicago history, I'll be the first to admit there's not enough data to *really* calculate my odds of surviving longer than a month, a week, even a few days, but in broad strokes the answer seems apparent. My chances are not great.

"Fuck it," I murmur to myself.

In the email's *To* field, I start adding the contact information for every press outlet I can think of.

♣ ♥ ♦ ♠

The files on Layne's computer are much too numerous for one person to comb through, but rest assured the major news teams quickly assemble a greatest-hits compilation the likes of which has never been seen.

The luck experiments are particularly gruesome, starting in ethically dubious territory and then quickly devolving from there. Plenty of them make the Alice Friedman videos look tame.

One subject was submerged in a tank of water until a rolling die produced his lucky number. After a particularly long session, the man survived, but not without life-altering brain damage. Another trial featured the identical twins of LPE victims, an attempt to see if rotten fate was in our DNA. The offer was a hefty sum of cash to spin a roulette wheel of medical procedures, ranging from routine check-ups to full eye removals. Many took the gamble and several lost.

Exploring hereditary bad luck, some unusually brutal experiments involved the children of LPE casualties.

Anyone who underwent a dramatic physical transformation during these tests usually disappeared not long after, loose ends tying themselves up in a suspicious double dose of misfortune. Nearly all the subjects were at-risk, low-income individuals coaxed in by the promise of financial support, which begs the question: What about the Survivor's Program?

It wasn't long before financial audits revealed the vast majority of donations and taxes collected for the Survivor's Program were not actually getting to the people who needed help. Instead, all of that money went into funding the LPEC.

Social media users did an incredible job of combing through data logs and reports, folks posting their findings on internet message boards for remarkably thorough analysis. These deep dives eventually worked their way back to the international media titans for repackaging and distribution.

It pains me to say it, but some of this stuff is fascinating.

Several reports are in-depth studies of every unlikely step that occurred to create a seemingly supernatural result. For instance, that chimp I encountered at the diner on May 23 was being transferred away from the Lincoln Park Zoo after multiple aggressive encounters with other primates. Typically, this transfer wouldn't have been routed through downtown Chicago, but a combination of road closures and one accidental wrong turn sent the truck directly into the city.

Someone ran a red light, which was malfunctioning due to a miscommunication in the maintenance schedule, and their vehicle slammed into the transport truck. This released the primate, as well as a handful of other aggressive animals.

The chimp made his way into the backstage area of a theater, which just so happened to be located within the same structure as our diner. He tried on clothes for two hours, hidden away and avoiding capture, but growing steadily hungrier and more frustrated.

This frustration came to a boil when he was finally discovered and reacted with aggression, grabbing a prop typewriter and flying into a belligerent rage.

The rest is history.

LPEC even started their report on the poolside disaster at the Great Britannica, written by none other than Agent Goodwin.

Apparently, four gamblers struck the mega jackpot in unison on a row of slot machines earlier that morning, and each winner's following actions played a major part in the disaster.

Player one, who was positioned on the far-left slot machine, suffered an immediate heart attack after recognizing his good fortune. He was rushed through a service hallway deep within the bowels of the casino, the fastest route for an ambulance pickup.

It was during this trip that security cameras captured the man's stretcher taking a corner too sharply, abruptly cracking a safety regulator for the wave pool's largest pressure tank.

Amid the chaos, nobody returned to fix it.

Player two celebrated on the pool deck—the same place where she'd eventually lose her life—popping a bottle of six-hundred-dollar Cobel Vineyards champagne with her friends and shooting the cork off like a rocket. Several stories up it would strike a window and crack the glass. The extreme heat of the day gradually took care of the rest, shattering the windowpane.

Nobody noticed, because that particular floor of the casino was under construction, and the falling glass landed in a bed of ferns and palms below.

Players three and four were caught on security cameras passionately kissing immediately after their big win, celebrating with an elated smooch that quickly evolved into something more. There's no evidence that these two players even knew each other before this moment, but I suppose winning $1.6 million is enough to put folks in the mood.

This lucky pair happened to be staying on the same floor of the casino as each other, a floor that was partially under construction at the time. In a fit of passion, they decided to spice things up by skipping the trip to either private room, heading for the restricted area instead. The duo admit to having sex amid the construction equipment, including a stack of square-cut sheet metal that could've easily slipped through the shattered window, drifting down to the pool below and splashing into the water unnoticed. It's here the metal squares settled over the wave pool's multiple safety drains, the suction tugging them into place.

A series of very, very, very unlikely events, but not impossible.

It's only been a few days since the files dropped, and the Great Britannica Hotel and Casino has been shuttered and a massive investigation into Everett Vacation and Entertainment has been launched. Hex International, the parent conglomerate that quietly hosts all these wriggling corporate tentacles, appears to remain unscathed.

I was intrigued to discover there are no LPEC dossiers about extraterrestrials in Area 51. It seems Layne really didn't know what we were in for on that horrifying night in the desert.

Other leaked documents are downright comical, beginning with concrete data and then gradually flying off the rails in brash moments of speculation and science fiction that could only thrive in a department free from oversight.

One such report was dedicated to determining the range and potential effects of larger plot holes, a term the media absolutely devoured. Based on LPEC's data, a massive, planet-sized tear into The Void (their capitalization, not mine) could cause astronomically rare global shifts that would last indefinitely. In this case, it's unlikely we'd even notice the opening.

This theory is terrifying, as is the concrete data to back it up, but where things get hilarious is when the author of this report starts hypothesizing about various effects. A world where all bigfeet (yes, he uses the term big*feet*) leave the wilderness and integrate into human society. Or my personal favorite: a world where all straight, cisgender humans become raving, murderous lunatics once a year, leaving the queer folks to fend for themselves.

I can't even *begin* to psychoanalyze the brain that came up with that one.

It's all a lot to take in, but I'm fascinated. I'm fascinated because, for the first time in four long years, I'm starting to participate in the big wide world.

I found one of Agent Layne's new-music playlists, titled *Layne 'Em Up, Knock 'Em Down,* and I listened to it nonstop on my journey back to Wisconsin.

♣ ♥ ♦ ♠

The leaker's identity has yet to be uncovered, at least publicly. Whether or not it stays that way is anyone's guess, and for all I know a government task force could be quietly mobilizing on the shores of Lake Geneva at this very moment. Regardless, I'm thankful for the time this has afforded me. I've got some business to take care of around the house.

As I stand in the doorway of my dilapidated home, the knob still busted thanks to my initial meeting with Agent Layne, I feel the slightest twinge of hope bubbling up within me. I find myself wishing for the very unlikely event that the LPEC is dissolved before they get the chance to retaliate, that their hands are simply too full to come after me.

Stranger things have happened.

In the meantime, I've got some living to do. I get some fresh trash bags out of my car and start filling them with junk from around the house, which is plentiful but not overwhelming. The larger issue is a thick layer of dust that's settled over everything, but with enough cleaning spray and some rags, I soon manage to get the living room looking halfway decent.

After this, I dismantle the handgun resting on my dining room table and place the components in separate bags to throw out.

All of this plot hole talk has got me thinking about a storytelling concept called Chekov's gun. It posits the idea that if you mention a gun in the first act, it has to go off later on. Like life itself, there's a momentum within every story, a preordained conclusion that everything will eventually guide you back to: a series of mysterious numbers, a lucky penny returning after years of circulation, the reveal of a tragic unknown history with a friend. These intricate tethers can make it hard to believe in free will.

But even if historical inertia means the gun will always come back, it can still represent something else when it does. Shooting a gun isn't the only meaningful thing you can do with it.

Opening the blinds causes golden beams of sunlight to bathe my home in a pleasant haze, flooding the setting with natural illumination.

It's a great feeling, but there's a lot more work to be done.

A lot.

Stepping into the backyard, my gaze drifts across the tangled weeds and tall grass that have overtaken everything. Unfortunately, in the few weeks I've been gone, things out here have only gotten worse, the summer heat baking my already unsightly flora and transforming it into a patchy plot of brown-and-yellow decay. I'm gonna need a trip to the garden store, I suddenly realize.

I'm about to head back inside and finish cleaning up the living room when I notice a strange gathering of outliers in the sea of beige. While the majority of my backyard has withered and rotted in the oppressive heat, one particular section is thriving, teeming with glorious wildflowers in a rainbow of hues.

I can't help stepping toward this little miracle, walking to the edge of the patio and gazing down at a colorful assortment of blooms. I gasp softly when I see what lies below them, however, an unexpected sight nestled in the dirt. The body of my cat friend is still sprawled out in the yard, her remains now mostly skeletal.

A death that had once been utterly devastating has provided unexpected results, serving as fertilizer and moisture to help this single patch flourish. The stalks jut up through Kat's bony rib cage in a shade of lush green, looking healthy and new in the warm sun. This display might sound macabre—and maybe it is—but it's also so much more than that.

Despite my efforts, I couldn't save my furry friend, but Kat saved these flowers, and these flowers will help out a handful of desperate bees who find themselves parched in this hellscape of a garden.

Butterflies, too.

These endless connections used to seem so chaotic and overwhelming to me. In fact, *they still do.* The world *is* a messy, clumsy, frustrating, outlandish place, and I spent a long time hoping to convince myself otherwise. I tried to find an ultimate order where there's no order to be found, because existence is just as sloppy and weird as it appears.

But it's also awe-inspiring and delightful and wonderfully strange.

There was a time when this made me feel worthless, like my place was infinitely small and devoid of importance, but after coming face-to-face with absolute *nothingness,* I know the truth.

I'm *something,* at the very least. I've defied the existential odds already, winning the trillion-to-one jackpot of even existing in the first place. My position within these trembling strings of fate may be infinitely small if you zoom out, but it's also infinitely large if you zoom in.

Nothing matters, but that's no reason to mourn. It's reason to celebrate. I'm here, whatever *that* means, so I might as well enjoy the ride.

With this final thought, I turn and head back inside. My old phone is still tucked away in the junk drawer, resting right where I left it. The device powers on, retaining a sliver of its previous charge from my last stroll down memory lane.

I take my phone and head back out to the patio, finding a seat on the stoop. I open my texts and start a new one, addressing it to Annie.

I'm sorry I disappeared like that. I fucked up. If you ignore this message, I understand. I'm guessing you've probably moved on by now, and I understand that, too. I don't expect anything, but if you ever want to talk, I'll answer this time. I'm so sorry.

I hit send, then abruptly realize it's been such a long time she might've removed my contact.

This is Vera, I add awkwardly in a second text, cringing as I send it off.

I set the phone down next to me and close my eyes, basking in the golden sunlight. The warmth feels incredible against my skin, washing over me in tandem with the gratitude that blooms at the pit of my stomach.

A gentle wind drifts through my peculiar little backyard, the sea of death and decay punctuated by a flourish of eccentric, colorful wildflowers that somehow makes it all worthwhile.

My phone buzzes.

ABOUT THE AUTHOR

Sam Rand

CHUCK TINGLE is the *USA Today* bestselling author of *Camp Damascus*, *Bury Your Gays*, and *Straight*. His books have been finalists for the Bram Stoker and CALIBA Golden Poppy Awards. Tingle is a mysterious force of energy behind sunglasses and a pink mask. He is also an anonymous author of romance, horror, and fantasy. Tingle was born in Home of Truth, Utah, and now lives in Los Angeles, California. Tingle writes to prove love is real, because love is the most important tool we have when resisting the endless cosmic void. Not everything people say about Tingle is true, but the important parts are.